THE LAST OF
THE DRAGONS
PAUL CARBERRY

Published in Canada by Engen Books, Chapel Arm, NL.

A CIP catalogue record for this book is available from Library and Archives Canada.

ISBN-13: 978-1-77478-112-8

Distributed by:
Engen Books
www.engenbooks.com
submissions@engenbooks.com

First mass market paperback printing: September 2022

Cover Design: Ellen Curtis

THE LAST OF
THE DRAGONS
PAUL CARBERRY

For Matthew LeDrew
Your encouragement is the reason (blame)
for each and every one of my novels.

"Crocodiles are easy. They try to kill and eat you. People are harder. Sometimes they pretend to be your friend first."
-Steve Irwin

PROLOGUE

Henry stood outside in the sweltering heat. Perspiration forming beaded on his forearms and flowed from his brow over his forehead. He dabbed at his forehead with a white handkerchief, saturating the fabric in flop sweat, then tucked it back into his blazer's chest pocket. A swarm of insects buzzed around his head in a low, droning murmur. With the wave of his hand, he tried swatting the mosquitoes away, which proved to be a fruitless gesture. Craning his neck back, he stared up into the security camera and brandished his security badge, desperate to escape the heat and wildlife. The flashing red eye of the camera followed his every movement.

The door opened with a mechanized swish to reveal sharp fluorescent lights shimmering off the marbled floor of the foyer. A glacial gush of conditioned air rushed out to greet Henry, a welcomed reprieve from the dense humidity. Without wasting another moment, he dashed inside, eager to get away from the jungle's torments. His briefcase swayed in wide arcs as he entered the climate-controlled building, his security badge affixed to a yellow lanyard held high beside his cheek.

"Good day, Mr. Collins," the security guard said from

behind a thick pane of bulletproof glass. He didn't bother to glance up from the newspaper sprawled out in front of him, the different sections of the paper spread out, taking up the entirety of his workspace. Tucked behind his right ear, a pencil worn down to the stub waited for its turn at the daily crossword puzzle in the entertainment section.

Henry waved his hand as he passed the security booth and walked through the metal detector. An alarm blared as he passed through. He craned his neck toward the ceiling and let out a deep sigh. "Again?" he groaned. "I thought we've been through all of this already. You will not keep me here all day again, will you?"

A crackle of static burst through the speakers overhead. "You're free to go, Mr. Collins. Mr. Anders is expecting you and gave us strict order not to keep you waiting." Even through the speaker, the security guard couldn't hide his exasperated tone.

Before he continued, Henry adjusted his tie, using abrupt actions to illustrate his dissatisfaction with the slight inconvenience. "Make sure you don't let it happen again," he said as he continued on his way, knowing the security guard had already turned his attention back to his newspaper.

The corridor slanted downwards at a slight angle, barely discernible to the untrained eye. Unless you paid close attention to the scant shadows cast by the light fixtures, you'd never notice. At the end of the hallway, he stepped onto a conveyor belt, glancing at his watch and tapping his foot impatiently as it carried him along at a snail's pace toward the laboratory. Bright fluorescent lights reflected off the pristine marble floor, catching in speckles of golden glimmer scattered throughout the design at random intervals. The temperature dropped drastically as the conveyor headed deeper underground. At the end of the corridor, a stainless-steel double door awaited him, the light glaring off the pristine surface. Henry stepped off the belt with practiced grace and made his way straight for the door.

There were no security checks here. Henry shoved his way through the double door and stepped into the quarantine zone. By request, they had left a chair for him in the center of the room. He sat down in the chair, placed his briefcase next to him on the floor, and waited for the uncomfortable part. Beneath him, the floor pulsated, and the walls reverberated as the pressure in the room increased. A current of wind rushed downwards from the ceiling, pressing him down into the chair. Then the pressure altered, and the wind drove upwards, forcing him to lean against the force so it wouldn't blow him over. Another blast of pressurized air blew from the left and then from the right. The process repeated itself, eliminating any foreign debris from his clothing, the pressure creating the suction of a vacuum. A sharp ding signaled the end of the process. A green light flashed above the entrance to the lab. Henry adjusted his suit once more and ran his fingers through his untamed hair before he thrust the door open.

"You know I hate all of this," he growled to himself as he entered the room.

Technicians sat in front of a row of computer terminals, working away, paying no attention to Henry's outburst. In the center of the room, a man wearing a lab coat busied himself recording data from the screens onto his clipboard as he studied the round incubator filled with wood chips. A robotic arm dangled into the habitat. Henry stared at the empty incubator with disdain, his blood pressure rising.

"Hey," Henry shouted in a demanding tone, grabbing the scientist by the shoulder to spin him around. "Where's the egg, egghead?"

Refusing to tear his eyes away from his clipboard, the man pushed his glasses up the bridge of his nose and said, "It's all in there." The man's pen scrawled across the page as he continued his work.

"Where?" Henry demanded. "Is this some sort of fucking joke? Can you fathom the dollar amount my client has tied up in this project?"

The man tapped his pen off the glass. The cavernous sound annoyed Henry. His eye twitched as his blood pressure continued to soar. Everything about his monthly visits to this lab irritated him. He hated flying into South Africa, despised the ramshackle hotel, and detested the helicopter ride over the sweltering jungle. And the worst part of the entire trip involved speaking to the smug scientists in this laboratory. Each one of them acted indifferently toward him like he didn't factor into the equation.

"It's all in there," he responded in monotone. "In pieces."

Henry squinted through the glass, beads of moisture obscuring his view. But even through the droplets of water, he could see the fragments of yellowish-white membrane scattered over the wood chips. Shards of the egg lay trampled over and pressed into the terrarium. The paper-thin membrane stretched out, loosely connecting the shell's segments into a macabre puzzle.

"It hatched?" Henry asked, hopeful this would be his last visit to this cursed building.

The scientist nodded his head and said, "Affirmative." And without another word, he turned and attended to his work.

A security door swooshed open with a metallic hiss. "How nice of you to join us, Mr. Collins."

Henry tried to ignore the sarcastic tone; he wouldn't get drawn into another fight. "Pleasure is all mine, Doctor Anders," he lied.

Filled with pride, Dr. Anders ushered Henry to join him at the door. "Quickly now, come. We have something extraordinary to show you."

Dr. Anders' stark white lab coat hurt Henry's eyes. The fabric was covered in a high-grade repellent liquid to repel any genetic substances from the specimens in the lab—an added layer of protection to prevent any of the valuable research from leaving the watchful eyes of the owner. He peered out over the thin frame of his black wire glasses at Henry, his eyes shifting back and forth the entire time. Anders ran his tongue over his permanently dry lips, a side effect of the air purity inside every square inch of the building.

Unable to contain his excitement, Anders rushed down the corridor, his lab coat billowing behind him. "I think you're going to be particularly pleased with how this turned out." Jubilation added a high-pitched waver to his tone. "Oh yes indeed, thrilled might be a better sentiment."

"Really?" Henry said, doubt rising to the surface. "Isn't that what you said the last time?"

The doctor laughed and said, "I believe that's what I say every time. My work is groundbreaking." His tongue matched his quickening pace. "Right this way now." He led them through another stainless-steel door. A vigorous blast of tepid air greeted them as they entered the examining room where a glass window overlooked a pen. Giant palm trees stretched to the ceiling, their vibrant green leaves clustered together, obscuring Henry's view. Lined along the glass front, two staggered rows of seats offered a view over the room below.

As Henry stepped into the room, a broiling heat assaulted him. Sweat flowed down his forehead and his dress shirt clung to his chest. "What the hell is this place?"

"Why, it's the nursery, of course," Anders replied in a knowing tone. "Take a seat. It's almost time for a feeding."

Filled with excitement and a sense of dread, Henry stood frozen in place. Something about all of this was wrong. The experiment hatched far too soon—the gestation period had been cut in half. "I have so many questions."

"Have a seat," Anders said, his tone demanding. He slid into his own near the middle and patted his hand on the seat beside him. "I can explain any questions you want to ask. But I think it would be best if I show you first."

Henry wandered over beside Anders, staring down at him. The doctor paid him no attention, his eyes glued to the viewing screen. With the heat affecting him, Henry dropped into the cushioned leather seat, allowing the fabric to absorb the full brunt of his weight. He loosened his tie, feeling his internal temperature soar out of control.

"Can I get a drink of water or something?" Henry asked, finding himself short of breath, the heat pressing down on him.

Anders pressed a button on the arm of his seat. A static crackle filled the room. "Debbie, could you bring some water into the Colossus viewing room, please? Our guest isn't used to this level of heat." A condescending snort escaped his pursed lips.

"Right away, Doctor Anders."

"Thank you," Henry said.

Anders nodded his head, then turned back to the viewing glass. "This is a remarkable breakthrough we have on our hands. We've created something far beyond our wildest expectations." Anders spoke with passion, his tone expressive and invested. "It will impress your client beyond their wildest expectations."

"You've mentioned that," Henry said, tugging at the collar of his dress shirt. He unfastened the top two buttons of his shirt and hauled the tie over his left shoulder. "Listen, can you just tell me what it is so I can go report back to my client…your investor?"

"I'll do you one better," Anders said, taking the cell phone out of the chest pocket on his smock. "This is Anders. Can we move up the feeding?" He paused as the person on the other end objected. Anders' eyebrows furrowed. "I realize that, but fifteen minutes early won't affect the feeding schedule." He ended the call without waiting for the person on the other end to protest.

Behind them, the door opened. Henry felt a gush of air suck out of the room, catching a hint of the chilled air from the corridor. A woman wearing a black skirt and white lab coat over a navy blouse entered the room, pushing a trolley in front of her. The front wheel wobbled and squeaked. "Gentlemen, I have chilled bottles of water. Or may I offer you a bottle of American soda?"

"I'll take a soda," Anders said with a smile. "I miss home so much. This is one of the few things in this lab that reminds me of Texas."

The woman dug through a container of ice and pulled out a bottle of Coke. Beads of condensation dripped down the glass. "And for you, sir?"

Henry licked his lips. "I'll have one of those."

With a beaming smile, the woman popped the cap off and handed him a bottle of Coke. It felt ice cold against his palm. Henry tilted his head back and drained half the bottle in one continuous gulp. He belched once then finished the bottle. "Can I have another?"

The woman laughed. "Thirsty?" Her hand vanished into the ice, rooting around at the bottom, and pulled out another bottle. "Here you go, sir."

"Thanks," Henry said with a thankful nod. He sipped a mouthful of soda from the bottle, savoring the bubbles and the sweet taste.

Without a word, the woman turned and left Anders and Henry alone in the room. When the door closed behind her, Anders turned to Henry and said, "She's the only other thing that reminds me of home. She's a real sweet Texas gal."

Henry found Anders' use of the word *thing* offensive, but he dropped it, not wanting to spend too much time in this room with this man. "When's the feeding taking place?" Henry asked, desperate to change the topic. As if on cue, a man wearing bright orange coveralls wandered into view, hauling a cow behind him on a leash.

"As you're aware," Anders said, laying his drink down on the floor in front of him, "we've spliced several strings of crocodile DNA together, most notably the American saltwater crocodile with the Nile. And, as I'm sure you're painfully aware, we've failed at this several times."

Henry nodded his head in agreement and bit his tongue. With the amount of money funneled into the research, "painful" wasn't sufficient to describe his client's attitude. "Yes, I'm up to speed on all aspects of the project—even the topics that I don't understand."

"Well then, I guess you understand the reason for our failures?" Anders asked, his tone accusatory.

"I wouldn't say that. But I know that you have had troubles with keeping the DNA together long enough to reach maturity," Henry answered with confidence.

"In amateur terms, yes," Anders said with a smirk. "We stumbled upon our solution by accident. But I recognized it right away."

"What's the solution?"

"We discovered the fossil of a *Deinosuchus* right here in our very own backyard," Anders said, bursting with excitement. "This colossal creature roamed the earth during the Cretaceous period, and we pulled enough DNA from the preserved bone marrow to genetically engineer something remarkable. I think you'll agree our product is truly extraordinary."

Two yellow flashing lights went off along the far wall, the arcs rotating in a thin beam through the dense jungle foliage. The man tied the leash off on a metal pole protruding from the ground, bent at a slight angle toward the wall. Agitated, the cow tried to pull herself free from the leash, her hooves scuffing over the damp soil. Once the worker had the rope secured in place, he ran back toward the viewing room, disappearing in a flash.

A dull, metal grinding noise rumbled as the back wall slipped open. Natural light flooded into the man-made jungle. The dank odor of swamp filtered in from outside. After a tense moment, a monstrous silhouette crept into view, forced to wait for the doors to slide further apart before it could trudge through. Henry stood up and leaned against the viewing glass, trying to get a better angle. A twenty-foot-long shadow vanished into the verdant foliage. The trees quivered as the predator stalked its prey.

Angry, Henry grunted in disgust and slapped his hand off the window. "Do your think I'm that fucking stupid? We asked for a newborn monster. And now you're trying to pull the wool over my eyes by manipulating the shadow of a full-grown crocodile?"

Anders chuckled and said, "I can assure you…this is the product your client asked for. And I think we can both agree, it exceeds expectations."

"There's no way I'm falling for this nonsense," Henry asserted. "I haven't been away long enough for a crocodile to grow that large."

"Mr. Collins, that beast you see before you is only three weeks old," Anders said, his tone firm. "And once it steps into the light, you'll know that this is no ordinary, run-of-the-mill crocodile."

"I saw the egg in the incubation chamber," Henry spat. "Are you trying to tell me you left that eggshell in there for three weeks to show me?"

Anders laughed as he approached the window. "Mr. Collins," Anders said, staring out the viewing glass, "your client is not the only one interested in what we've created. That one down there is yours. We already have a buyer for the baby born today. If you're not interested, we have others in line who will take it in a heartbeat. Decide before you leave here today whether your client wants to purchase or pass up this opportunity."

Anger flowed through Henry, his blood pressure soaring through the roof. Before he could unleash his fury, the predator lunged at the cow in a flash of savagery that demanded his full attention. His jaw hung open as he watched the genetic freak devour the flesh from bone in a grotesque display of unrivaled power. Hardly able to believe his eyes, he blinked and examined the mutant before him. Without a second guess, Henry knew what he needed to do.

"I'll see that they wire the rest of the money into your company's account," Henry said, his tone riddled with awe as he handed over the briefcase. He pulled out his cell phone and went through his contact. "And I'll make the arrangements to have it delivered to my client by the end of the week."

DAY AT THE BEACH

Samuel Grant leaned back in his beach chair and nestled his toes into the warmth of the sand while he read his sons-in-law's latest novel. As the setting sun melted into the horizon, shades of orange and pink bled into the ocean. But now, impending clouds drifting over the Gulf of Mexico cast a dreary glow over the Florida Keys. A cold breeze whistled as waves pounded the beach with a relentless fury. The ocean exhaled a strong and overpowering stench of deep brine, churned up by the strong winds, suffocating the stiff aroma of his drink.

When he reached the end of his current chapter, he slipped the bookmark between the pages and closed the book, careful to place it on a dry spot on the flimsy plastic table beside him. He leaned over the chair and grabbed his glass of whiskey, the ice clattering as he took a sip. Overhead, a plastic kite rustled boisterously in the wind; the cheerfully dyed bird-shaped kite fluttered in the swift current, accompanied by children's laughter. Intrigued, Samuel watched with a child-like sense of awe. Having lost track of time, he finished the last swig of his whiskey in one gulp. The chilled amber liquid delivered a pleasing warmth throughout his body.

Drowned out by the thunderous roar of the ocean, the growing crowd surprised Samuel. With the last rays of daylight fading, he took a moment to enjoy the view. For most of his married life, it had been his dream to retire to the Florida coast with his wife, Amanda. They lived in Big Pine Key for three years together before she passed away from a heart attack. There were no warning signs, and she was an avid jogger. But that's the problem with genetics—some people are just born with hidden defects.

He knew she wouldn't have wanted him to dwell on it, but he never moved on. Every day since he got over the shock of her death, he came back to the same spot on the beach where they would both read their books. It came as a surprise when their son Daniel announced that his husband William was publishing a book. That was almost ten years ago, and seven books ago. All of them made it to the bestsellers list, all of them steamy romance novels. Typically, not Samuel's first choice, but Amanda couldn't get enough of them, and reading them made him feel close to her. And he still brought her chair with him every time so he could pretend she was sitting there next to him, reading along as she hummed the latest catchy tune on the radio to herself—often off-key, but always energetic. If the beach was empty, which it often was, he would even pour a drink of her favorite wine for himself before chasing it down with his favorite whiskey.

Lost deep in his thoughts, he didn't see the Frisbee until it thumped off his chest and landed in his lap. Surprised, he lurched backward in his chair, spilling his drink over his shirt and shorts.

"Sorry, mister," a college kid called out. She shuffled

toward him, her feet dragging through the sand, the wind blowing her hair over her eyes. "That one got away from me."

All Samuel could do was laugh. "The wind is strong tonight." He held out the Frisbee for her. For a moment, she didn't seem to notice; a vacant stare dawned on her face. After an awkward pause, she snatched the Frisbee and stuffed it under her arm.

"Is that the latest Compton book, *Sailor's Salt?*" She reached out and picked up the novel. Her face blushed a brilliant shade of red. "Is it as hot as the last one?" she giggled as she admired the two shirtless men on the cover. When she finished ogling the models, she flipped the novel over in her hand, her eyes darting back and forth as she read the description on the back.

Samuel chuckled. "I think it's sizzling."

"My dad would hate knowing that I read these books," she said. "And he would have something to say about you reading it at the beach." She opened the cover, squinting to read the raving reviews on the inside cover in the dying light.

"Well," Samuel paused, "I guess he's entitled to his opinion, but..."

"Oh," the girl interrupted, "no, he isn't. I love my dad, but he's a backwards asshole." She rolled the book over in her hand, admiring it. "You don't need to waste your breath on a politically correct statement. I'll say it for you...He's an asshole."

Samuel laughed. "Just misinformed. But yeah, I guess you would call him an asshole." They both shared a laugh. "Do you want to know a secret?"

The girl sank into the empty chair. Samuel grimaced for a moment, biting his tongue, and suppressed the urge to tell her to get out of the chair. There was no way she could have known it belonged to his deceased wife. Plus, she was young enough to be his granddaughter. She eyed him intently, the book clutched tight to her chest. Samuel fought his eyes as they wandered down her cleavage, willing them to meet the dreamy gaze of her ultramarine eyes. Lost in her beautiful gaze for a moment, Samuel forced himself back into reality.

"Dean Compton is my son-in-law," he said. "And they dedicated this one to me."

"That's so cool," the girl gushed. She opened the cover again. "It's nice to meet you, Mr. Grant. But they made the autograph out to Amanda. Who's that, your wife?"

Samuel ignored the sadness in his heart, taking a moment to compose himself before speaking. "That's right, it's Mrs. Grant's book. I locked mine up in a shadow box."

In a moment of recognition, the girl sat up straight in the chair. Her pupils enlarged in the dying light, forming two drops of oil threatening to engulf her deep blue eyes. She darted up and stared at the chair with a guilty expression on her face. "Forgive me. I should have known this seat belonged to someone else. Hope she doesn't mind."

"I'm sure she doesn't," Samuel lied. If his wife had seen that, jealousy would have soured her for the rest of the evening.

With a sly smile, she walked back toward her friends. "I'm sorry about your shirt." Samuel admired her toned body as she left, wishing he noticed her earlier when the sun still cast its brilliant rays over the beach.

"That's alright," Samuel drawled, trying to sound natural despite his racing heart. He stood still until she vanished into the shadows before turning his attention back to his little area. Unfortunately, the stain on his khaki shorts, dark against the light tan fabric, formed a wide arc like he'd pissed himself. Embarrassed, he packed up his stuff and started making his way back toward the boardwalk. Besides, with the day changing into dusk and the approaching storm, he wanted to get a head start on getting his house prepared for the approaching hurricane. Even though his home was perched on a high bluff, the wind would wreak havoc on his windows if they didn't get the storm shutters secured in place before the wind really picked up. And flood waters found a way into his crawl space every time it rained.

It must have been past 7 pm because the dull glow of the automatic arc sodium lights was already on. He cursed under his breath at the busy crowd on the boardwalk. Tonight was the last night before Hurricane Rose was set to lash out at the Florida coast tomorrow evening. Everyone was getting out to enjoy the calm before the storm. He glanced down at his shorts again and realized he must look like a drunk who pissed himself. If it wasn't for the overpowering salt air, he would have smelt like it. He never mixed his whiskey, just one of his rules from his days in the corps that he never let go.

Without thinking about it, he strolled along the riverbank all the way back to the bridge just before the parking lot. He diverted from the wooden planks and walked along the muddied edge. In the darkness, he missed the tipped-over sign, the reflective yellow paint hidden beneath a layer of mud. But because the sun had dipped below the horizon, the faint light never illuminated the reflective border of the sign meant to draw attention. Or the words scrawled in red across the sign: *Beware of Dangerous Wildlife*.

He strolled away from the crowd, the sounds of laughter and chatter fading behind him. A savage wind howled, shaking the palm leaves into a racket. The banks of the riverbed were wide and flat near the mouth of the calm river. As he made his way further along the bank, the slope increased steadily, and the sandy surface turned into mud, his feet slipping out from beneath him with every few steps. Away from the lamp posts, and with the dense jungle enclosing him, the night fell over him like a blanket. Taking a glance over his shoulder, he couldn't see anything except the pale glow of the lamps along the boardwalk. All around him, frogs croaked and crickets chirruped. Even though he was only half a mile away from the boardwalk, he imagined himself in the depths of the darkest jungle.

The moon crested the horizon, its frail silver glow is still weak, offering only a faint trace of light to navigate by. Steep embankments towered over the calm surface on either side of the babbling stream. "Damn," he muttered to himself, deciding to make his way to the top of the bank. It would be difficult to move around the dense foliage. But at least he wouldn't wind up falling into the river. He noticed a small tree just above it, its gnarled roots stretching down toward him. If he could reach the roots, he could haul himself up over the ledge instead of backtracking.

With a leap, he jumped up the side of the bank, his feet sliding out from beneath him. He reached out for the root. The slick surface slipped out of his grasp, and he collapsed face-first into the muddied bank. A sour taste flooded his mouth as the impact drove mud over the back of his tongue. With nothing to brace himself, he tumbled into the water with a splash, cursing the entire way down. He landed in the murky bed of the river and felt the mud squish beneath him as it fanned out into the muddied water. Desperate to get rid of the filthy swamp water in his mouth, he cupped his hands and drank from the river. Filled with grit, the water did little to flush the taste of the swamp from his mouth, only adding to his misery.

Another boisterous splash filled the night air. Nearby, a flock of birds fluttered from the trees into the night sky. Once more, he cursed under his breath. The stale stench of the swamp water filled his nostrils, as a mouthful of filthy water filtered down into the back of his throat. Once he suppressed his coughing fit, he placed his hands into the muck and pushed himself up, noticing that his backpack was much lighter.

He unslung the bag from his shoulder, finding that his wife's chair was missing from the loose straps that trailed down into the water. The toggles bobbed along the surface. It didn't take long to find the missing folding chair. A sliver of moonlight reflected off the steel arm. Only a foot deep, the soft riverbed made it arduous to traverse. And the muck sucked his feet deep beneath the surface until it coated his shins. Every step required his full effort and attention. Behind him, something disturbed the natural rhythm of the current. Distracted, the soft splashes went unnoticed by Samuel.

It didn't take him long to catch up to his wife's chair. The gentle calm of the river moved along without a ripple on the surface, virtually still in the tiny alcove where it was caught in a tangle of branches. If it had been daylight, he would have noticed the ripples coursing over the surface, closing in on him.

Samuel bent down and reached into the water, snatched the arm of the folding chair, and yanked it from a cluster of branches. Surprised as the chair slipped from the tangle with ease, he stumbled through the water. His fumbling feet splashed through the current, drowning out the sounds of the low, guttural growl.

When he turned to head back to the shore, a blur of motion caught the corner of his eye. An enormous black reptilian mass maneuvered through the water with surprising agility. Half hidden beneath the river's surface, jagged scales protruded from the murkiness. Before he could react, the water separated as an explosion of river water blinded him. A searing pain radiated from his calf as serrated teeth tore through his flesh, tearing muscle and ligaments from the bone. A terrified scream escaped his throat, choked out by the river as he slammed into the rippling currents. But no one heard his desperate plea for help.

In the back of his mind, he conjured images of some insidious creature. With its jaws locked over his leg, the creature spun, pulling Samuel into a death roll with it. The horizon and murky depths of the shallow water swirled in his vision, blending into a maddening, chaotic image. He cried out, and his lungs filled with more disgusting swamp water as the river rushed into his gaping mouth, the air drawing the river down into his lungs with force. Desperate, he tried to lash out against the beast, flailing his arms as his vision continued to whirl around him. The meaty side of his fist struck stony scales, bloodying the pads of his hands as the toughened armor tore his fist into ribbons of red, mangled flesh.

The intense pain in his knee gave way to a loud, wet pop as the knee tore from its socket. Mercifully, Samuel found himself free of the creature's death lock. Survival instincts took over, and he lurched forward, trying to get to his feet. His left foot was planted deep in the mud, but he stumbled back into the river when he tried to plant his right. There was nothing from the knee down. Blood gushed from the yawning wound. The current spread the gore downriver in a swelling red stain. Behind him, the disgusting sounds of chewing echoed from the apex predator's mouth, wet and sucking, gargled and grotesque.

Samuel screamed into the silent night for help, his voice drowned out by the raucous winds and joyous chatter at the beach. No one heard his final, agonized cries as the creature stalked him toward the muddy bank. Samuel's fingers clawed into the muck, bits of decaying bark and soil crammed beneath his fingernails. Too afraid to look over his shoulder, he hauled himself toward the muddy bank, his eyes fixed on the dangling branches. He felt the immense presence of the creature as it scurried toward him. The water splashed and the ground trembled as the creature exited the water.

Jagged claws shredded the flesh of Samuel's left leg, dragging him beneath its gigantic, scaly frame. Spoiled, hot breath poured from the pit of the creature's stomach. Filed, yellow-stained teeth rimmed its massive jaws. Ropes of bloodied saliva sprang from the predator's mouth as a roar cut through the phlegm that coated its throat. A sickly, feverish yellow eye glared down at Samuel. Its jaw raised high into the air, gaping wide, its gums coated in Samuel's blood. The beast's jaw clamped over Samuel's head, severing his spine with brutal ease.

CATCH AND RELEASE

Art wiped his forehead with the back of his sleeve. Heat billowed from the fishing vessel's engine block as he toiled to fix the problem. He wasn't much of a mechanic, but he couldn't afford to pay anyone to resolve it for him. With the approaching hurricane and the cargo in the immense wooden crate below, he found himself desperate to get underway—he even contemplated praying.

He fidgeted with the numerous toggles, not knowing the correct sequence, and pressed the red ignition button. The diesel engine sputtered and choked, spewing black plumes of undulating smoke. Art cursed and threw the wrench back into the toolbox, the metallic racket drowned out by the mechanical grinding. For a moment, the motor screeched a high-pitched, sputtering squeal as the entire engine rattled against the bracket. Then, as if taking pity on Art, the noises calmed, and the motor settled into a working groove.

"Thank fuck!" Art shouted in triumph and pumped his fist. He glanced over his shoulder at the wooden crate that filled the cargo hold of his ship, ordinarily reserved for the day's catch. But these were desperate times. Once he made this delivery, he would never put himself in this situation again—no matter how much money they paid him. Now he regretted answering the phone call from Mr. Collins. With no one around to hear him but the diabolical occupant of the crate, he felt ridiculous, letting out a triumphal cheer, pumping his fist in the air. But he no longer cared about his fellow passenger's opinion.

Art was feeling stressed ever since that oddball Anders had stepped foot on his vessel. Anders gave him strict orders on how to care for the genetically engineered freak. And enough food to feed an army to keep the creature alive for the journey from the lab in South Africa to the States. He even had Art sign a plethora of confidentiality forms before loading the creature onto Art's fishing vessel. Whatever slumbered inside that crate, Art would never be allowed to tell another soul.

The past year had been rough. Even with the payment received from his new arrangement under the table, he couldn't afford to lose another fishing vessel. He didn't have any other way to launder the money from his lucrative side hustle. After spending months in jail last year for possession, and missing the commercial season, his money bled out of his account. To make matters worse, his girlfriend emptied their joint bank account, leaving him with nothing but a severe case of the clap. His supplier refused to deal with him after getting caught, leaving him scrambling to find a source of income.

With no one in the state of Florida willing to deal with him, he found himself forced into a corner, trafficking for a Columbian drug lord turned connoisseur of exotic animals. A cartel in Mexico had once let him run drugs up the eastern seaboard all the way to New York. Now, they refused to trust him with any more of their product because of his inability to escape the cops and his loose tongue. But the creature in that crate proved far more dangerous. He climbed the ladder into the cabin, eying the locked crate with the tranquilized beast worth over twenty million dollars. He couldn't afford to fail again. Now, with Hurricane Rose threatening, he scrambled to save his ship. And the vicious reptile in the crate. If he made it far enough north before the storm hit, he would find shelter in a cove from the rough seas. Then he would make his way back down into the Keys once the waters calmed and into the Atlantic.

He eased the throttle forward, not wanting to stress the engine. The choppy waves rattled the fishing vessel, threatening to push the engine past its limits and beyond Art's ability to repair them. If he couldn't make it to calmer waters in time, his backup plan would be to abandon ship and get as far away from that savage freak of nature in the crate. And if that abomination got loose, he wouldn't be the only person in danger; they would need a swat team to kill it.

A blanket of darkness encompassed the sky. Pale moonlight glowed from behind a patch of clouds overhead, offering a scant trace of light to navigate by. His spotlight wasn't working, and his running lights were sporadic. He would have to stay up all night to cover the distance he had lost since breaking down.

The boat struck something solid, the hull shuddered against the impact. "Christ," Art swore. He walked over to the railing and peered over the side, expecting to find the side of his boat torn open by a jagged rock. There was nothing there except the inky waters rocking his boat. "Must have grazed it," he said to himself. As he turned to head back into the cabin, a loud splash caught his attention.

When he glanced over the side, the blackness played tricks on his eyes. A slithering caudal fin swept beneath the boat, heading toward land. It slammed against the hull with a thunderous blow that shook the decking. Art dashed to the other side, trying to glimpse the creature swimming past. Nothing but open water between his ship and the shore. Another violent knock jarred the boat, forcing Art to brace himself against the ramshackle wooden railing.

"What the hell?" Art mumbled, his jaw hanging open. A sliver of moonlight caught in a glassy, soulless eye. His heart leaped into his throat, blocking the free flow of air, choking him. A gray shadow stretched beneath the surface twenty feet, the rolling waves exposing the mammoth girth of the hideous shark in frightening intervals. The creature studied Art for a moment before disappearing beneath the choppy waves. Reports of giant sharks on the Eastern Seaboard had been on the rise for months.

Art raced into the cabin and pushed the throttle full ahead. Heavy vibrations rattled the ship as it sped across the waves. He didn't care anymore if his fishing ship fell apart. All he wanted was to get away from the freakish monstrosity. Thick plumes of blackened smoke belched from below deck. The fetid stench of diesel tainted the salt air, filling the cabin in a foggy haze. The polluted air stung his eyes. Tears welled in the ducts, pooling in the corner, clouding his vision. He coughed violently, spitting a thick wad of phlegm into his palm.

"Jesus Christ," Art said, throwing the door open and stumbling outside, trying to catch a breath of fresh air. The vegetation along the shoreline blended into the dusky horizon, creating a swirling backdrop of blackness. Disoriented, Art never noticed the warning buoy. His boat motored straight ahead with no one at the helm, on a collision path with the craggy island.

The rocks tore into the hull of the ship. Wooden planks cracked and splintered into slivers. The exploding fragments of wood sprayed in a wide arc. One sliver caught Art's shoulder, piercing through his subtle flesh with ease. He brought his hands up to the wound, the tacky warmth oozing through his fingers.

The aft end of the boat caught the rocks, jolting the fishing vessel abruptly. With his hand protecting his shoulder, Art didn't brace himself for the impact. He hurtled over the railing, spinning head over heels before plummeting into the ocean. Shocked by the precipitous temperature change, Art's hands left his shoulder as he trod water. His work boots felt like two lead weights tied to the end of his legs, straining every muscle in both thighs.

The engine continued to struggle, dragging the boat along and tearing the side wide open. A deluge of water gushed inside, the boat listing heavily to the port side. Art rolled over on his back and kicked himself away. The mast of the ship slapped against the water as it capsized. A giant tidal wave crashed over Art, sending him hurtling through the water, gasping for breath. His backside collided with something hard and rigid. When he righted himself, he found himself among the jagged rocks that housed the buoy.

Desperate and propelled by adrenaline, Art pulled himself up onto the buoy. Rusted out and covered in barnacles, the metal surface nipped at his exposed flesh. He sat with his back against the frame of the buoy and watched his ship sink below the surface in a spectacle of smoke and bubbling water. The life raft bobbed upside down in the water, drifting aimlessly amongst the detritus.

The wind whipped over the surface of the ocean, carrying the deep salt air with it. Chilled to the bone, Art wrapped his arms around his chest in a clumsy embrace, trying to rub the warmth back into his body. A trickle of blood oozed down his shoulder, the sharp pain a dull throb now. With his fears forgotten, he readied himself to leap into the water and swim for the raft. If he could overturn it, he would find his way back onto dry land.

Fear gripped Art's chest as broken fragments of the crate floated to the surface. "Oh, dear God," he muttered to the heavens, his head tilted up toward the sky. The caudal fin cut through the choppy waves with ease, pushing through the debris. From his position, Art watched in horror as the shadowed form beneath the surface swam with a sinister grace, powerful and methodical.

Art stood up and climbed higher onto the buoy. The rusted edge cut into his hand, tearing ragged hunks of flesh from his palm as he hauled himself up. He sat on a beam that ran horizontal to the base. His gaze wandered toward the shore. Fixed on a wooden shack at the top of a cliff, he scanned the immediate area for any signs of movement. He wasn't sure, but he thought he saw someone on the property. Trying to get their attention, he waved his arms over his head, crossing them back and forth as he shouted out for help.

When he turned back toward the ocean, it didn't take him long to spot the circling shark. From his new vantage point, he had a clearer view of the shark's daunting form. Its tail sliced back and forth, elegantly propelling it through the ocean current.

But something else caught his eye, a second shadow lurking beneath the surface that dwarfed the mammoth shark. Art screamed for help, hoping that the wind would carry his cry to the shore. Behind him, the ocean erupted into chaos. Terrified, Art trembled as he turned to witness the horror taking place down below.

***

The dark blue color evaporated from the water as the monster glided toward the camouflaged silhouette of the tiger shark above. Drifting toward the surface, the creature's jaw unhinged, opening wide, ready to strike at the exposed belly. Unaccustomed to the ocean, the force of the current threw it off its projected course. At the last moment, the shark thrust its mighty tail, propelling it out of harm's way as the heinous beast exploded out of the surface.

An avalanche of water sprayed in a dazzling arc. The ancient reptile never left the ocean completely. Its gruesome jaws and upper body lunged out of the water before slamming back down into the waves with a thunderous splash. Bubbles churned in the water as the beast sank back under the surface. When they cleared, the creature spotted the shark circling. It tried to keep up with the swift movements, but the tiger shark was too agile for the methodical movements of the creature out of its element. With the battlefield a distinct disadvantage for the apex predator, the beast used its colossal size and ferocity to scare off the shark.

With every passing circle, the tiger shark narrowed the gap between them, getting a better picture of its adversary. As the shark swam into clear view, the predator got a better view of its opponent. The black stripes that covered the creature's gray scales filtered into view, becoming an asymmetrical pattern, as if drawn freehand by an artist experimenting with different brushes. Curious, the tiger made one last rotation, studying the alpha before scuttling away, vanishing with one mighty thrust of its tail.

***

Shivering in fear, Art watched in horror as the scaled reptile erupted from the ocean. A downpour of salt water drenched the buoy, splattering against the metal frame in a torrent of dull thuds. The vociferous spattering sounded like thunder in his ears, and the salt water stung his eyes, rendering him blind and deaf. Art pinned his body against the metal frame, grasping his arms around the metal beam in a bear hug, holding on for dear life.

In the pandemonium, Art couldn't get a clear picture of the monster. There were only two things he could be certain of from his brief glimpse: it was a reptile and it was enormous. When Art mustered the courage, he opened his eyes and gazed out over the ocean. His body shuddered with terrified apprehension. There was a giant circle of churned-white water that stood out against the vivid blue surface. His eyes darted back and forth, frantically searching for any sign of the ungodly creature.

Overhead, seagulls congregated, cawing incisively. Certainly no expert in animal behavior, Art remembered something his grandfather told him once upon a time. Seagulls had a sixth sense for opportunities to earn a free meal.

Art's gaze wandered over the expanse of deep blue ocean toward the shore, speculating where that reptilian creature could be lurking. The waves carried white tops toward the shore in rolling swells. As the undulating motion of the ocean pounded the buoy, the metal structure listed at a steep angle. He stared out toward the endless ocean. Threatening storm clouds approached, dark gray and ominous. A flash of lightning snaked through the bleak sky. Wind carried the first signs of rain from the storm, far ahead of Hurricane Rose. The first warning of the dreadful weather approaching.

Art knew he couldn't stay here much longer, the waves already crashing over the base of the buoy, sending a shiver through the entire structure. But he didn't think he'd be able to make it to the shore with that predator lurking in the depths. Tears tracked down his cheek as he struggled to decide on how he wanted to die.

THE KEYS TO THE KINGDOM

Exposed portions of the ancient Key Largo Limestone coral reef formed the basis of the Florida Keys. A series of coral cay archipelago located off the southern coast of Florida enjoyed a tropical climate closer to the Caribbean than to the rest of mainland Florida. There were several small transitional keys and islands composed of sandy accumulations of limestone grains produced by plants and marine organisms deposited around small areas of this exposed reef. Tourists could frequent beautiful beaches throughout the day and the Middle and Lower Florida Keys were among the few remaining dark-sky locations accessible by car. These brilliant southern skylines offered an unobstructed view of the Milky Way, free of light pollution. That, along with its distinctive flora and fauna, made it a popular tourist destination. A diverse range of both temperate, such as red maple and slash pine, and tropical flora like mahogany and Jamaican dogwood were common throughout the keys. It was also the home to many unique animals, such as the Key deer and the Key Largo woodrat.

Connected by an overseas highway dubbed Seven Mile Bridge, the inhabitants of the Keys could travel from south Key Largo to Key West, passing through all the densely populated cities along the way. These islands formed along the Florida Straits defined one edge of Florida Bay, dividing the Atlantic Ocean to the East from the Gulf of Mexico to the Northwest. Within the Keys, a large section of the mainland belonged to the Everglades National Park. In Monroe County, Big Pine Key was home to over 20,000 residents of the United States. Within Big Pine Key was the Blue Hole, an abandoned rock quarry, and the only freshwater lake in the Florida Keys. It was home to various wildlife, such as birds, snakes, alligators, and green iguanas. Tourists could find the visitor center for the National Key Deer Refuge in Big Pine Key. Built atop a hill that overlooked the Blue Hole, the Big Pine Sportsplex was home to many national sporting events since the COVID-19 Pandemic. Because of its breathtaking scenery and isolated location, it became the ideal location to host events and maintain control over any potential outbreak.

The visitors' center for the Blue Hole National Key Deer Refuge was nestled amongst verdant foliage below the Big Pine Sportsplex. Hidden amongst a tangle of palm trees, bushes, and overgrowth, the red tin roof of the visitors' center poked out of the jungle ceiling. And once the last of the tourists visiting the Florida Keys left, avoiding the upcoming hurricane season, the building became a frequent hangout for drug users and the homeless. The new residents of the visitors' center knew the workers' schedule and made themselves scarce on the weekends when the park opened again. Now, with the storm closing the park for the weekend, the building was full. Travelers from all over the keys had settled here by the hundreds.

A single trail leading through the dense foliage wound up the hill, the falling rain already turning the hard-packed dirt into a slippery muck. This access road, wide enough for a single vehicle, was the only escape from the Blue Hole. Hurricane Rose approached, bringing with her treacherous flood waters, torrential downpour, and a gigantic reptilian beast. And the diabolical abomination brought its insatiable appetite with it.

IN A RUSH

Unable to go back to sleep after Daniel's work phone woke them up, William headed down to the kitchen while his husband showered. Daniel took the call in the hallway, keeping his voice hushed, believing that his partner was still asleep. William couldn't hear the one-sided conversation clearly, but enough to realize that whatever the dilemma was, Daniel was being called in early to deal with it.

Since the Florida coast stayed balmy all year round, it encouraged homeless communities to migrate to the streets. While not high on the city's priority list, Daniel remarked that getting them off the streets to someplace safe before the level-five hurricane arrived would ultimately get addressed. And assuming that was the reason for Daniel's early morning rise, William decided to help by getting breakfast started. Water gushed and gurgled down the drain and into the ancient plumbing system of their condo as Daniel shut off the shower. William knew from experience that it would only take him about fifteen minutes to get dressed. That wouldn't give him much time, but he wanted to make sure his husband got something to eat before he headed out for what would undoubtedly be a long day.

William shuffled down the hallway, admiring the random collection of art hanging from the walls. Each piece evoked a memory of a vacation or sporadic day trip to some nearby exotic location. They often found themselves on a friend's yacht traveling toward some new adventure or heading out on a fishing trip for marlins or sharks—one of the many benefits of living near the Gulf of Mexico. To William, this hallway was a stroll down memory lane, bringing him joyous memories every time. But the kitchen always seemed to bring him back to reality. He abhorred cooking, preferring to order out. He tried to avoid the stove at all costs, and it went days without being used. But the coffee machine was a different story.

The first thing he did as he entered the kitchen was to open the bag of coffee beans, inhale the invigorating aroma, and scoop a cup of them into the grinder. As he flicked the switch, the obnoxious rattle of the blades roared until the beans had been ground into a fine powder. He dumped a generous helping of coffee into the filter, not bothering to measure, and switched the machine on. The water reservoir gurgled, drawing water through the tubes, then the first drips landed in the empty glass urn. William wandered over to the fridge and considered preparing eggs, but the early dawn grogginess deterred his ambition, and he closed the fridge door. Instead, he opened the brown paper bag from the local bakery. The savory smell of chives wafted into the kitchen. Daniel took out two of the cheddar bagels, placed them into the stainless-steel toaster, closed the bag back up, and proceeded to the fridge. Rustling through the shelves, he found the garlic cream cheese behind the orange juice. He didn't bother to put the bagels down yet, waiting for Daniel to finish his morning routine.

Behind him, the welcoming aroma of woodsy coffee filled the room as the percolator gargled the last drops into the urn. He shuffled across the kitchen to the cupboard and pulled down two mugs, pouring his own all the way to the rim. Daniel took cream and sugar in his, so he left enough room in his mug before placing the urn back. He took a sip of the bitter coffee, reminding himself not to let Daniel choose the brand the next time they visited the supermarket. William sat at the kitchen table, keeping the window in his peripheral, and turned on the news. He turned the channel to the local news, but he didn't need anyone to tell him the forecast. Outside, the wind boomed against the side of the building, tossing the first specks of rain from Hurricane Rose against the glass. Below him, a concrete jungle sprawled out all around him. They were miles away from the coast in the heart of Big Pine Key. Still, he predicted evacuation orders to be issued soon. Just last year, they'd received two. And Channel Five had already anticipated this storm to be far worse than anything they experienced last year.

The noise of Daniel rummaging through his dresser drawer signaled to William it was time to put the bagel into the toaster. By the time the toaster popped, Daniel had walked down the hallway and into the living room. William recognized the urgency of his steps, and that he would head straight for the porch and out the door before without saying a word. So, he spread the cream cheese onto Daniel's bagel, threw it in a paper bag, and poured the coffee into Daniel's thermos.

"Hey, I'm sorry," Daniel said when he noticed William walking toward him. "In a rush, sweetheart." His hair, still wet from the shower, shimmered pitch black, hiding any traces of gray that had crept in over the last three years; it reminded William of when they first met.

William handed over the paper bag and thermos, embracing Daniel with a tight hug. Heat from the shower radiated from Daniel's body. His shoulder holster dug into William's chest, but at least Daniel's service pistol remained locked away at the precinct. "I know, dear," he said, taking a step back. Daniel was scrolling through his phone, his gaze fixed on the screen. "What's wrong?"

"Did my father call last night?"

William shook his head. "No, he didn't. Were you expecting him to call?"

"It's just strange he didn't call to remind us to batten down the hatches," Daniel chuckled. "You know how he is. I can hear him now, going over his checklist and ensuring everything is in order."

William smirked and let out a hearty burst of laughter. "You'll always be a kid to him. I think it's kinda sweet," he added. With a watchful eye, he watched Daniel check his screen again before slipping his phone into the pocket of his black-uniformed pants. "Is everything alright?"

"I tried calling him a few times." A worried expression crossed Daniel's face. "I'm sure it's nothing." He hesitated. "Would you mind checking in on him if you can't get in touch with him?"

Unable to ignore those grayish-blue eyes, William nodded his head. "Of course." How could he say no, even if he wanted? "I'll take the truck down right after lunch before the storm gets too bad."

"Thanks, dear." Daniel leaned in and gave William one last hug before opening the door. "Just be careful. We've been told that they are on standby to declare a state of emergency. The latest reports are predicting the storm is going to land a devastating blow to the Keys."

"I'll be careful," William said. "Love you."

"Love you more," Daniel said as he left.

William wandered back to the kitchen table and continued to watch the news as he finished his bagel. The rain fell harder now, splattering against the window in big oval drops as the wind drove it in from the ocean. The morning was growing dim as the clouds rushed in overhead. During a commercial break, William tried calling his father-in-law, but he didn't answer. When he finished his coffee, he grabbed a quick shower and get dressed. He needed to get to his appointment with his editor so they could go over the revisions on his latest novel. Then he would drive over to Samuel's house before it got too late. It would be an hour's drive to the coast where his father-in-law lived in this weather. And another twenty minutes to reach his place near the beach. Before he got ready for his shower, he sent a text to his editor, hoping that they could meet earlier, freeing up his morning to head over to Samuel's before lunch. He didn't want to get caught near the coast in this storm.

While he was in the shower, an alert highlighted in red scrolled across the television screen, warning viewers of the treacherous condition of the ocean. Waves preceding Hurricane Rose had already battered the coast, causing several ships to crash off the southern shore of Big Pine Key. By the time William got dressed, he realized he still had time to waste before meeting with the editor. He grabbed another cup of coffee and sat at the kitchen table to watch some television. On the television, he surfed the channels, stopping when he saw a familiar face. A woman wearing an orange wool knit cap with long, jet-black hair flowing out of it stood in front of a Canadian Coast Guard Ship. Her puffy red jacket concealed any figure she might have had, turning her body into a block. Ice formed on the fur around her collar. Vapor accompanied her every word as she spoke to the reporter about her expedition in the Arctic.

When "Kate Hamilton" appeared along the bottom he recognized her as one of the fabled survivors of the claimed megalodon attack off the coast of Newfoundland six months ago. No one ever provided any proof or explanation of the events, only conflicting stories and tall tales of a cover-up by Labrynth Oils remained, most notably the unexplained and often debated way that television star Andy Grant had disappeared into the Atlantic, his body never recovered. They made him out to be an action hero, battling an ancient sea monster to save everyone. The only problem with the story was that no one could produce any evidence the massive shark existed. Another tall tale from those crazy Newfies.

Ridiculed by the media for her outlandish claims, Kate Hamilton now led an exploratory expedition through the Arctic in search of oil for the same company she accused of covering up the shark attack off the coast of Newfoundland. William laughed at the irony and thought that it would make for a great story if she only took the job to sabotage Labrynth Oils as revenge for what she claimed they did. He considered writing a novel about that and laughed out loud at the prospect. "That would be silly," he said to himself.

His phone buzzed, interrupting his train of thought. His editor was available to meet right now at the coffee shop just around the corner. William turned off the television and grabbed his jacket before heading out into the rain.

PRIMAL INSTINCT

As Hurricane Rose approached the Florida coastline, the brewing storm churned the waters with savage ferocity. Waves over five feet tall smashed onto the beaches. Already within the clutches of Rose's formidable force, the nutrient-rich waters from the ocean floor ascended to the surface, which began a lethal chain reaction. Generated by the storm surge, Rose drove gallons of saltwater into the freshwater area of the Blue Hole. All animals had a built-in instinct that allowed them to predict evolving weather patterns. When barometric pressure dropped ahead of a hurricane, some sea creatures sought shelter within deeper waters. Others remained within their natural habitat. For apex predators that chose to remain closer to shore, this created an imbalance in the food chain, forcing the creature to seek another food source.

Hurricane Rose drove millions of gallons of saltwater into the wetlands that protected mainland Florida from the ocean. The wildlife was driven deeper inland by the influx of saltwater, forcing the predator to give chase. The creature that had feasted on Samuel had a ravenous hunger. Ordinarily hard-wired to remain patient and opportunistic, the fear induced by the storm, and lack of options, drove the ancient animal to attack everything it came across. The alpha predator, disoriented by the storm, tracked inland, lured towards civilization by the scent of prey. And its extraordinary ability to take down animals of great size made it a formidable predator. Honed by millions of years of evolution, this new iteration would sit alone at the top of the food chain, both on land and at sea. No other predators could rival the beast that lurked in the shadows, stalking its prey as Hurricane Rose pushed the murky waters inland. Animals close enough to sense the ancient beast's presence fled, trying to find high ground on the other side of Big Pine Key. Strange noises filled its reptilian ears. Not accustomed to the boisterous racket of the city limits, but not afraid of them, the monstrous creature crept toward the concrete jungle in search of prey.

FOLLOWING ORDERS

Slurping his coffee as he waited at the lights, Daniel embraced the jolt of caffeine as it coursed through his veins. Traffic was heavy today. Everybody was out at the last minute, stalking up on provisions before the stores shut down. Rain pattered off the windshield with heavy thumps, propelled by the ferocious winds. The street lights swayed perilously. Powerful metallic groans screeched as the poles tottered back and forth, the light housing swaying at the mercy of the gales. There was no need for the wipers yet; as fast as the rain could fall, the wind swept it up and over the hood of his Ford Mustang.

He took a bite of his bagel and the melted cream cheese dribbled over his chin just as the light changed. The car behind him laid on the horn. Daniel was in uniform, and even though he wasn't in his police cruiser yet, he had to restrain himself from raising a middle finger to the driver behind him. He eased off the brake, rolled through the intersection, and turned down King Boulevard toward the Fifteenth Precinct. The car behind sped straight through the intersection, the driver shaking his fist at Daniel as he passed. He couldn't help but laugh as he watched the man's angered expression twist into dread as he recognized the uniform.

It was a straight drive all the way until the station., and with scarce traffic, it didn't take long. The industrial business district didn't bother to open today. Mostly car dealerships and industrial shops lined the streets. No one would rush out to visit these stores until after the storm, often after companies have paid the insurance money out. He pulled into the precinct and parked next to his partner's Harley Davidson, which had remained behind since last Tuesday. Harold was single and enjoyed driving around in his police cruiser, garnering the respectful gaze of the local females as he made the drive along the beach toward his home. Not wanting to get soaked, Daniel dashed across the parking lot toward the entrance. Before he reached the door, it swung open. Harold stood in the doorway with his raincoat zipped up to the chin.

"Thanks, man," Daniel said, reaching out and taking the edge of the door in his grasp. Harold stepped aside, allowing Daniel to get out of the elements.

"Grab your rain gear and let's go." A frown curled Harold's bottom lip. A set of unfamiliar keys dangled from his thumb inside the silver key ring.

"What about the captain's briefing?" Daniel asked, pausing before heading toward the locker room.

"He already moved ahead with it," Harold said, his hands fidgeting with the keys. "He's not mad you're late. Hell, he even mentioned you came in on your day off."

"So, what's the problem?" Daniel made his way down the corridor, Harold walking alongside him. When he entered the locker room, he noticed how bare the lockers were. Only two of the lockers remained filled with gear, his own and Ortez's, who was out of the country on vacation. With all the rain gear removed from their pegs, it was hard not to notice that everyone else was already out there. "How bad is it?"

"There was an accident last night," Harold said, his tone grave. He paused before continuing. "Some idiot crashed their fishing boat off Key Largo, near the guiding buoy."

"Someone we know?" Daniel asked, feeling a sense of creeping dread.

"Some ex-con who just got out of jail," Harold responded, his tone full of venom.

"So," Daniel paused, "what's the problem?"

"They sent Cheryl and Tim out to investigate earlier this morning," Harold said, fidgeting with something inside his locker. "We've lost communication with them, and they've been out of contact since 3 am."

"Fuck," Daniel sighed. "Has anyone gone to check up on them?"

"The brass spread the unit too thin. And then they ordered an evacuation on top of everything else going on. They've already alerted the national guard, and they are organizing relief efforts as we speak. Captain gave us strict orders. He said he'd go check on them himself and meet up with us later." Harold rushed to get out all the information, his words slurring together as if he were drunk. "Since we were the last team to head out, we're taking the bus to transport any homeless people we can find to the shelter."

"Where's the shelter being set up?" Daniel entered his locker combination, the door swung open with a rusted squeak.

"They're using the multiplex sports facility just off Kensington Street."

Daniel threw his rain slicker over his uniform and grabbed his hat. "Isn't that a little close to the wetlands?"

"Yeah," Harold sighed, "but the captain says because it's on top of Kensington Hill, it's the safest place left where we can still provide all the necessary amenities. There are several shelters throughout the town. But they're already full." From his expression, Daniel could tell Harold didn't agree.

"What do you mean, already full?"

"Money can buy you a lot of things," Harold said, disgust heavy on his tone.

Daniel rolled his eyes and shook his head. "But didn't they pass a law a few years back stating you couldn't purchase spots in emergency community shelters?"

Harold nodded his affirmation. "You're correct. However, they didn't purchase bunks in the shelters. They made sizable donations to town hall for future considerations. I guess they're cashing them in today."

"Fucking Christ," Daniel muttered.

Harold asked, "Do you want to drive the bus?"

"You drive," Daniel reached into his pocket. "I need to make a phone call to my husband."

"That's a good idea," Harold agreed. "I expect the power to go out at any minute now."

They hurried down the hallway toward the garage, their rubber boots squawking on the tiled floor. The precinct remained deserted. Outside, the rain thrummed against the roof and battered the side of the building. With the wind howling, the lights flickered as the power lines danced in the wind. They both gave a nod to Seth as they passed his office just outside the garage. He waved back, a fragile smile twitching on his weathered face. No longer able to work the streets, Seth handled the squadron's vehicles and kept them maintained year-round. The garage was empty except for the bus. Harold hurried inside, and the diesel engine started with a growl. The tight confines of the space amplified the boisterous grumble. Seth stared out at them from his tiny office window and worked the controls of the garage bay door. It opened with a thunderous clatter, the metal gears grinding. The panels of the door bounced up and down as it slid along the track. Wind-driven rain forced its way inside the garage. Small tributaries snaked across the floor, converging toward the drain built into the floor.

One giant windshield wiper tracked across the window. the arm reached down from the top of the window, and the large black blade endeavored to keep the driver's side window clear. Daniel called his husband, but the call went to voice mail. He cursed under his breath, waiting for the beep. "William, as soon as you get this, I want you to drop whatever you're doing and head to the Big Pine Sportsplex. I'm sure you're already at dad's by now, so don't let him talk you into staying there. Just do whatever it takes to convince him he needs to leave with you." Daniel paused. "I love you."

***

Captain Kyle Krusneski cursed out loud and pounded his fist against the dashboard of his truck. The abrasive pattern tore the skin from his knuckles, leaving behind flaps of dead skin. Angered and disheartened, he discovered Cheryl West's squad car abandoned in the parking lot leading to Golden Sands Beach. Waves pounded against the barricade, flooding over the tires of the cruiser before retreating. He picked up his radio, a buzz of static emitting from the cab's speakers. With the send button pushed, it interrupted the static warble, allowing him to speak into the receiver. "Come in, Officer West," he requested, his tone steady yet harsh, panic playing with his emotions. "Can you hear me? Come in, Officer West." He released the send button and a flood of static filled the cab.

Outside, the wind howled across the raging waves, carrying salt water from the ocean over the shore. The saline water left white streaks behind on the squad car's front window. Every procedure in the book told Kyle to call for backup. He backed up his truck and pulled in closer to the police car. Too high up, he struggled to see much through the windshield at this angle. Ignoring his better judgment as a police officer, he pushed open his car door, not bothering to call in his location in case something went wrong. The wind pushed the door back at him with unexpected force. With a sharp smack, the door slammed into his knees, the plastic cracking and splintering. This time, he kicked the door open, pinning it against the car with his foot before making his way outside. He used his back to brace the door, the wind driving it into his hip as he peered through the window.

Empty coffee cups and takeout bags littered the backseat. There was a half-eaten Boston cream donut left behind on the dashboard. Yellowish-white cream spilled over the dusty dashboard, oozing from the bite mark. Years on the streets kicked in, and Kyle pictured the scene as evidence of a satirical crime scene. The mud-caked floor was covered with more garbage. It was a wonder West could press the accelerator down to the floor. He made a mental note to bring it up with her after this was all over.

He used his radio to call Officer West again, this time hearing his own voice echo back to him from her squad car. Her receiver was dangling from the curly black cord, obscured by a brown takeout bag. "Christ." Kyle thumped the roof of her car with his fist. He added another mental note to ensure he spoke with Ben. How this ever passed inspection was beyond his comprehension.

Something wedged between the concrete pillars separating the beach from the parking lot caught Kyle's eye. A reflective strip captured and magnified the dull sunlight as the raging tide retreated. The tide rolled in over it, vanquishing it from view, then slid back to reveal it again. A poor attempt at the S.O.S signal, but it caught his attention. Despite the rough current flooding through the barrier, Kyle couldn't leave without checking it out. The reflective tape was far too familiar to ignore.

Now, as the waves crashed into the concrete barricades, arcs of white froth exploded high into the air, the wind tossing it around in all directions. Kyle shielded his eyes, wading through the deepening water as he approached the mysterious object. There was a nylon fabric wrapped around it, the retreating water tugging at the black garment. A wave smashed against the barricade, submerging the object beneath a raging, muddy current. Kyle reached out, grasping the cement with his bare hand, waiting for the tide to retreat. Something deep inside warned him not to touch the mysterious object.

When the water rushed away, it left behind a layer of silt and muck. Even Kyle held his breath as he reached out, grabbing the swatch of fabric. He tugged at it, and it held fast between the cement barricades. Kyle yanked it again, tearing the fabric, exposing the ghastly ashen flesh of Cheryl's severed arm. Bile surged from his stomach, burning his throat, and it spewed from his pursed lips. Thick ropes of vomit dangled from his mouth, the wind taking it away once it rolled down his chin.

As the wave washed over Cheryl's severed arm again, Kyle heard a solid thump on the other side of the barricade. He gathered his courage and leaned over the side. More vomit exploded from his stomach. He hurled over the cement barricade. The haggard remains of Cheryl's body stained the cement barricade, her lacerated carcass pinned against the roadblock. Everything below her ribcage was missing. Sand and seaweed settled over her severed spine, making it look like the rest of her body remained buried beneath the beach. Strands of shredded flesh flapped from the gnarled wound and bone-white shards of ribcage poked out from beneath the bloodied jacket.

Before Kyle could turn to leave, he bent over at the hips and emptied his stomach. His mouth burned with the vile, acidic fluids. He wiped ropes of vomit away with the back of his hand. The gushing water washed it away, leaving behind a film of silty sand and some of the thicker chunks of vomit on the cap of his work boots. He stared down at the ruined polish, trying anything to distract himself from his worst fears. An officer down and one missing. Even though his stomach was empty, he felt the muscles clench and turn over. Waves of nausea washed over him.

A faint sound carried on the wind. Muffled by blustering gusts, a desperate cry for help swirled through the air. It was impossible to tell where it was coming from. The storm diluted the plea and distorted the source. Kyle's mind raced and his heartbeat quickened. With his hopes raised, he cupped his hands and called out, "Officer Robichaud!"

The wind threw his voice back at him, taunting him with the cries for help that came from somewhere nearby. "Tim, are you out there?"

Before he continued his search, he radioed back to the station to explain the situation. But because it wasn't an emergency, the ambulance would attend to more dire situations across the Keys. After the call ended, he cursed repeatedly, letting his frustrations out. With all the emergency services dealing with destruction from Hurricane Rose, he marked the roadblock with police tape, secured what remained of Cheryl in a body bag from the back seat of his truck, and threw up one last time.

If it wasn't for the broken cries that rose above the crashing waves, Kyle could have taken better care of Cheryl. But he had to salvage this horrendous situation with at least something good to feel about. He leaped over the barricade, timing his movements to align with the retreating tide. The beach was shifting beneath his feet and his legs appeared to fall out from underneath him as the sand washed out from beneath his boots. Nearby, the cries rose out. "Tim, hold on!" He recognized the voice and dashed toward the craggy outcrop where the voice was coming from.

A WRITER'S BEST FRIENDS

William pushed the door to the coffee shop open, glad to get out of the blustering wind and rain. A bell jingled a charming, welcoming chorus overhead. Everyone's heads turned toward him. The barista behind the counter greeted him with a beaming smile as she frothed milk at the stainless-steel espresso machine. He waved back and tipped his hat to her. His eyes wandered around the room, spotting the regular customers in their usual spots and the day shift toiling about their daily routines. When they noticed him, they said hi or expressed their love for his latest novel, engaging him in small talk about it. Everyone here recognized him as a celebrity, and it did wonders for his ego. But it also made doing personal things a chore.

He made his way into the cloakroom, found the corner, and took an exaggerated time to hang his coat so that he could check his phone. After listening to the voice mail from Daniel, a wave of guilt washed over him for having kept his appointment with his editor. For a moment, he considered heading back outside and getting into his truck to make the drive to Samuel's place before the storm got any worse. Instead, he tried calling Daniel back, but the call went to voice mail. He didn't bother to leave a message. Instead, he ended the call with a regretful sigh—he felt awkward talking on the phone in public. Being a minor celebrity meant people were interested in every conversation, no matter how personal, and William didn't want his message to get analyzed today. With his head tilted down, he headed back into the coffee shop, greeted by the strong, bitter aroma of the espresso machine.

Nestled in the corner in a booth, his editor Brad sat, staring up at the bleak horizon as the rain splattered against the glass. Brad had let his beard grow out since the last time they met. It covered his neck and rested on his chest, the coarse black hairs splayed across his checkered dress shirt. Clutching his cup of coffee in both hands, Brad took a sip without taking his gaze from the outside. Across the table from Brad, a second cup of coffee waited for William along with two hazelnut creamers and a packet of Splenda propped on a saucer next to the cup. He let out a deep sigh, knowing that the flavored creamers were a harbinger of bad news. Brad must have some gruesome dissection to pass along about the latest novel, trying to soften the blow with literal sweetness.

"Hey, Brad," William said with a tentative pause. "How are you doing?" Accustomed to his usual hard-backed chair at the tables up front, William sank deep into the cushion.

"What's up, Will," Brad said. He picked up his briefcase and dropped it on the table with a loud thunk. The buckles opened with a satisfying metallic snap, revealing a neat stack of papers, two leather-bound journals, and an assortment of fancy pens inside. "Long time no see. How's everything been?"

William drummed his fingers off the table, a nervous habit. To steady himself, he picked up the coffee and poured the creamer and sweetener in. At least it occupied his idle hands. "I'm good, Brad. How are you and the wife?" He took a sip, bracing himself for the bitter news to come.

"Divorced," he stated. Clearly bitter, his lips curled into a snarl.

William said, "I'm sorry to hear that. Hope you're doing okay."

"Honestly, I think it's for the best." Brad took out a black journal and opened it to a bookmarked page. "Let's get down to business, shall we?"

William hung his head down, staring into his coffee as he stirred it, mesmerized by the cream as it swirled into the black liquid, forming an expanding cyclone of white that blended into a light brown. "I'm sorry... I didn't realize that you two were having issues."

"It's fine. Really. I haven't been telling people because I'm not ready to broadcast that aspect of my life to my clients just yet."

William glanced up from his cup, looking at Brad through the rising steam. "We can reschedule. I'm not in a rush to get this novel out."

"Haven't you been talking to your agent lately?" An astonished expression settled over Brad's face. "Melanie, isn't that her name?"

William shook his head. "Not in the last few weeks. Should I have heard from her?"

"I'm sure you will in the next day or so," Brad said, the words blending together as his accent came out. He does his best to contain a smirk.

William couldn't help feeling left out. "Do you know something that I don't?"

"I'll get her to call you." Brad took out his cell phone and sent a text. His giant fingers make the phone appear comically insignificant. Once he hit send, he took a long sip of his coffee, smacked his lips, and continued. "So, let's talk about the latest Sailor's Salt." Brad slid the journal across the table toward William.

William studied the page. Four notes directed William to the pages where the editorial changes awaited his revision. "Only four mistakes?"

"That's right. I guess you've been listening to your critics. This is by far your best grammatical effort. Nearly perfect, actually." Brad motioned toward the journal with his index finger, mimicking turning the page. "The problem I have with this book is that you focused too much on your critics and strayed away from what you're best at, telling a fascinating story."

William turned the page, finding it filled top to bottom with notes. He continued to flip the pages. There was paragraph after paragraph of suggestions for pages. "What is this?"

"Will," Brad paused. He scrunched up his face, his beard twitching. "I'm not trying to be mean. But I think you've spent too much time trying to please the critics. You've left out what makes the Sailor's Salt novels great. Passion. There's none of it. And to top it off, the plot is predictable, and the pacing is horrible."

William let out a deep sigh and slumped back into his seat. He took a sip of his coffee, finding it extra bitter. The rain pattered against the window and idle chatter swelled in the shop. "Is it that bad?" William thrust his finger at the journal.

"No," Brad interjects without hesitation. "It just needs more work put into it. Some tender care is all it needs. Listen to me." Brad hesitated, ensuring that he had William's full attention. Once their eyes locked, he continued. "You're not the first author who lost his way trying to appease his critics. But let me give you some advice. You can't forget about all the things that made you famous. People read your novels for the sexual tension and thrilling adventure. It's great that you've improved your writing skills. Honestly, I'm impressed that you honed your skills this much from one book to the next."

"Thanks," William interrupted.

Brad thumped his finger off the journal. "Take this home and consider this an excellent first draft. There are a lot of great things in here. All that's missing is the heart."

William closed the journal. The cover slammed shut with a dull thud, the harsh sound reminding him of a prison cell door. "I think my problem with all of this is I'm bored with Sailor's Salt. You know, I suspect I need a break to help clear my head." William paused, waiting for Brad to interrupt. Brad listened, sipping his coffee, but his eyes remained locked in an attentive gaze. William continued. "I saw a program on television just before I came over. Do you remember that scientist from Newfoundland that claimed that a megalodon attacked the Canadian Coast Guard ship? And that Labrynth Oils covered it all up so they wouldn't share any of the responsibility for the disaster?"

Brad shook his head but said nothing.

"Well, she's working for that company now. Up in the Arctic on some exploratory expedition. I thought to myself, wouldn't it be great if her plan is to sabotage the expedition as some form of revenge? Then I laughed at myself. No one would believe that story. What do you think? Would it make a great novel?"

Brad chuckled, a wide grin crossing his face. "There's actually a cult following for novels just like you described. Some of them are exceptional, and some of them are terrible. As long as you don't replicate Benchley's *Jaws*, and embrace just the right amount of hokey, you can pull it off."

Intrigued, William asked, "Are you trying to pull one over on me? People read this sort of thing?"

"You betcha. And I consider myself one of those people. So, here's what we're going to do. You're going to write that story. Melanie would loath the idea, so don't bother telling her. It can be our secret. When it's finished, give it to me and I'll read it over. If it's got potential, I'll help you out. I can reach out to some other agents I've worked with who will take on that genre. Worst-case scenario, you get your mind away from Sailor's Salt for a bit and you get to have a little fun with something new. Then, come back to the series, refreshed and ready to go for book nine."

"That's great," William said, excited and invigorated. He tucked the journal under his arm and grabbed his coffee cup. "Thanks, Brad." William turned and waltzed through the maze of tables and chairs toward the entrance.

"I'm still going to need those edits back," Brad called out. "I still want to get paid, you know."

William pushed the door open and stood in the entrance. The wind gusted into the coffee shop with a drizzle of rain. "I'll have them back to you by the end of the month." William left and the wind slammed the door shut behind him.

***

The bus barrelled down the freeway, every seat occupied. A buzz of nervous chatter cut through the uneasy silence. Harold hummed to himself. But it wasn't the song on the radio—some old Beatles tune—and it was driving Daniel nuts. A gust of wind hammered the side of the bus, causing every window to buckle and rattle boisterously.

Standing up on the hill, the Sportsplex towered over them, watching the coast from up high. Harold slowed the bus and got ready to take the exit ramp. The brakes squealed and screeched, while the engine fussed as he changed gears awkwardly.

"Are you sure you can drive a stick?" Daniel laughed.

"Hey man, you've driven with me before and you still asked me to drive. I'm thinking you don't know how to drive a standard transmission." Harold didn't bother with his blinker and took the turn a little too sharply. A frightened gasp sucked the air out of the bus as it rocked hard to the right.

When the bus evened out, Daniel said, "Easy does it now. You realize we are here to keep these people safe?"

"To serve and protect," Harold answered, giving Daniel a mock salute.

The road wound up the hill and cut out of view. Rivulets of water were tracking down the gutters already. Harold ground the gears as the bus lurched up the asphalt.

The engine revved, stressed from being in too high a gear. It took a moment for Harold to correct gears, the metallic grinding of metal becoming a shrill caw that silenced everyone on the bus.

"I'm going to ask for a different partner when we get back to the station. This is embarrassing." William patted Harold on the shoulder. "Besides driving, it's been nice working with you."

"Ah shut up," Harold grumbled.

With a sly grin, Daniel turned around and faced the crowd. "Don't worry everyone. We'll have you at the Sportsplex in a few minutes, and I promise that someone else will drive you back to the city."

Raucous laughter erupted from everyone except Harold. He shook his head. "You can be a real ass sometimes."

"I take that as a compliment," Daniel agreed.

***

By the time William reached his truck, his rain jacket was slick with a fine layer of mist. He stepped up into the cab and slammed the door shut behind him. Hunched over the steering wheel, he turned the key and the engine grumbled to life. Samuel had helped him pick out the new truck, and the thought reminded him to check in on his father-in-law.

"Alexa, call Samuel." The Bluetooth connected to the console and the phone rang, the sound echoing through the speakers. After several rings, the call went to voice mail.

"You've reached Samuel Grant. Sorry, but I'm unable to take your call at the moment or I caught the caller ID before

answering. Leave a message and I'll get back." A sharp beep blared through the speakers.

"Hey Sam, it's William." He felt stupid saying his own name, but old habits died hard. "Can you call me as soon as you get this? I'm on my way to your place now, and I'm not turning around until I hear from you."

William reached out and touched the red icon on the screen, ending the call. With the call ended, he switched over to satellite radio. A familiar song mixed with blasts of static barked from the speakers, the station already flickering in and out from the storm's interference. With a sigh, William put the truck in reverse and backed out of his spot and turned out of the parking lot. Traffic was abundant on the main road, and William stared at his phone, willing it to ring. He didn't want to make the trip to Samuel's in this weather or traffic. But he couldn't break his promise to Daniel.

He noticed another missed call from his husband. "Alexa, call Daniel." The phone rang seven times before William told Alexa to hang up. "We just can't seem to get on the same page today," William added with a contrite sigh.

***

With the last of the passengers off the bus, Daniel exhaled a sigh of relief. The wind howled on top of the hill, booming against the side of the Big Pine Sportsplex. Rain splattered off the concrete walls and blacktop. Harold had vanished inside the main doors with the crowd. Daniel wandered over to the railing at the edge of the road and looked out over the Blue Hole National Key Deer Refuge. Luscious swampland stretched out, pushing back against the concrete wasteland that had expanded into the wetland in recent years. Giant palm trees and impenetrable vegetation harbored the ground below. The series of circular, red tin roofs of the deer refuge was the only sign of human life. Nestled in the heart of the jungle, the tourist attraction offered an escape from city life.

Nearby, the Blue Hole stood out in sharp contrast against the lush green palm leaves and dense brush. Daniel couldn't imagine a more beautiful sight than that brilliant shade of blue that only nature produced. Even in the storm's drab, overcast shadow, the Blue Hole continued to be a vibrant beacon in a sea of emerald jungle.

"Hey, Daniel," Harold called out from the door of the bus. "Let's go. We still have one more stop to make."

Daniel stared down at his phone, noticing that William had returned his call. He hit redial, but the phone didn't ring. He got a text message back from William's Alexa. *The customer is on another call and can't talk right now. Hit one to leave a text message.* With a regretful sigh, Daniel turned back toward the view one last time before heading back to the bus. After the storm, Daniel would never want to see the Blue Hole ever again.

AROUND TOWN PART ONE

Amy sat beneath the awning of the entrance to the hotel, the dark sky casting long shadows over the street. Tucked in between the wall and a large cement potted palm tree, she prayed the doorman wouldn't spot her again. He'd warned her twice already and promised the next time he spotted her he'd call the cops. There was no mercy to be found in him. Even with the torrential downpour, he refused to let her "sully" the entrance to this fine establishment. Not a single guest arrived to check in, and no one dared leave the shelter of the hotel.

Waterfalls poured from the edge of the awning, splashing off the pavement with a maddening racket. She could have handled sleeping in the dampness. In fact, she had been doing just that for most of the last year, but that relentless patter of water prevented her from getting any sleep. Her sleeping bag was still relatively dry, but the cardboard beneath was already waterlogged. And it wouldn't be long before the fabric would absorb more than its fair share of the rainwater, ruining another sleeping bag for her. With the streets deserted, nothing blocked the gales as they swept through the streets, swaying the light poles. It rained so hard that the raindrops appeared to be defying gravity, ricocheting off the asphalt and hanging in the air before the wind whisked them away.

The impending clouds were slate gray and swelling with gloom, casting a dismal shadow over the city, leaving the horizon a dreary shell of its usual sunny self. The color drained from the buildings, and water drenched the palm leaves, adding a touch of gloom to the verdant greenery. Even the cherry red Mercedes parked across the street turned a drab, lifeless maroon beneath the storm clouds.

Something set off a car alarm on a nearby street. The blaring noise lasted for a few minutes before the owner shut it off. Amy guessed that a fallen tree branch or some form of detritus set it off, and it would only be the first of many occurrences today. She'd lost her home during the last year's hurricane season, each storm battering her house with unrelenting fury, draining her finances until there was nothing left in her bank account. A tear welled in the corner of her eye. The memory of her former life made her depressed. Despite her education and experience, living on the streets made it difficult to hold down a job, and even harder to get a new one.

A low, hissing growl floated into Amy's cerebellum, carried there by the wind. The sound grew closer. She sat up, pressing her backside against the wall, her heart thrashing in her chest as the approaching noise grew louder. Not caring anymore, Amy ran for the door and pushed it open. A flood of cooled air-conditioned air greeted her.

"You can't come in here," the doorman groaned from the desk. He was leaning on the counter, his undone black vest revealing just how scrawny he was. When Amy stepped inside, he pushed himself off the counter, a scowl contorting his face into something sinister. "I'm not asking you again."

Amy turned to face the street and tiptoed to the side of the door, facing the tall window. Her eye caught the flutter of a scaled tail as it slithered out of view. Something bumped against the car parked beside the curb. It rocked back and forth as the alarm blared.

"Please," Amy cried out, her voice panicked, "there's something out there."

"Not my problem," the concierge said, seizing Amy's arm, his nails burrowing into her bicep. She yanked her arm backward, and he fell forwards into her, bracing himself against the door frame. "Listen to me." His voice was on the verge of a scream. "Don't make me hurt you." He whispered the last part.

"Aaron," a woman's voice called out from behind the desk, "let her go." A tall, thin woman stepped out from behind the counter. Long curls of chestnut brown hair rested on her shoulder. "There's no one coming here today, so there's no reason she can't stay."

Aaron hesitated, eying Amy with disdain. He let go and shook his head. "If she steals anything it's on you. I want that noted down somewhere." Storming off, he slammed the *Employees Only* door behind him with as much strength as he could muster.

"Why don't you have a seat in the restaurant." The woman pointed toward a set of double doors. "The buffet is almost closed but there's a lot of food left. It's just going to go to waste, so help yourself and I'll be right in."

Amy took one last glance over her shoulder. A gust

of wind rattled the glass door. Stray palm leaves and garbage fluttered against the glass, pinned in place like posters advertising for Hurricane Rose. Somebody turned off the blaring car alarm, and there were no signs of the monster she believed she saw. It must have been her imagination running wild. Drawn into the room by the smell of cinnamon and coffee, Amy left her worries behind and headed into the dining room.

***

Jake held the phone away from his ear as Ms. Shelton demanded that as the building superintendent, he check the circuit breaker in the basement. Her drunken words rambled together, incoherent and full of spite, barking orders that only a dog could understand. He waited for a pause, not daring to interrupt, so he could assure her he would run down right now and check. Pointless as it may be, at least it would stop the verbal berating and misplaced fear. Hurricane Rose had knocked out power to the city block over an hour ago, and there was no way he was going to start the generator just yet. With only fourteen hours of gas, he was going to wait until nightfall before he powered it up.

"Are you even listening to me?" her shrill voice came through the line. And that damn dog of hers yapping in the background made him cringe.

"Yes, ma'am," Jake answered, placing as much politeness as he could muster into his tone. "I'm heading down there right now." He opened the closet door and pulled out his rubber boots. The basement was dank during the best of days. Built directly over the city's sewage system, it was common to find puddles of filthy brown water near the metal grates on the floor. They'd built Sunrise Apartments on the outskirts of the city limits, near the wetlands, and the designers believed this would be the best way to avoid flooding out of the building.

There was an unusual moment of silence on the other end of the line; even the dog was respecting the pause. Then she spoke. "The storm will not affect me up here?" Her voice worked to disguise the slight tremble rising from the pit of her stomach. "I can feel the building swaying," she added.

Sunrise Apartments, built over ten years ago, was long past settling, and Hurricane Rose was pushing the limits of the architecture. "You're going to be just fine, Ms. Shelton," Jake assured her as a gust of wind slapped the side of the building. The steel girders groaned, yielding to the pressure. It would bend but not break. Now Jake spoke to persuade himself. "Would you like me to come check on you after I've finished in the basement?" After another elongated pause, he waited for her response. This time, the dog was barking its head off. "If you're still there, can you please say something?"

"Yes," her voice sounded distant, distracted. "Are you looking out the window right now?"

Jake sauntered toward the window. "What's going on out there?" He jerked open the window and nearly dropped his cell phone. Hurricane Rose had transformed the streets into raging rivers. Murky water flowed between the cars, creeping up and over the vehicle's tires. "I'm going to call you back, Ms. Shelton." His thoughts raced toward the basement. If the sewers grates hadn't discharged the flood waters back into the building, it would be a miracle. He ended the call, grabbed the flashlight from the kitchen table, and ran out into the hallway. Shadows cast the corridor into gloomy darkness. Only the emergency exit lights offered the faintest trace of light near the stairwell. As he made his way down the stairs, he tried to remember the last time he'd changed the batteries in those emergency light power packs.

On days when the power was out, Jake was glad he lived on the second floor. He reached the basement in no time and wasn't breathing too hard. It took him longer to find the right key to the basement door than it did to reach it, and by the time he opened the door, his breathing was back to normal. When he opened the door, the stench assaulted him. He gagged and pulled his shirt up over his nose to filter the stale stench of mineral water, copper piping, and the putrid odor of sewage. "Goddamn it," he muttered to himself as he watched the brown water bubbling up from the center of the floor.

He took out his phone and called Ms. Shelton back. She answered on the first ring. "Ms. Shelton, if I get the power back on, you need to boil as much water as you can."

"Why?" Her voice flooded with panic. "What's happening?"

"Just trust me," he said, turning the flashlight on and directing the beam down the stairs. "I'll be up to your apartment to explain. Please have a cup of tea ready and a sink full of hot water to wash up with." He ended the call and made his way down the basement stairs, his eyes locked on the generator. It was still dry, sitting on an elevated platform, but the water would soon reach it. Distracted by the task at hand, Jake never noticed the grate floating beneath the stairs, or the busted bolts next to it.

***

Wendy stood beside the patio door, blowing smoke through the screen as she waited for her dog, Bud, to finish his business. Thunder rumbled in the distance, and rain pounded the wooden boards of her deck. Her husband was upstairs, attempting to patch a leak in the roof. Bud kept trotting back and forth on the top step, refusing to go on the wood, and afraid to get his feet wet. "Just go already," she hollered at the dog. Then, as if offended, Bud turned his head and gawked at her in disbelief as the rain soaked into his fur, making him look like a drowned rat.

She was suffering a lousy day and needed relief, no matter how much her husband hated the stale stench of cigarette smoke in the house. Besides, she was doing her best to keep it outside, and she just remembered the candles in the cupboard above the microwave. She slid the screen over the dog's leash, the thin fabric preventing it from shutting completely, and laid the handle over the latch before heading over to grab a candle. In the dull glow of day, the spark was a radiant flash of yellow and orange, settling into a bright reddish-yellow flame. The vibrant scent of lavender filled her nostrils.

Now her husband was thumping a hammer against the boards in the roof, each pounding thud a sharp stab of pain. Outside, the dog was growling, adding to her compounding headache. She wanted to cry, growing frustrated with everything around her. Something had to give. She was on the verge of having a mental breakdown.

From outside, the dog let out an ear-splitting bark. "Would you shut up?" she screeched, swiveling around to face the patio door. When she stared outside, the dog was nowhere to be seen. His leash trailed from the post, over the steps, and vanished into the murky water building up on their lawn. She eased the screen door open. "Where are you, Bud?" A flood of panic forced her outside, her socks soaking up the water from the storm as she crossed the patio. She grasped the dog's leash and yanked it backward. Expecting Bud's weight, she fell backward, her feet slipping out from beneath her, landing hard on her backside.

A bloodied collar landed in her lap. She picked it up and turned it over in her palm, finding only a single tuft of black fur remaining. She let out a scream, scrambling toward the screen door. Her hands slipped over the slick decking, and her knees refused to lock in place when she tried to get to her feet. Fear forced her to crawl to safety, too afraid to glance over her shoulder. Her vision narrowed on the door handle. When she reached the door, she tumbled inside and slammed it shut behind her. A flash of lightning lit up the street. For a moment, she thought she could see a pair of yellowish-green eyes watching her from the murky water. She rubbed her eyes with her hands, and when she looked again, nothing was watching her.

"Honey," she called out, her voice quivering. She pushed herself into the corner of the cupboards, unable to shake the strange sensation of something stalking her from the shadows. "Get down here," her shrill voice carried upstairs.

***

"Sure, Ted, I'll take your shift," Erin said into her cell phone while lying in bed. She rubbed her forehead, regretting that last glass of red wine before bed. "No, I really don't mind pulling a double. I actually love staying at the lodge in this weather. It will be peaceful." She rolled over into Sharon's spot, relishing in the faint warmth left behind. "Really, don't worry about it. And you're sure that the homeless people are all going up to the shelter?" Erin nodded her head when Ted confirmed as if he could see her. "Just do me one favor. Don't tell the boss about me bringing Sharon and we can call it even."

Erin slid her legs out of the sheets, placing her feet on the bear rug at the side of her bed. "Great. I'll see you tomorrow then." Without waiting for Ted to respond, she hung up her work phone and plugged it into the charger. Her eyes wandered to the digital clock on Sharon's nightstand and groaned when she noticed she had slept in.

She rummaged through her dresser, sliding the drawers open and slamming them shut as she went about hauling out a change of clothes and her uniform. With the hurricane approaching, she knew the park would become deserted by supper if not sooner, and she could get into comfy clothes for the rest of her shift. She grabbed a change of clothes for Sharon just in case and made her way into the kitchen.

"Hey, sleepy head," Erin said, her voice echoing in the empty kitchen. She examined the counter, finding the bread bag left wide open and the container of butter without its lid laid out next to the toaster. When she tried to place the lid back on, she found the butter a melted mess, the heat from the toaster having sped up the process.

"In a rush, I guess," she said to the empty apartment. She tried to find the plastic clip for the bread, searching around the plates and cups left on the counter waiting to be loaded into the dishwasher. When she couldn't, she spun the bag around and laid the bread on the top loop to keep it sealed. She fished the lid to the butter out of the sink and laughed, realizing that none of the dishes had made their way there to be rinsed.

Erin microwaved a bowl of instant oatmeal—apple cinnamon, her favorite. The spicy scent permeated the kitchen as she waited, the small of her back leaning against the counter as she stared out the window at the rain. Rivers snaked down the window, streaking left and right without rhyme or reason. When the microwave dinged, she retrieved her oatmeal and strolled into the living room, not bothering with the television. She enjoyed the soft sound of the rain pattering off the glass. Ever since she was a little girl, the methodical cadence of heavy rain brought a sense of serenity.

She laid her oatmeal on the coffee table next to Sharon's collection of dishes from the week and headed back into their bedroom. A smile raised her lips when she found the sheets a jumbled mess from the night before. Upside down and leaning against the wall, the night lamp teetered precariously between the nightstand and the gravity. The cord for her phone trailed from the nightstand to the floor. She pulled on the chord, relieved to feel the heavy weight at the end as she hauled her personal phone up from the floor.

"Are you still free this afternoon?" Erin hit send and

unhooked her cell from the charger. Heading back into the living room, she waited impatiently for Sharon to respond. Slumped into the living room chair, she picked at her oatmeal and listened to the rainfall.

Erin's phone chirped. *"Depends. Are you still taking me to the Blue Hole National Key Deer Refuge?"*

"And what if I'm not?" Erin's finger hovered over send, hesitating before hitting it.

A series of dots appeared on the screen as Sharon prepared for her response. *"I think we destroyed the bedroom last night."*

Erin burst out laughing, her body flushed hot with the memories of last night. It took her a minute to think of a witty response. *"If I need to take you somewhere special every time we break the bed, I'm going to be poor."*

In an instant, the phone buzzed back. *"Will they have room for both of us at the poor house?"*

"Where can I pick you up?" Erin turned her attention back to her oatmeal while she waited for Sharon to respond.

"I'm at mom's house. It's her birthday, remember?"

Erin let out a defeated sigh. *"Why didn't you wake me?"* She dropped her bowl down on the table. It landed with a loud bang on the glass.

"You looked so peaceful sleeping there. Like an angel."

"I'll be over right after my shower. Did you want anything brought in the overnight bag?" Erin gathered the morning dishes from the coffee table and raced into the kitchen with them. She placed them in the sink and ran the hot water, squirting dish liquid into the sink as it filled. After they soaked for a while, she would load the dishwasher.

"Some of that wine from last night. If there's any left. And you can bring the speaker if you want to listen to music."

Erin only needed to listen to the rain falling on the tin roof of the Blue Hole National Key Deer Refuge. But she knew Sharon would enjoy the music, so she brought both. As the sink filled, she wandered over to the wine rack and grabbed a bottle of red and a bottle of white. If no one would be around, they would enjoy a drink with supper to kick-start their romantic getaway. And she knew one bottle wouldn't go far between the two of them.

"I'll be there by 10."

In a rush, Erin finished packing the bag and jumped into the shower. Still locked in the gun safe, her holster and pistol remained in the closet. As a wildlife ranger, she had never drawn her weapon or given it a second thought. She left it behind as she rushed out the door.

WAKING UP

Art shielded his face against the wind-driven rain, the droplets pounding his body in a barrage of frigid ammo. At the mercy of the gales, the buoy rocked back and forth as the waves crashed over the base, white foam spraying into the air in violent arcs. Overhead, the encroaching black clouds cast a drab shadow over the slate-gray ocean.

Surrounded by water, Art found himself dehydrated. "Ironic," he muttered to himself. With his throat dry, his voice came out in a harsh and raspy bark. He tried catching raindrops on his tongue, but the wind carried brine from the deep sea, making the air bitter. His stomach ached from the salt water that lined his throat and nostrils and filled his lungs, making him lightheaded. If he didn't get off this buoy soon, he would pass out.

A flock of seagulls landed on the buoy, cawing at him. Some of the braver ones pecked at him, not wanting to wait for him to die before getting a taste. A silent scream caught in his throat and died on his dry lips. Forced to swat the gulls away, he grasped the buoy with one hand, his grip fleeting. The gull squawked at him, lurched forward, and nipped at the exposed flesh on his thigh. Art screamed as pain radiated from the bite.

Angry, Art swiped at the seagull, lost his balance, and slipped from his perch on the buoy. Then he plummeted into the water headfirst, his vision filled with air bubbles and frothing water. The brine stung his eyes, blinding him. He kicked furiously toward the surface, his arms stretched out over his head, guiding his way. Relief flooded him as his arms shot through the surface. He gasped for air, sucking in the saltwater in his panic, making his stomach ache.

Desperate, he swam back toward the buoy, but his arms and legs struggled to work in tandem. Out of sync, he scrambled toward the bobbing metal island, keeping his gaze fixed on the rusted red metal. But a powerful wave swept him toward the shore, whisking him away from the buoy in the powerful current. He tried fighting it to no avail.

Stuck in the middle of nowhere, his eyes wandered all around. A dull, drab horizon and murky waters hid salvation from his view. As he peered down into the water, the sea appeared to be a crystal-clear emerald, but he couldn't even see his own feet. His heart pounded against his ribs, out of rhythm, thumping wildly one moment, then skipping a beat the next. Lactic acid flooded his muscles, his legs becoming useless dead weight. Aching with exertion, his shoulders knotted and burned. With no other options left, he swam toward the shore.

GIMMIE SHELTER

Back within city limits on their second trip, Harold pulled up alongside the abandoned Labrynth Oils storage facility. Once a thriving pillar within the community, it offered hundreds of jobs to the locals. But as soon as the oil dried up off the coast, Labrynth Oils pulled out and disappeared without a single word. Workers appeared one morning and discovered the gate locked. Labrynth had taken all the salvageable industrial equipment under the umbrella of darkness. Only the unwanted office furniture and some worthless filing cabinets remained.

Now, it was just another red-bricked building at the end of Cober Lane to weather away with the other derelict buildings that cluttered the slums. And provide a gathering place for the homeless and drug addicts. The police overlooked the ill-fated congregation because it kept them off the streets. Daniel even remembered his captain telling them to avoid nosing around down there, saying, "out of sight, out of mind."

"Alright," Harold left the engine to idle, "let's head inside."

"Do you think they'll even come with us?"

"Some of them will," Harold answered candidly. "And

that's all that we can do. The strung-out ones will resent our presence. Years of drug abuse can make people paranoid. So...you should do the talking."

A wave of anger flooded Daniel's system. "Why? Because I'm black? And you think all drug addicts are black?"

Harold's guilt-ridden expression turned his cheeks a blazing red. "You know, I don't think all drug addicts are black, Daniel. I'm just..." he sputtered, "...statistics don't lie."

"I'm not having this argument with you today." Daniel stormed down the steps and stomped toward the broken gate. Raindrops bounced off the pavement, splashing back up at him, soaking him to the bone from the knees down. The wind rattled the gate, but the chain held it in place—a seemingly endless battle that would rage on with no winner. Harold's boots splashed through the layer of water forming on the roads, debris from the storm clogging the drains throughout the city. Daniel slipped inside the gate, turning to face Harold. "Why don't you go back and get the bolt cutter? It will save us time getting people through this gate."

"I'm sorry," Harold whined.

"Just go." Daniel turned without saying another word.

The Labrynth Oils logo hung over the door, the sun having beaten it down over the years, leaving it all but faded from its former vibrant glory. He pushed the front door open and was greeted by the putrid stench of human waste, mold, and alcohol. Broken syringes and various drug paraphernalia littered the corridor. "Florida State

Police," Daniel called out, announcing his presence before heading further into the building. Daniel could hear people rustling and scuffling in a mad dash from within. "I'm here to bring you to safety. I'm not here to arrest anybody." The frantic sounds continued. "Hurricane Rose is approaching, and we need to get you somewhere safe."

Beads of water dripped from the ceiling, and rivers ran down the weathered walls. Several large puddles had formed in the entrance, one of which ran the length of the hallway along the right-hand side of the wall. Shattered windows allowed the wind to drive the elements into the abandoned factory. Colorful graffiti vandalized the walls; the crudeness of the images stole any attempt at being art. Some of it was directed toward the former occupants, Labrynth Oils. Daniel also found several racial slurs that he'd never even learned before scrawled across the offices, each one disturbing and hateful.

The first curious resident staggered into the hall. Dressed in a tattered gray hoodie and faded blue jeans, the woman eyed him suspiciously. There was a dried vomit stain from the collar down to her knees. She looked in his direction with a blank, bloodshot stare.

"Ma'am." Daniel used his softest tone, worried that she was going to bolt at the sight of the uniform. "I'm here to bring you to the emergency shelter."

"I ain't in trouble," her raspy voice croaked. Her deep southern accent made the word come out as *trobah*.

"No, I'm only here to help."

The woman ran her hand through her tangled hair and scratched her scalp. "I guess so." Her drawl ran the words together. "Lots of people come'round here before offering to help me. You can't do no worse than any of them, I suppose."

"Can you round up your friends?" Daniel asked as she shuffled away, her boots scuffing across the wet cement.

"None of us got friends in here," she laughed. "That's why we are all here. We ain't got nobody, mister. This way, we can have each other. But we ain't friends, no sir. Say, is there going to be food where we headed?" Her dark brown eyes showed a hint of hope behind them, her lips curled into a faint smile.

"Three meals a day, ma'am." Daniel had no clue, but if it helped to get them to move faster, it was worth lying about it. "And snacks too."

The woman disappeared back into the room. Her tired voice called out, and an indecipherable grunt answered her agitated call. Daniel walked down the corridor, finding the rooms vacant. Only the foul body odor lingered, along with some soiled clothing and other disgusting refuse. A powerful gust of wind rattled the eaves. The metal screeched and groaned, and for a moment Daniel was sure the roof was going to lift off. Outside, the chain-link fence shrieked in protest. Beneath the savage orchestra of the storm, a panicked rhythm of footsteps rumbled toward the building. The boisterous beat of mismatched marching demanded attention, drawing the inhabitants that had been lurking in the shadows along the old storage bins. They wandered toward the giant receiving doors, resembling a pack of zombies drawn toward the sound of the living in one of the George A. Romero movies.

With every passing second, the sound grew, and the foundation shook. It became apparent that those weren't human footprints, but something that reminded Daniel of a herd of buffalo. One of the homeless men opened the exit door next to the loading bay. With surprising speed, he lurched backward as a deluge of water flooded into the building around his feet. The door swung hard against the wall, knocking chunks of debris into the gushing flow. The thunderous stampede boomed as gazelle galloped inside the Labrynth Oils storage facility, narrowly avoiding trampling the people gathered around the door.

Rushing forward, Daniel dragged the strung-out addicts from harm's way. A frantic animal thumped into Daniel, knocking him into a heap of trash piled on the floor. It frightened him, and he'd have a sore ribcage from where the gazelle struck him tomorrow, but he had avoided a serious injury. Jumping to his feet, he ushered the crowd toward the front gate. The herd gathered in one of the large empty rooms. Spooked by the storm, they refused to settle and avoided the rising water. At least they were out of the way.

A blast of wind greeted Daniel as he pushed the front door open. Harold was still cutting the lock from the front gate, the gales and downpour of rain giving him trouble. Beads of water poured from the brim of his hat as he struggled to hold both the gate and bolt cutter in place. Startled, he didn't hear Daniel approaching and jumped when Daniel asked if he needed help.

"Could you hold the gate steady?" The irritation in Harold's voice was thick. They worked together to open the gate, while the storm worked against them. Some of the building's inhabitants made their way outside. Not prepared for the weather, the residents were wearing nothing but their tattered rags and worn shoes. They didn't seem to mind the rain. Maybe it was the prospect of a hot meal or a roof that didn't leak over their heads. Either way, more people than Daniel could have expected were cooperating. The lock snapped with a high-pitched snap, and the wind threw the gate wide open.

"Get those people on the bus," Harold said, almost yelling to be understood over the high winds.

Daniel reached out and grabbed Harold by the cuff of his jacket. "Where are you going?"

"I'm going to do a quick sweep of the building before we go." Harold's gaze wandered down, fixated on his boots. "I'll just be a minute." Daniel knew Harold felt ashamed of what he'd said earlier and didn't need to press the issue any further.

Daniel nodded his head and let Harold go. He walked back to the bus, pushed the door inwards, and climbed inside out of the elements. People shuffled aboard, sitting in random seats, closing their eyes to get some rest as the comfort of heat washed over them. Rain pattered off the roof in a mesmerizing rhythm. It was almost hypnotic despite the chaos brewing outside.

Outside, a booming crash of thunder drowned out a blood-curdling scream from within the Labrynth Oils building as Harold vanished inside.

***

Wave after wave crashed onto the beach, the flood of water threatening to sweep Kyle's feet out from under him. Plumes of white foam sprayed high into the air as the ocean slammed against the craggy shore on the south side. Known for its prominent cave systems, Kyle realized exactly where to go. "Hold on, Tim," he hollered. Tourists flocked from the world over to visit the network of caves that littered the shoreline along Big Pine Key. Over the years in his role as a civil servant, Kyle had been called to aid in the rescue of many foolish, amateur spelunkers who had decided to explore; a lack of respect for the tides often caused dangerous situations for the unprepared.

His foot struck solid rock, but the slimy surface sent him stumbling forward. Kyle thrust his hands out to break his fall. His hand struck the craggy surface below, narrowly avoiding bashing his face off the ground. Surprised, the ocean forced a mouthful of salt water down his gullet, gagging him. He spat out a mouthful of brine, choking on the bile racing up his throat.

"Help me," Tim's voice came in loud and clear, echoing from within the cave.

With renewed hope, Kyle lifted himself up. Standing on the edge of a jagged cliff that jutted up from the beach, the entrance was just below. The surging waves roared into the mouth of the cave. Treacherous currents flooded inside the entrance. As the tide rolled out, rapid swirls of water oozed back into the ocean. Proper procedure dictated he call for backup, but there wasn't enough time for that.

"I'm coming, Tim!" Kyle yelled. He leaped down without thinking, determined to rescue his friend. The sand shifted beneath his feet, working against him. He felt like he was running the wrong way up an escalator. Wind whistled into the cavern, booming off the rock face. A faint trace of daylight shined against his backside as darkness enveloped him.

"I'm up here, Captain," Tim called out, his voice labored. Exhausted gasps filled the space between every word.

The narrow entrance shrouded everything in darkness. "Where?" Kyle yelled. Frustrated, he slammed his fists against his thighs. "I can't find you," he snapped. Outside, the ocean roared. The entire cave trembled. Loose pebbles and small boulders fell from the ceiling and smashed against the rocks below.

"Follow my voice, captain," Tim answered, his voice fading. "Walk forward…if you keep your hands up, you'll touch the ledge in about five feet."

Kyle wandered deeper into the cave. Vibrations rumbled toward him as the next wave funneled into the entrance. A wall of water slammed against the back of his legs, shoving him down face first. This time, he couldn't brace his fall. His head smacked off the hard-packed rocks below, opening a savage gash on his forehead. Disoriented by the blow, Kyle found himself at the mercy of the ocean. It flung him against the wall, pinning him there as the salt water gushed over him. He held his breath, his arms frantically scouring the wall for something to grab onto. His fingers found a crevice, and he pulled his head above water.

"Are you okay, captain?"

Kyle spat out a mouthful of ocean. "I'm fine." He pulled himself up onto the ledge, rolling over onto his backside to catch his breath.

With his eyes adjusted to the dim light, Kyle could see the blood-soaked bandage wrapped around Tim's leg. "Jesus Christ, Tim, what the fuck happened to your leg?"

"There's..." his voice trembled, he swallowed deeply before spitting out, "...something out there." His finger pointed out at the vast ocean.

"What?" Kyle asked. He patted his chest. A wave of relief washed over him as he patted the radio, finding it still secured in his vest.

"Some gnarly sea beast," Tim gasped. "Something lurking in the water."

"Did it bite you?"

"No, but it wanted to." Tim raised his voice. "It chased me and Cheryl into this damn cave. I smashed my ankle off a rock. She picked me up and somehow lifted me onto this ledge, sacrificing her life to save me. The beast snagged her, dragging her outside the cave."

"Did you see what did it? It couldn't have been a shark this close to shore?"

"I've never seen anything like it before in my life," Tim coughed, spitting a wad of phlegm onto the rock. It was thick with blood, landing with an audible smack against the ground.

Kyle turned on the radio, and a burst of static shrieked inside the cave. He turned the dial to the emergency channel. "Come in. This is Captain Krusneski." Static blared back.

"It's no use." Tim held up his radio. "I've tried. The signal is being blocked by the cave."

"Christ," Kyle snapped. "I'll carry you out."

"We have to be quick." Tim rolled onto his knees.

"I know," Kyle agreed. "Those flood waters are going to cut us off soon if we don't get moving."

"I'm not worried about that." Tim angled his head

so that his right ear faced the entrance. "Don't you hear that?"

"The roar of the ocean," Kyle answered, confused by Tim's frightened tone.

"Not that," Tim replied, holding his finger up to his mouth. "Listen," he whispered.

At first, only the pounding of the raging ocean waves crashing against the shoreline and the booming wail of the gale force winds thundered in his ears. Then something else rose above the deafening roar of the storm, demanding an audience. A low guttural growl came from the darkness.

BLEEDING TIME

The windshield wiper thumped across the glass, the motor working at full capacity, but it struggled to keep up with the downpour. Violent winds lashed out from the ocean with enough force to keep William's grip on the wheel so tight his knuckles turned white. Under diminishing weather conditions, he found himself forced to keep far below the speed limit, adding an extra thirty minutes on the highway to his commute. Maybe even more on the way back if the intensity of the surging waves continued to increase at this rate. His lane remained empty for as far as the eye could see, nothing but free space ahead. Beside him, traffic clogged the outgoing lane. He assumed people weren't waiting for the evacuation orders and got out while they still had plenty of time. William reached over to the radio and was about to search for the news when his phone went off. Connected to the dashboard by Bluetooth, the display switched from the radio over to his phone's screen.

William stared at the dashboard. The incoming call display flashed his agent's name, Melanie, forming a bundle of nerves in his stomach. In his experience, unless she was expecting the next manuscript from him, she never called.

She wasn't one for small talk, and his latest book was just released last week. Then he remembered Brad mentioned he should expect her to call from her. In fact, it had surprised him he hadn't heard from her yet. He reached over and accepted the call, hoping that he wasn't too late, and he wouldn't receive a dead dial tone for his efforts.

"Hello, Mel." William tried to sound casual despite the fluttering sensation in his stomach.

"Mr. Compton," Melanie's voice was chipper, "how's Hurricane Rose? Has the weather turned bad there yet?"

"Yeah," he mumbled, unable to produce anything intelligent to say. This was a strange phone call coming from Melanie. "It's picking up now."

"Well, I hope you stay safe." She talked with an unusual measure of compassion. When his father died, she had sounded like a robot programmed to offer sympathy—and not one of those well-designed robots with all the bells and whistles.

"Listen, I need to talk to you about the next book. I had my meeting with Brad earlier today. And we both agree it's going to need a little more work before it's ready. So, I'm reluctant to admit that it will not be ready on time."

"Oh, I already know that. Brad told me when I called last week."

Confused by Melanie's tone, William asked, "So you're not mad?"

"Mad?" Melanie snorted. "Not at all. Besides, I wouldn't know what to do with all that money you're bringing into the firm."

William choked back laughter. Being an author paid the bills and some extravagance, but it wasn't lucrative by any means. "Thanks. I mean, I wish it was more. I would love to move out of this damn condo and into my own place."

"My sister is in real estate. A branch of her company is based where you live. I can get you a number."

"That's way out of my budget right now. There's no way I would be able to afford a house," William answered with a sigh.

"You couldn't afford anything yesterday," Melanie said.

"What?" William asked during a pregnant pause, hoping that she would fill in the void of silence. "Please, just tell me what's going on."

"We have a lucrative deal in place to adapt your Sailor's Salt novels into a series on Netflix," she said, excitement bursting off every word.

"That's incredible!" William shouted, unable to contain himself. He was ecstatic.

As Melanie filled him in on the details, William continued his drive. Oblivious to the outgoing traffic. He ignored the blackened clouds marching in like an army from the ocean. Distracted by the tremendous news, he missed a call from his husband.

***

Cursing at herself, Erin stared at the dashboard, her mind willing time to run in reverse. Already fifteen minutes behind schedule, she found herself stuck in traffic far from her destination, crawling forward at a snail's pace. A blaring horn behind her pierced into her skull, trying her patience, bleeding it dry. She rolled down her window and gave the guy the middle finger. "Fucking asshole," she shouted into the wind. The man wouldn't be able to hear her, but her facial expression conveyed her sentiment.

Erin's phone buzzed in the cup holder. In the dead of traffic, she unlocked the screen and read the message from Sharon. *"Where are you?"*

"Sorry, stuck in traffic."

The man behind her laid on the horn again, letting it blare until the piercing sound died out with a whiffling buzz. With her last nerve wearing thin, she adjusted her rear-view mirror, giving herself a better view of the driver behind her. An older man with white hair and liver spots sat behind the wheel, his mouth twisted into a snarl, pressing his lips tight against his teeth. He hammered the steering wheel with the palm of his hand in three short bursts.

"Mom said it's not a big deal if you can't make it on time. I told her you worked late last night."

"I shouldn't be much longer. Tell her I'm almost there."

Erin watched as a vigorous flurry of wind rattled the traffic light. The metal frame swayed with the wind, bobbing up and down as the light turned green. The flow of cars opened up, allowing Erin to move toward the intersection and get into the left-turning lane. She hunched over the steering wheel, willing the green turning arrow to last a little longer so she could get through.

Cars trickled straight through the intersection as the arrow faded and the green circle lit up. Erin pounded her fist off the dashboard as the left-turning lane came to a dead halt, with one car ahead of her. The old man behind her laid on his horn again. Erin stuck her head out the window and screamed, "Fuck off!" The wind pelted her with rain, the air heavy with the stench of brine and sea-weed.

When she turned back to the road, the car in front of her made the turn just as the light turned yellow. "Fuck it," Erin grumbled, accelerating through the red light, car horns blaring at her as rubber screeched over the wet asphalt at the intersection. She peeked over her shoulder at the elderly man's car as she drove off with a smirking grin on her face.

***

Samuel Grant's house rested just twenty feet away from the peak of a cliff overlooking the ocean. On most days, the view sprawled out over the pristine emerald waters of the Gulf of Mexico. But not today. It was utter chaos on the horizon. Lightning snaked through the black clouds all along the Gulf skyline, which was as dark as the night sky. The first thing William recognized as he pulled into the driveway was the state of the house. With a hurricane approaching, William would have bet on Samuel to have his home weatherproofed. There wasn't a single storm shutter latched. They banged against the side of the house with a thunderous clatter as the wind ravaged them. All the windows remained intact, but it would only be a matter of time before it happened.

William pulled in behind Samuel's Ford Ranger and turned off the engine. The radiator knocked as it cooled down. Raindrops beat against the roof of his Dodge Ram and pattered off the windshield. After a moment, he noticed that Samuel's car was absent from the driveway, and he had even left the garage door open. William took out his phone, dialed his father-in-law, and again it went straight to voice mail. With no other options, he decided not to waste any more time sitting in the driveway. If luck remained on his side, Samuel would be asleep in his bed, sick with the flu. With nothing to block the elements between his vehicle and the front door, he readied himself to head out into the storm. When he opened the door, the wind caught it and yanked it from his hand. He cursed himself for not expecting it and jumped down from the cab of his truck. Leaning into the wind, William made his way toward the front door, calling out to Samuel, but the blustering wind snatched the voice from his throat. Not bothering to knock, William tried the doorknob, finding it locked. He knew his father-in-law kept a key for the kitchen door tucked away inside the light fixture, so he made his way around the patio, toward the cliff side.

A booming crack of thunder exploded over the Gulf. Momentarily mesmerized by the raging waves below, William leaned over the railing. Waves crashed into the craggy bluff below, sending up large plumes of white, foamy water. Hidden below the surging waters, the ocean spilled over the beach and flooded the road, reaching all the way to the old boathouse that housed Samuel's fishing vessel.

Samuel's neighbor, Mr. Burke, was outside with a hammer, nailing boards over his rain gutters. Mr. Burke served with Samuel in the Marine Corps and had lived in that house since before he joined. After the war, Mr. Burke found God and grew apart from Samuel despite how close they lived. Neither man was to blame as their friendship deteriorated into distant acquaintances, but they were still civil to each other, and would even share a beer over a Rays' game on a sunny afternoon. William never understood the game of baseball, or the interest it garnered, but Daniel shared his father's interest in the game, and William found himself caught in the Sunday afternoon routine far too often. Unfortunately, this would not be one of those lazy afternoons shared with a few cold beers and an endless barrage of snacks that found its way out between innings.

No matter how severe the storm became, or if they issued an evacuation order, Mr. Burke would refuse to leave. William could hear him as clear as day inside his head: *"I didn't serve my time in Afghanistan to let a little bad weather force me from my home. After everything I've been through, God wouldn't let anything bad happen to me."* Built at the crest of the next valley, Mr. Burke's home was situated just above the rock levee that protected the road from the surging waves. For now, the levee was still holding, but it wouldn't be able to withstand the relentless barrage forever; nature would win this round. White foam sprayed over the man-made rock wall as the waves pounded against the barrier. William didn't think the wall would still stand after the storm, but he was sure Mr. Burke believed it would triumph against Hurricane Rose. His home had stood on that cliff for over sixty years before the city limits expanded, encompassing him within them.

William glanced at his watch, noted the time, and gave himself ten minutes to have a quick look for Samuel. The key wasn't inside the light shade, but when he looked down, he found it lodged between two beams, the key ring too wide to slip between the crack in the boards. He picked up the key and dashed inside the house, trying to keep out as much rain as possible.

"Hey, Dad!" William yelled, his echo dampened by the raging storm. "Are you in here?" He tried the light switch in the kitchen, but the electricity was out. There were still dishes from last night's supper in the sink, something William found odd. Samuel was a neat freak and stuck to his routine with a regimental approach. Samuel had left the living room window curtains open, providing a view of the driveway. Streams of rain washed down the pane glass, distorting the vehicles parked there.

"Are you upstairs?"

No response. He checked his watch and cursed at himself, his heart rate increasing to a gallop as time ran out. If he wasn't in his bedroom, he might be down in the cellar, working away at one of his projects. Forced to decide, he dashed up the stairs, his footfalls dampened by the lush carpet. As he dashed down the hallway, he found the bedroom door wide open, revealing the inspection-ready bed—crisp sheets tucked neatly into hospital corners, pulled so tight you could bounce a dime off them. Folded at the foot of the bed, the duvet formed a precise rectangle that mirrored the shape of the bed. This level of attention to detail was one of the few habits Samuel had never abandoned since his days in the Marine Corps.

"Hey, Sam," William called out as he approached the bedroom. He poked his head into the bathroom. Drawn close, the shower curtain offered a panoramic view of a mountain landscape, but the water wasn't running. Not wanting to leave any stone unturned, William walked around to the far side of the bed and checked the floor. Empty, which brought about a flood of emotions washing over him in a cascade of disturbing conclusions: relieved that Samuel wasn't a stiff corpse on the floor after having dropped dead of a heart attack, but dreadful of the unknown whereabouts.

William decided he shouldn't waste any more time here. Whatever was wrong, staying here and getting caught in the storm wouldn't help. He headed back downstairs, locked the patio door, and left the key on the marbled kitchen counter next to the coffee maker. As he crossed the living room, he heard a loud crashing bang from the basement.

"Sam!" William yelled. "Is that you?"

He ran to the basement stairs, scrambling down the dilapidated staircase. The basement was flooding with muddied water that seeped in through the unseen cracks in the weathered cement walls. The shelving unit was knocked over. Power tools and some projects Samuel worked on in his spare time were floating in murky, foamy water. When he reached the last step, water was splashing up over the board. It didn't take long to find the source of the bang. The basement door swung back and forth with the wind, banging off the frame and siding in a maddening crescendo.

"Fuck," William cursed to himself.

He couldn't bring himself to leave the basement in such a state, even though he didn't want to deal with this right now. Guilt forced him to wade into the water. It was frigid and filled with debris as the water rushed over his hiking boots, William wondered why he hadn't bothered to put on his rain boots. For the last time, he glanced at his watch. "Better get moving," he said as passed the collapsed shelf.

He thought about righting the shelf, then decided against it. All he had time for was to close the basement door on the way out. He made sure it was closed behind him and ran to his car. His ten minutes were already up.

***

Erin leaned over the steering wheel, pushing the pedal to the floor. The tires kicked out a wide, arcing spray of mud behind the jeep. All around her, the wicked gales shoved the trees toward her, scraping the windshield with stray branches. Erin rocked back and forth, encouraging her jeep to make it through this rut before the torrential downpour turned the dirt road into a slick mud trap.

"Come on, Betsy," Erin said aloud.

"So," Sharon said, "this is Betsy." She laughed. "That explains a lot and saves us an awkward conversation."

"What?" Erin asked, oblivious to the context of Sharon's comment.

"You've been calling out Betsy's name in your sleep," Sharon said, sighing, knowing the joke didn't land.

"No, I haven't," Erin said, defending herself.

Suddenly, the front right tire dug into the gravel, gaining enough traction to catapult the jeep forward. As the back tires popped out of the rut, the cab lurched violently. The steering wheel drove into Erin's gut, winding her. Somehow, she kept the jeep on the road. With the deteriorating weather, time was becoming a factor. If the jeep got stuck on this road, it would be a twenty-minute walk to the Blue Hole National Key Deer Refuge.

Sharon's head thumped the soft top of the jeep. Absently, she rubbed the back of her head, her fingers vanishing into the deep chestnut curls.

When Erin caught her breath, she laughed. "I'm sorry," she reached over and placed her hand on Sharon's knee. She traced the inside of Sharon's exposed thigh with her index finger. When she reached the torn fabric of her jean shorts, she worked her fingers beneath.

Sharon shivered, gasping, "You tease." She reached down and grabbed Erin by the wrist. "Don't start something you can't finish." Without letting go of Erin, she moved her hand back down to her knee.

"Just giving you a preview of what to expect when we get there," Erin said, winking at Sharon. Driven wild by the danger, she forced the jeep over thirty. The tires slipped in the mud, causing the jeep to swerve back and forth.

"Slow down," Sharon demanded, strengthening her voice. "We can't fool around if we're dead."

In the silence between them, the rain pattered off the soft top. Pouring from the sky in sheets, the speed of the rainfall blended the sound into a constant drone. Each squall of wind circulated falling water from the palm leaves and splattered it over the windshield. The wipers swept across the window, working hard to keep up. "I'm just fooling around," Erin whispered, breaking the silence, her voice suffocated by the storm.

A blustering gust of wind rocked the jeep. In the distance, a palm tree cracked in half. The splintering wood exploded outwards in a barrage of wooden projectiles. Erin bumped her head off the roof, jumping at the sharp sound. At the bend, the top of the tree collapsed onto the road. She eased off the gas, allowing the jeep to coast the rest of the way. "Help me move that branch," Erin said.

"Please," she added.

"Why did we think this would be a great idea?" Sharon protested, crisscrossing her arms over her chest.

"If I recall," Erin started, "you thought it would be nice to be alone in the jungle, away from the turmoil of the city, to experience this storm. Besides, the electricity in our apartment would go out, anyway. And there's a generator here we can use." Erin shoved her door open, using her shoulder to brace the door against the wicked winds. Instantly, the rain soaked Erin head to toe. Her tank-top clung to her body, forming a second skin. Mud splashed beneath her feet, the road slick with rivers of rainwater running over it. Her glasses slid down her nose. She pushed them back up out of habit, knowing full well they'd become a nuisance soon enough. If she hadn't been in such a rush this morning, she would have worn her contacts.

When she glanced over her shoulder at Sharon, she winked. Despite the terrible conditions, she allowed a smile to form on her lips. Sharon grinned back. Her curls, flattened by the rain, draped over her face. She peered out from behind the veil of hair. With a graceful sweep of her hand, Sharon's hazel eyes were on full display. Even though they'd been dating for years, Erin couldn't help but feel jealous of Sharon's curves and natural good looks, even amid this chaotic scene.

Splinters of the broken palm tree trunk lay scattered across the road. Palm leaves glistened in the rain, catching the faint trickle of daylight through the blackened clouds. They got to work shifting the downed tree to the side of the road. A boom of thunder resounded overhead, and the earth shuddered. Hidden by the deafening roar rumbling in the sky, a guttural growl rose from the bushes.

"What the hell?" Sharon asked, her jaw hanging wide open as she caught the tail end of the disturbing noise.

"I don't know," Erin answered in a low whisper. "But I'm not going to stick around to find out. Let's get that tree branch to the side of the road and get out of here."

WASHOUT

William drove down the winding hill, the towering bluff blocking the roaring wind. At the bottom of the hill, the road stretched across a low valley. Voluminous white spray soared over the rock levee that protected the road from the ocean. The surging salt water was finding its way past the barrier as the road disappeared beneath the frothy waters. On the other side of the valley, the road leading to Mr. Burke's house had turned into a waterfall. The ocean had torn down the garage at the back of Mr. Burke's property, and flotsam drifted in the raging water.

"That stubborn fool," William muttered to himself.

He waited at the top of the hill, letting the engine idle as he gauged the current. If he timed it right, he could make it most of the way across the dip in the road before the surge of water gushed across the highway. When the tide rolled out, he watched in fascination as the faint traces of the reflective yellow paint on the road appeared in the dull daylight. As the tide rushed forward, the muddied water blurred out any signs that a road even existed. Above him, the power lines swayed wildly as the gusts of wind hammered the coastline.

When the water level reached its peak, William floored

the accelerator. As the black arm of the RPM gauge approached the top of the red warning limits, the engine grumbled in protest. His Dodge rumbled down the hill. The back tires swayed from side to side on the wet pavement before catching their grip, and the rear end of the truck straightened out. As the front grill of the truck collided with the unexpected depths, filthy water exploded over the front window, smearing the glass in brine and grit. The wipers skittered over the dirtied surface. For a moment, the truck drifted toward the levee, the force of the retreating wave carrying him with savage ferocity. The cab of the truck seemed to float on top of the surface for an eternity before it rocked, the tires gaining traction on the asphalt just before the edge of the road.

Never once taking his foot off the gas peddle, the engine roared, and the tires screeched against the pavement. All at once, the Dodge hauled itself forward in a jerking motion, accelerating down the dangerous strip of road. Where the road crested, the next hill seemed impossibly far away. It took the Hemi engine ten seconds to reach sixty miles an hour, which felt like an eternity to William. The muddied water retreated, but he couldn't see the lines on the road beneath the deepening layer of encroaching saltwater. His vision narrowed, fixed on the rise of the road just above Mr. Burke's driveway. If he crossed the final 100-stretch of road quickly, he'd be out of the water and on dry land before the next surge.

A thunderous wave pounded the levee. Thick, white foam pelted the windshield, the wipers leaving streaks behind as they struggled to keep his line of sight free. The wind howled overhead, and the water level surged exponentially.

"Fuck!" William pounded his fist against the wheel as he felt the cab of the truck defying gravity once more. The back end went first, and the truck swung ninety degrees until he was facing the rock wall. He watched in horror as the tremendous surge of ocean swept the top layer of rocks over and onto the road with a booming crash. The tremendous force of the ocean dragged his truck backward, carrying several rocks toward the truck. Suddenly, the rear tires slipped off the road and the truck slipped into a small ditch.

There was nothing for William to do but close his eyes and pray for the best. A metallic thunk rattled the undercarriage of the truck. His head smacked the steering wheel as the violent force shook the cab. Metal crunched beneath him as the Dodge skidded further into the ditch. When he opened his eyes, he was staring up at the swirling storm clouds. The boisterous sound of gushing water filled his ears as the ocean rushed back toward Hurricane Rose.

"Get out of there," a faint voice called out.

Dazed and confused, William couldn't tell where the sound was coming from. He rubbed his forehead, expecting to find blood on his fingers when he pulled his hand back, but there was none there. Frigid water dripped into his lap from a crack in the windshield. William just sat there, trying to regain his wits before the next surge plowed through. With the levee already crumbling, the next wave would deal a devastating blow.

The door groaned open. "Come on," someone said. Mr. Burke was standing on the runners, leaning into the cab. "You got to get moving, son," he said as he fumbled with William's seat belt. "Snap out of it!" he screamed as the roar of water gushed past them.

Without the seatbelt holding him up, William fell into Mr. Burke and they both tumbled onto the road. William landed on top. Burke gagged as he sucked in a mouthful of water, pushing William off. "Jesus Christ, son," he choked out.

Somehow, William found his feet and reached out his hand to help his savior up. The gritty, surging ocean sloshed past his feet, tugging at him, urging him to come with it. "Sorry," William stuttered, yanking Burke to his feet.

"Run, you fool," Burke shoved William toward the embankment.

Without a second thought, William sprinted toward safety, both men's footfalls splashing in the retreating water. The rain was falling sideways in sheets, pelting them as they struggled to get to higher ground. Burke kept stride with the younger man, only falling a few feet behind. William's leg muscles ached, and his lungs burned. The roar of the ocean thundered against the rock wall, and a rumble shook the road beneath their feet. A flood of water rushed toward them. Just as William was about to lose hope, he stumbled forwards as his toe struck the rising pavement. Hope fueled William, propelling him forward. The tug of the water brushed past his boots as he made his way up the road and toward Mr. Burke's house. Unable to contain himself, he let out a triumphant scream.

A screech of terror answered. When William turned around, Mr. Burke was nowhere to be seen. "Where are you?" he yelled into the raging storm, the wind whisking his voice away.

The ocean surged past the levee, the rocks all but vanishing beneath the churning waves as they rushed inland. A swatch of Burke's yellow rain slicker floated on the surface, smeared with gobs of deep red blood. William raised his hand to his face to stifle a scream as something beneath the surface emerged from the murky waters. Greenish-black scales rose out of the water in a thousand blades, and a set of reptilian-yellow eyes focused on William. Before he could see the monster rise from the depths, he turned and raced toward Mr. Burke's home. Behind him, the ground rumbled with a series of rapid thumps as the ancient creature gave chase.

***

Caught up in the current, Art found himself trapped in the relentless cycle of the tide. At the mercy of the elements, his energy was depleted. He bobbed with the swell of the tide, white caps crashing over him, the ebb and flow of the tide pulling him back and forth. Out of the corner of his eye, Art spotted debris drifting along, stuck in the same holding pattern.

With the last of his strength, Art swam toward the debris of his sunken ship. Gasping for air and his heart racing in his chest, Art realized he would only get one chance. If he timed it right, the tide would do most of the work for him—but one lapse in judgment would result in a fatal mistake. The saltwater stung his eyes, and the brine soured his stomach as the ocean forced itself down his throat.

A wave rolled toward him. He swam toward it so that it wouldn't sweep him too far off course. The swell lifted him up, giving him a momentary glimpse of the shore. Before sinking down into the trough, Art drifted along the crest atop the wave, taking in the glorious vision of green ahead. The view gave him false hope.

The churning water knocked the wreckage around, broken boards battering against the hard plastic keel of the ship's capsized life raft. Exhausted, Art felt himself sinking beneath the surface, powerless to resist the call of the sea. With fatigued muscles, he kicked and clawed his way back to the surface. As he breached, he smashed his head off a wooden beam. A tepid trickle of blood beneath the hairline dribbled down his face, the saltwater diluting it and stinging at the wound.

Dizzy with pain, Art flailed his arms and wracked his knuckles off the beam. He embraced the excruciating throb as he dug his nails into the board, dragging himself to it. Using the crux of his elbows to hold him up, he laid his arms over the floating wood. With the aid of the flotsam, Art allowed himself to relax. Lactic acid flooded into his legs, cramping his muscles. His quadriceps flexed and tensed, the fibers separating, pulling them apart. If his arms failed him, they'd drag him down to the bottom.

He tried to kick his legs to propel himself toward the shore, but they refused to cooperate with the signals sent from his brain. Pulling himself out of the water as much as he could, Art leaned his chest across the beam. Despite the pressing situation, his legs needed to rest. Tossed around by the waves, Art drifted in the middle of the bay, waiting for his legs to recover enough to make another attempt at reaching the shore before the brunt force of Hurricane Rose arrived.

Underneath him, the alpha predator stalked the strange shape along the surface, unafraid, curious, and ravenous.

PREDATOR

Hidden at the edge of the muddied flow of water, the twenty-seven-foot creature topped the scale at just over 25,000 pounds. The beast lurked amongst the shadows, concealing itself just below the surface, waiting for its opportunity to feed. Driven mad by the storm, the ancient survival instincts hard-wired into its DNA switched to their primal function: to hunt. With its heightened senses enraged by Hurricane Rose, the beast relentlessly stalked any signs of prey. With fear pushing away hunger and cravings driving it mad, the creature was emboldened. After being taken from its natural habitat and drugged, the creature's appetite had grown out of control. And the storm was wreaking havoc on the food chain, scattering the various animals in all directions away from their natural habitats. Forced into the concrete jungle, the predator reacted furiously at the strange noises and overload of electric impulses, throwing caution to the wind and pressing the attack.

The bite-sized prey it had devoured earlier did little to satisfy its gigantic appetite, so the predator pursued vibrations coming from somewhere nearby. As it made its way inland, the water level decreased, and soon its horrendous scales and jagged teeth would become exposed, its advantage taken away. It knew it should wait for the surging storm to flood this strange place, but Hurricane Rose had already scrambled its thoughts. Besides, the beast sensed other predators forging their way deep into the city. And it didn't want the competition to devour its source of food before satisfying its hunger.

With an attuned sense, the beast could perceive others of its kind nearby, fleeing from its path, giving the alpha predator a wide berth. Driven by primal instinct, the predator picked up the pheromones of a nearby male, keeping the potential mate close. Once it satisfied its hunger, the beast would fill its primary aim: it would procreate.

***

Its nostrils flared, filling the creature's brain with the unusual aroma of its prey. Hidden in the darkness, just beneath the raging waters, the predator stalked the strange animal. Always an opportunistic hunter, the reptilian creature headed toward the cave entrance. Thousands of years of evolution and hereditary instinct had honed its skills. It would ambush its prey where the entrance narrowed, using the raging waters to its advantage. Moving swiftly against the current, the massive predator moved into position.

Powerful waves crashed into the mouth of the cave, the strong currents pelting the beast with debris. Hardened scales easily defended against the assault, deflecting the will of the ocean with ease. Its prey struggled against the surging waters, stumbling toward the waiting ambush. Muddied waters gushed over the creature's scaled backside, camouflaging it in the dim light. Its prey was close now. The beast could feel the vibrations on the ground as it stumbled toward its demise.

The beast's jaw unhinged, its upper row of teeth ready to snap closed with incredible force. A booming scream echoed off the cavern walls and the strange animal ran back into the depths of the cave. Patient, the beast boded its time. Either they'd be forced to leave through the exit, or the water level would rise enough for the beast to move on the offensive. It wouldn't let another opportunity pass.

AROUND TOWN PART TWO

Jake tugged at his belt, hitching his pants as he stood up, scratching at the back of his head with the wrench as he peered at the generator. A flood of water gushed into the basement from a crack in the foundation, whirling just below his knees. His toes were numb from the frigid flood waters pouring into the room from deep underground, his calf muscles heavy with the coldness. The platform budged after spending the last ten minutes unscrewing the bolts that fastened the bracket to the far wall, tilting the unit downwards, providing the proper angle to allow him to attach the wires to the primary power system. Once Jake secured the last wire into place, he placed the wrench back into his tool belt and allowed the platform to fall back against the wall, thudding against the cement blocks with a thunderous crash.

He manipulated the toggles into their correct positions and grasped the pull cord. With a strong yank, the generator grumbled and sputtered. For a moment, the basement lights flickered then abruptly died. "Damn it," he mumbled under his breath. After another pull, the generator rumbled steadily, settling into a powerful, growling purr. Electricity hummed emphatically after the prolonged absence.

"That's better," Jake said, turning around. Focused on the stairwell, his feet snagged under something beneath the filthy water. His hands shot out to brace against the fall, and they scrapped over something ridged, tearing the palms of his hand wide open. A terrified scream escaped his lips as his eyes fell upon the scaled torso of a crocodile. Twelve feet long and two feet wide, the slithering creature blocked his path to the stairs. Its jaws snapped open and growled at Jake.

He jumped to his feet and scurried backward, trying to put some space between himself and the savage beast. "Get out of here!" Jake screamed. The shrill sound of his own voice sounded foreign in his ears, almost alien.

The gator scurried through the water, displacing waves throughout the basement. It threw its head back, letting out a hissing howl. Yellow teeth lined the creature's jaw. Designed to blend into the murky water, its green hide slithered beneath the surface. Before the creature reached Jake, he leaped up onto the platform. It rocked beneath him, and his arms dashed out to his side, struggling to re-gain his balance. Blistering heat from the generator seared the back of his leg, singing the hairs through his jeans. The generator sent a constant stream of vibrations cours-ing through the platform, which quickly worked its way up Jake's leg and into his abdomen.

The crocodile rammed its snout into the platform's leg, sending a jolt that wobbled the wooden structure. There was a sharp snap as a crack splintered the leg. For a second, Jake thought he would plummet into the wa-ter below. When he didn't, he let out a burst of laughter.

"You're just someone's discarded pet," he chuckled. "Nobody wants you. They flushed you down the toilet to live with the other shit."

With the water level rising fast, Jake didn't want to swim toward the exit with that creature. Despite the beast's smaller stature, its fanged, razor-sharp teeth and jagged claws would cut through his flesh with ease. Jake studied the crocodile, trying to determine its ability to navigate the flooding waters. It moved with astonishing grace, stalking Jake from below.

Jake's gaze shifted to the stairs and saw the basement door hanging open. If he reached the top of the stairs, he would slam it closed behind him, locking the crocodile in the basement. He needed something to distract the creature long enough to give him time to make his move. His eyes scanned the room, searching for anything he could use to give him an advantage. Then he remembered his tool belt—the hammer. He tugged the clawed hammer from his belt, enjoying the weight of it in his hand, and instantly felt safer. If something went wrong, it would double as a blunt weapon, and he wouldn't think twice about using it.

As he unbuckled the tool belt, the uneven weight caught him by surprise. The left side dipped and swung, dispersing a pouch full of screws over the water. Intrigued by the commotion, the crocodile veered directly toward the sinking screws. Not allowing himself to overthink it, Jake leaped from the platform. He landed in the water with a deafening splash. Behind him, the platform collapsed into a splintered heap. The generator crashed into the water. As the water fried the wires, the power cut out, causing the electricity to die. Too afraid to glance over his shoulder, he bolted for the staircase, the sole of his work boots sloshing through the deepening waters.

Submerged beneath the muddied water, Jake's right foot slammed hard into the first step. He tripped up the stairs. The edge of the stair banged against his shin, sending a wave of pain up his leg. Instincts drove his limbs, and he scurried up the steps without getting to his feet, knocking his elbows and knees off the wood without acknowledging the pain. With the doorknob within reach, he lunged forward, hauling himself to his feet. Not looking back, he slammed the door behind him.

As he caught his breath, he leaned against the basement door and allowed his racing heart to steady. A creaking door opened down the hallway, catching his attention. Someone's familiar voice called out his name over and over. Far too winded to respond, he ignored the man calling out.

"What the hell is wrong with you?" Mr. Marshall snapped, appearing in front of Jake. "Are you deaf?"

"What is it?" Jake panted.

"I said," Mr. Marshall grunted, "what are you going to do about the water on the floor?" He swept his hand toward the hallway. A trickle of water seeped down the tiled hallway, puddling around Mr. Marshall's door. "What the hell have you been doing all…"

"Oh fuck off," Jake cut him off.

"Now you listen…"

"Not going to happen," Jake said, speaking with a false cordial tone. "The shop vacuum is in the basement. You're free to use it." Before Mr. Marshall could say anything, Jake headed toward the staircase leading upstairs.

He heard the basement door open, and the top stair creaked. Then Mr. Marshall's shrill scream echoed throughout the building, followed by the basement door slamming shut.

"Jake," Mr. Marshall called out breathlessly. "There's an alligator in the basement."

"It's a goddamn crocodile," Jake corrected him.

"What are you going to do about it?"

As if he had never heard Mr. Marshall, he added, "In a while, crocodile," as he stomped up the stairs, laughing to himself.

***

With the outside world shut out, Amy sat with her back to the window, slumped deep into the cushioned chair. In front of her, a plate loaded with three waffles, crisp bacon, sausage links, and hash browns, all smothered in sweet maple syrup, demanded her attention; her mouth watered at the sight of the food. The wind howled all it wanted, booming off the hotel with tremendous force. And the rain fell from the very heavens, spattering against the windows in a rhythmic melody. Nothing would stop her from eating this food.

Despite the power being out, the stainless steel basin had kept the food warm enough to leave a comforting tingle in her stomach. Saliva filled her mouth as she took a bite of bacon. Amy stabbed at her plate, piling an assortment of food into her mouth. Sweet, salty, and savory danced across her palette. The more she ate, the hungrier she became. Unable to control herself, she shoved forkfuls of food into her mouth, only taking a moment to chew before swallowing lumps of food down her throat. Months of living on the streets had made her ravenous.

"Can I get you anything else?" a server asked, appearing out of thin air. Dressed in a black pinstriped suit and silver tie with his hair slicked back, and his mustache fashioned into a thin curl that stuck out over his cheeks, the maître d' could have been ready for a c-level executive meeting. "Perhaps something to drink?"

"A coffee would be nice if it's still warm," Amy said, feeling guilty about asking for something else after being given so much. But she deserved it after everything she'd gone through, even if these people had nothing to do with her recent string of bad luck.

The server left and returned with a coffee urn, placing a saucer and mug on the table just to the left of Amy's plate. With a flourish, the server turned over the cup and poured the coffee from high above, a long, brown waterfall cascading into her mug. An enticing aroma of macadamia nuts and cocoa wafted from the urn. "Should I leave room for milk or sugar?"

Amy shook her head, mystified by the server's mannerisms.

"Very good, ma'am," he said, filling her cup. Bubbles danced on the top, congregating around the edge of the rim. A faint wisp of steam rose from the mug, spiraling into the air and vanishing from sight after traveling a few inches.

Amy almost choked on a bite of chocolate chip waffle, her hand darting up to cover her mouth. Wide-eyed, she stared up at the server with a confused expression.

"Is everything alright, ma'am?"

"Yes, everything is perfect," Amy responded. "It's just that no one's called me ma'am in ages. Too long if you ask me." Amy cut up the waffle into smaller, bite-sized pieces as she spoke, too embarrassed to match his gaze.

"My pleasure. If there's anything else you may want, don't be shy. Darrell is my name. Just call out and I'll be right over." He winked and left without giving Amy a chance to say thank you.

Darrell sat at an empty table by the window, staring out at the rain and drinking from his own cup of coffee. His left leg hung over his right knee, and he scratched at his calf. With no one else in the dining room, Darrell seemed to enjoy the quiet. He picked up a newspaper, opened it to the sports page, and hummed to himself as he read.

Amy turned her attention back to the food, devoting her time to devouring it before someone realized she didn't belong here. The clamorous sound of the double doors swinging open caught Amy's attention. Carrying a clipboard against her chest, the woman from the lobby made her way across the room toward her.

"Hi." The woman greeted Amy with her arm extended in a handshake. "My name is Jessica, but my friends call me Jessie."

Amy fumbled with the napkins, her fingers sticky with maple syrup, and reciprocated. Amy swallowed a mouthful of food. "Thank you so much, Jessie."

"Again," Jessica laid the clipboard on the table with a hollow thump, "I'm sorry about the incident earlier in the lobby. Certainly no reason for Aaron to behave in that manner." She unfastened the clip and slid a voucher across the table. "This is a free night's stay in our Queen's

Suite. It's already paid for, but the occupant never arrived. Their flight got canceled because of the hurricane." She gestured toward the window, the view outside confirming her statement. "It was Aaron's turn to claim any empty vacancies. But because of his behavior, I'm letting you have it."

"I don't know what to say." Amy paused. Overcome with emotions, she became anxious and joyous, waiting for it all to come crashing down around her. "Thanks." She couldn't properly articulate her gratitude, and her inability to express her genuine appreciation bothered her.

"Think nothing of it. With the power out, this food would just go to waste," Jessie said. "And don't worry about room…"

A crashing, clattering bang disrupted Jessie. Glass shattered and steel clanged and skidded across the tiles.

Jessie swung around toward the source of the clamorous racket. "Oh my God, Darrell," she laughed, "you scared the shit out of me."

A serving tray lay turned over at Darrell's feet as food splattered over his shiny shoes and a puddle of coffee expanded over the tile. He stood back onto them, staring out the window, his hands concealing his mouth. Faintly, Amy could hear the frightening growl from outside that caused Darrell to freeze. But she couldn't see anything through the rain.

"Are you alright, Darrell?" Jessie asked, stepping toward him, her eyes never once wandering toward the window.

The rain hammered the window, and the wind boomed against the glass. Darrell raised his arm, pointing a trembling finger toward the outside. "I think…" he paused, his voice catching in his throat. "I saw a dragon."

Jessie burst out laughing. "Don't be ridiculous," she said, slapping him on the back.

Outside, the sound of crunching metal rang out as a car alarm blared to life. Tremors rumbled the ground, pounding blows that galloped toward them. Amy raced over beside Darrell, trying to glimpse the frightening beast outside. Another car alarm went off, the horn honking in long bursts. Water obscured the view outside as a car rocked on its tires, the windows exploding inwards as the back end of a vehicle swung around.

"Oh my God," Jessie sputtered, gawking at the ancient reptilian monster outside.

***

"Where are you, Bud?" Wendy screamed into the wind, a strong gust whisking her voice away as if her words were weightless. "Stupid fucking dog," she muttered under her breath, the fear inside of her morphing into anger. She pulled her rain jacket tight against her body, feeling the wind assault her with pellets of rain. Despite the heat of the day, she shivered and considered heading back inside to get warm.

Rainwater gushed down the street, the sewer spewing filthy water into the streets from the gutters. For no reason at all, she headed up the winding hill, following her gut instincts without question. One of her neighbors was in their shed, busying themselves with a generator to prepare for the impending power outage. As she made her way up the hill, the wind blew with relentless fury, swaying the trees hard to one side with no reprieve.

Wendy cupped her hands and called out to her neighbor, "Hey, Bill! Have you seen my dog?"

He left the safety of his shed, his hand raising to protect his face as he stepped into the blustering weather. "Your dog is missing too?" he asked, clearly distraught.

Wendy stepped into Bill's driveway so she wouldn't have to yell. "Yeah, he must have hurt himself slipping out of his collar." She held up Bud's blue studded collar so that Bill could see the deep crimson stain.

"Oh dear," Bill sighed, "that looks terrible. You think he broke his collar and ran away?"

"Uh," Wendy paused, scrunching up her face as she suppressed the lingering thoughts from her mind. "What do you believe happened?"

Bill gestured toward his fence with a flick of his wrist. "Something destroyed my fence trying to get at the dog."

"The wind?"

"Definitely not the wind," Bill answered, his tone grave.

Perplexed, Wendy stared at Bill. "What do you mean?"

"There's no way wind caused that damage because whatever came through the fence shattered the boards inwards against the wind. The only thing that gives me any hope is that Chester doesn't have a leash and, hopefully..." Bill paused, staring into his backyard. "Chester will be back after he's done chasing some squirrel around." Lost in thought, Bill wandered aimlessly back into his garage to tinker with the generator, abandoning the conversation without another word.

"If I see him, I'll let you know," Wendy said, gave a

wave that wasn't reciprocated, then headed back to the road to search for Bud. The gusts of wind strengthened at the crest of the hill, forcing Wendy to lean into them to battle the gales. She turned back, hoping that she would have a better vantage point from the top of the hill. A threatening cluster of black clouds loomed just beyond the edge of town—Hurricane Rose knocking at their door. Lightning flashed but the dark skyline swallowed the brilliant sparks of white before they struck the earth.

A roaring clap of thunder rumbled in the distance. Wendy felt the ground tremble as if frightened by the heavens. She didn't know how much longer she could keep searching for her dog. With time running out, she doubled back over her tracks, keeping to the opposite side of the road. Her eyes scanned everything, scouring for any sign of Bud, anything. When she came to the intersection just above her home, she decided she'd make one loop of Portland Street, where she took Bud for walks every morning. Portland Street formed a pleasant loop that started above her house and wrapped back around to the bottom. "Maybe Bud would have gone somewhere familiar?" she suggested to herself.

Halfway down Portland Street, she noticed that something had left a deep indent in the grass, leaving a trail of mud that led over the embankment and into the ditch. It must have been a car, the width and depth much too big to have been anything else. Wendy raced toward the scene, expecting to find a car turned over in the ditch.

Filled with concern, she shouted out, "Is anyone down there?"

Stepping off the road to examine the impression, Wendy's foot slid on the slick grass beneath, sending her careening down a small embankment and into the ditch. She broke her fall with her hands as the flood waters soaked her to the bone. When she tried to get up, she slipped once more in the muddied earth, a hunk of sod sliding out from beneath her, and she landed hard on her backside. Gritty water filled her mouth as she plunged into three feet of water that had collected in the drainage ditch. She sat up, the current pounding against her as the drain of water ran toward a culvert at the bottom of Portland Street. In a fit of rage, she punched her fists into the water and screamed.

"Fucking dog," she snapped and cried.

When she tried to stand up, the current knocked her off balance. Wendy lunged for the bank, gasping for breath. On her hands and knees, she crawled up the bank, slipping on the slick surface. To steady herself, she dug the tips of her shoes into the softened earth, making shorter, safer movements.

Behind her, something interrupted the current as the drain water gushed down the hill, blocking the flow. Wendy turned toward the sound of sloshing water and screamed. Beneath the murky surface, something scaly slithered directly toward her. Terrified, she abandoned her slow and steady pace for a jumbled flurry of scrambled movements.

An intense, searing pain flooded her lower leg, and she observed herself being hauled down, the grassy bank growing larger as she dug her nails into the muddied bank. She turned just in time to witness the yellowish-white belly of the monster attacking her. Its armored verdant head deformed as its savage jaws clamped on her leg. Wendy battled against the creature's movements. With its teeth clamped into the subtle flesh of her calf, the crocodile ripped a hunk of meat from her leg as it tumbled back down into the gushing muddy water.

When she found herself released from the predator's death grip, Wendy scrambled up the embankment. An overwhelming surge of relief flooded her as her right hand slapped the concrete sidewalk. When she sought to get to her feet, the pain in her leg flared. She plunged forward and rolled into the street.

A truck slammed on its brakes, the rubber tires screeching as the Ford Ranger skidded to a halt inches from her face. "Hey, lady, are you alright?" a woman called out from the driver's seat.

Wendy heard the woman's feet splash onto the road as she jumped down from the cab. Exhausted and out of breath, Wendy pushed herself to her feet, using the grill to haul herself up. "Help!" Wendy shouted, her hoarse voice sounding alien in her head.

"Oh my god," the stranger gasped, "did I hit you?" She rushed to Wendy's side to help her to her feet.

"Get me out of here," Wendy sobbed.

"You're bleeding…"

"Now!" Wendy screamed, spittle flying from her lips.

The woman helped her to the passenger side, opening the door for her and guiding her into the seat. Once Wendy found herself inside the cab with the door shut, she breathed a sigh of relief. The stranger hopped in the driver's seat and put the truck in gear. She passed Wendy an old rag from the glove box. "Use this as a tourniquet to help stop the bleeding."

"Thanks," Wendy uttered, her voice fragile as the pain radiated from the bite mark and raced through her body. She tied the rag off just below her knee, feeling the pressure as she yanked it as tight as she could.

"What the hell happened to you?" she asked as she drove down Portland Street.

"I think a crocodile bit me."

"What do you mean? It's pretty obvious it bit you." The stranger gawked down at Wendy's leg with a distressed expression.

"I mean, it could have been an alligator," Wendy answered and laughed as she blacked out from the immense pain.

FEED

Art swayed with the crashing waves, bracing himself against the drifting wreckage. The current slammed him into the beam at the crest and trough of each wave. Each impact compressed his ribcage, driving the wind from him. The ocean took every opportunity to explore Art's lungs, giving him a ghastly preview of drowning, teaching him every excruciating detail that awaited him.

A snaking shadow swept through the darkened waters beneath Art, twisting as it slithered by. The predator encircled him, each rotation getting tighter as the creature searched for an opportunity to strike. As the creature rose, the shadow loomed larger, more detailed. It passed directly beneath Art, dwarfing him.

With his gaze fixed on the shore, Art never noticed death's shadow stalking him. His mind wandered with joyous thoughts of the sand beneath his toes, strolling over the beach toward the road. Occasionally, he would glance out at the drab horizon at Hurricane Rose, making sure he had time before her arrival. He didn't want to get caught out in the open waters with her. Without a care in the world, he kicked his feet, aiding the propulsion of his make-shift raft, the current doing all the work.

If Art had seen what lay beneath the surface, he would have gladly opened his mouth and answered the call of the sea. But a painful death waited enthusiastically for him.

***

The pull of the tide grew stronger, overpowering the alpha predator. She needed to get to land soon, or she would waste her energy out here and fall victim to the determination of the storm. It couldn't wait any longer to feed. Making one last pass, the drab light did little to help distinguish the features of the prey above, an oddly shaped shadow that formed a cross. The beast had seen nothing like it before. But her nostrils picked up the familiar stench of edible flesh.

Rain pounded the surface with a constant hammering drone. A strange scent bled into the ocean similar to urine but soured by a familiar aroma—fear. The creature floating along the surface thrashed, churning the water into a froth of bubbles as it floundered along the waves. Wounded, the animal's frantic action produced minimal movement. The predator dove, making a wide looping circle, keeping its reptilian eye on its prey, allowing it to spend its energy. A frantic flailing of limbs was enough to signal to the beast that the time to strike had arrived.

With a powerful thrust of its tail, the beast diverted from its course, rising toward the surface with a tremendous burst of lightning-quick speed. After spending hours encased in the darkness of the depths, the drab daylight transformed into a blaring glare. Guided strictly by scent, the alpha propelled toward its prey with unfathomable speed. A deluge of saltwater filled the creature's gullet, giving it the extra buoyancy it needed to land the killing blow.

***

Oblivious until the last minute, Art thrashed his legs. After the prolonged burst of exertion, his feet felt like two lead weights attached at the end of his legs. The wind howled around him; a harsh whistle that joined in the cacophony of the crashing waves that hammered the shore. A flock of seagulls flew out from the shore, circling overhead. The pitch of their call changed, growing shriller and more incisive. Blended with nature, the calamitous roar of Hurricane Rose drowned out the rush of water beneath him.

Before he knew what hit him, Art exploded from the ocean in a frothy spray. For a moment, he hovered over the waves, defying gravity. He had a bird's-eye view of the ocean and enjoyed being weightless, untethered from the hellish nightmare waiting below. Then, in a split second, everything came crashing down around him as he plummeted back into the ocean with tremendous force. His back snapped backward, but his hips smashed into something hard and rigid, snapping his spine with a crackling crunch. A jolt of pain raced through his body, every pain receptor in his body firing at once until he thought he would pass out from the overwhelming agony. But Art would not be so lucky.

A painful scream tried to escape his throat, but the seawater silenced the agonized sound. The faint noise bubbled to the surface, the dull sound dying as it reached the air above, swept away by the wind. He tried to hold the last of his breath in his lungs. They ached and burned as his body consumed the rest of the oxygen lingering in his lungs.

Numb from the waist down, the beast dragged Art toward the sea floor as the pressure in his abdomen increased. Through the dim light, Art could see a long snout clamped over his hips and stomach. Mangled teeth protruded from the diseased gums, bloodied and blackened. A trail of blood drifted upwards, fanning out as the monstrous jaws hauled him down with ease. Searing pain filled his abdomen. Blood flowed freely from his stomach, pouring out of the punctures from the razor-sharp teeth holding him in place. Entrails spilled from the wound as the teeth shredded his stomach into ribbons of red flesh. A cloud of blood and half-digested food washed over his face in a putrid shower.

The pressure compressed the plates of his cranium into the cerebral fluid of his brain. His eyes bulged from their sockets. A thick gush of blood expelled from his nose. He felt himself drifting toward oblivion as the jaws snapped shut over his chest, crushing his rib cage. A jolt of pain shocked him into consciousness long enough to allow the sea to flood his lungs. Welcoming the briny water into his body, Art thankfully drowned before the monster finished eating him alive.

TRAPPED WITH THE DEVIL

William sprinted up the hill, gasping for air; he kept glancing over his shoulder, praying he would find Mr. Burke chasing after him. But he knew that some horrendous creature from the depths of the ocean had feasted upon the army vet's flesh. And deep down, he knew he would be next if he couldn't get somewhere safe. He had to get as far away as possible before the sea monster finished its minuscule meal and turned its attention toward him.

When he reached the driveway, he turned back toward the hill one last time and wished he'd just kept going. A twenty-foot crocodile sat in the middle of the road with the fluorescent yellow strip running beneath its belly. The beast's snout raised in the air, swaying left to right, its nostrils flaring as it snorted, sucking in droplets of water from the air.

Frozen in place, William watched as the creature honed in on his scent despite the gales. Rain hammered off the roof of Mr. Burke's car and spattered across the windshield, the hollow patter of water cascading in an isochronal rhythm. A shrill scream cut through the boisterous racket of the storm. Torn from his trance, William spun around, desperately searching for the source of the distress call. The panicked plea for help vanished, whisked away by a powerful gust of wind.

"Mrs. Burke?" William called out, trying to remember if she even existed; he couldn't remember for the life of him. Not recognizing his own voice, it took William a minute to realize that he had been the one screaming.

The house stood vacant, silent except for the rattle of the gutters and boom of the wind against the siding. He turned to race toward the two-story New England-style home and bumped his hip off the fender of the old Chevrolet in the driveway. Checking the driver's side door, he found it locked. His heart sank in his chest.

The crocodile growled, demanding William's full attention. Without warning, the predator dashed toward him with a scrapping clatter, its claws shredding the asphalt as it closed the distance between them with surprising quickness. With nowhere else to go, William rolled over the hood of the car. The aluminum hood buckled and clunked beneath his weight. Before he reached the other side, the crocodile rattled the car with a thunderous impact, tossing William off the hood and onto the soaked lawn. He landed against the sod with a wet *thwump*.

Scrambling to his feet, William scurried toward the porch. The crocodile's webbed feet pounded the ground, navigating its way around the Chevrolet. When he reached the porch, his left foot stubbed the first step. He bashed his shin off the edge, let out a pained yelp, and stumbled forward. But he maintained his momentum churning toward the front door.

A moment of panic gripped his heart tight within its

grasp as William tried to turn the knob and it didn't twist. He threw his shoulder into the door with all his might, and the sound of wood splintered cracked in his ear. But there were no visible cracks anywhere to be found on the door, a sore shoulder the only reward. To dry his hands, he rubbed them against his jeans then tried the doorknob once more. It twisted beneath his grasp. The door swung inwards, and he stumbled into the house and tripped over the welcoming mat, his shoes scuffing over the rough surface.

He turned just as the crocodile lumbered up the steps. The entire foundation of the house trembled. William drove his foot into the door, slamming it shut just as the beast rammed its armored head into the wooden slab. A cracking boom rang out. Black spiderwebs spread over the door as the wood splintered inwards.

"Goddamn it!" William yelled. "Go away!"

Another booming thump rattled the door, but it held intact—at least for now. He knew it wouldn't hold forever. If that predator wanted in, he'd break that door down sooner rather than later. Not sticking around to watch helplessly while the beast forced his way inside, William got to his feet and searched for the way upstairs. Outside of the porch, the short hall branched off into a foyer that led to three separate rooms. He traveled through the living room on the left-hand side. Framed pictures of Mr. Burke's time in the Marines adorned the walls. A small tube television sat on an end table in the room's corner. As he rushed past the bay window, he couldn't help noticing the view out over the Atlantic The emerald waves roiled and churned up thick white froth as towering waves slammed the craggy hillside below. Seafoam mounted up into the sky until the winds could carry it away, the spray leaving salt stains on the large panes of glass.

Behind him, the door splintered into kindling as the crocodile burst through. Shards of jagged wood skittered across the floor and spilled into the foyer. Fear fueled William's muscles with adrenaline, his legs pumping as he raced toward the kitchen. He slipped on the linoleum and slid across the room. His side slammed into the counter. A whimper escaped his lungs in a gush of air. Above him, the dishes clattered in the cupboards.

The crocodile trundled through the house, its claws clacking off the wooden floor in a maddening crescendo. William made his way toward a door in the far corner of the kitchen, pushing aside his agonizing pain. He threw the door open and sent the doorknob smashing into the drywall. Dust sprinkled over the floor.

"Fuck," William cursed in frustration as he stared down into the basement.

He turned around and backtracked toward the living room, praying that the beast continued toward the dining room, drawn to the garbage can where remnants of Mr. Burke's last meal still gave off a strong odor. Before he left the kitchen, a wooden knife box caught his attention. William pulled a long serrated knife from the block, the weight reassuring in his hand.

As soon as he rounded the corner, the crocodile lunged for him. Jagged teeth shredded through the flesh of Williams' thigh as the snout snapped shut. He screamed out in agony. Waves of searing pain radiated from the torn leg muscles. A deluge of blood oozed from between the clenched teeth, squirting over the floor in thick globs. Blinded by pain, William momentarily forgot about the kitchen knife until he went to grip the door frame. The stainless steel blade smacked off the molding, sending a jolt up his forearm.

The crocodile rolled over onto its side, hauling William with it. Desperate, he lashed out with the blade, stars dancing in his vision, his head swimming. He felt the blade sink into supple flesh with a wet, sickening pop. Tepid liquid gushed over his hand and splattered on the linoleum tile with a disgusting plop. As his vision cleared, he saw the knife protruding from the creature's skull, the blade buried an inch deep in the eye socket; puss and a string of coiled optical nerves oozed from the gory hole.

William felt the pressure on his leg evaporate, replaced immediately by a flood of pain. His momentum carried him into the door frame as the crocodile rolled onto its backside with a crashing boom. His vision narrowed, burning white light closing in from the edges into a tight circle. A guttural growl emanated from the pit of the creature's stomach. Unable to see, William stumbled away from the terrifying roar, his hand out in front of him, trying to find his way back toward the basement door.

Glimpses of the kitchen floated through his vision. His fingers cracked off the fridge, and he stubbed his toe into the wall before he found the doorway again, his hand discovering the rail. After the first cautions step, he scampered down the staircase, slamming the door shut behind him. When he reached the bottom, the rail ended before the last step. In his head, he had reached the basement floor. His knee locked, expecting to contact the concrete.

Instead, he plummeted forward, crashing to the floor in a heap.

Without bracing his fall, he smashed his head off the concrete and slipped into a deep state of unconsciousness.

***

A thunderous growl boomed overhead, rustling William out of the abyss and into a semi-state of wakefulness. Confused, he didn't recognize his surroundings, or how he had gotten into this strange dungeon. Sawdust coated the floor, and the fragrant aroma of cut pine overpowered the damp stench of the permanently wet cement. Water bubbled up through the porous surface of the floor. Nearby, wood groaned and creaked with a sense of pressing urgency. William searched the strange, cavernous space for the source of the distressing noise.

Tiny slits on the far wall, open to the elements, allowed a sliver of dull daylight and a heaping gush of flood water through. The horizon was an all-encompassing expanse of slab black granite speckled with gray and navy blue. Filthy rainwater trickled down the wall in tiny rivers that changed directions, snaking back and forth, falling to the floor, gathered around a rusted-out grate, and soaked into the bare earth below. A foul stench belched from the muddied hole.

His head throbbed and his vision blurred with each pounding pulse. With a grunt, he got to his feet, bracing himself by leaning on a worn workbench. He could feel the deep grooves and divots beneath his palm as he wandered aimlessly toward the staircase, his hands fumbling over metal tools. But he never picked one up. William stumbled toward the staircase, the hissing sound growing louder. His heart froze in his chest as he stared beneath the stairs. A thousand shapes lurked within the shadows, waiting for him to run up the stairs, allowing them to reach out and nab him, so they could drag him down to hell with them.

There were no other exits from the basement. He had to climb those stairs. A feral scream escaped his throat as he took the first step and glanced up. Wedged between the door frame, a freakishly enormous crocodile snapped its jaws at him, ropes of saliva dangling from its jowls. One clawed paw dangled over the first step; shards of splintered wood tracked down the steps. Its yellowed underbelly bulged over the top step and the green-scaled armor pierced the molding, sawing into the wood as it pressed itself into the tight confines, threatening to break the door down with every thrust of its body.

William backed away, his backside colliding with the workbench. Metal tools fell over the side and clattered against the floor. The boisterous racket caught his attention. A black handle poked out from beneath the bench, and a flat sheet of steel vanished beneath the bottom wooden shelf. He dropped to his hands and knees, grabbed the handle, and hauled a handsaw out from underneath the workbench. Wear and tear were visible over every jagged, rusted tooth of the saw blade.

A deep, booming crack exploded from the top of the staircase, sending a barrage of wooden shrapnel down the steps and over the floor. The staircase swayed and shuddered, struggling to withstand the tremendous weight of the beast. It made it halfway down before the staircase imploded, collapsing upon itself.

Stunned from the fall, the crocodile remained beneath the debris. The pile heaved and flowed with the creature's shallow breath. It shifted around beneath the boards, revealing the greenish-black reptilian skin of its backside. Primal instincts took over William, driving him forward, the saw brandished over his head. He lunged toward the pile and swung the blade down in an arc. The teeth bit into the hardened scaled armor, and a splat of blood splashed upwards, coating the rusted metal blade in thick, black globs of blood.

Enraged with the pain, the crocodile swung its tail, sweeping the debris toward the near wall, forcing William to jump over it. As he came down, he landed awkwardly on a board, sending him stumbling backward and toppling over the creature's tail. His backside slammed into the cement wall with an audible smack, compressing his ribcage and driving the air from his lungs in an exaggerated gasp.

With its snout wide open, the crocodile twisted its neck. One pale yellow eye glared at William. A blackened slurry of blood, puss, and optical nerves oozed from the other eye socket and down into its jaws.

"No fucking way."

William reached out and found the ragged edge of what remained of the staircase. With a tenuous grip, he pulled himself off the ground and tucked his knees into his stomach as the creature's jaws clamped shut with an audible snap.

Unable to hold on any longer, William's grip slipped, and he collapsed on top of the crocodile's head, the hardened scales driving into his backside. The beast trotted forwards, hoisting itself up onto a low bench. William tumbled backward, rolling over the freakishly long backside before careening off the side and landing on his side in the debris. An agonized yelp escaped his lungs as a sliver of wood slashed his stomach open. Blood soaked into his shirt as the fabric clung to his skin. He held his hand over the wound, assessing the damage through the cotton, keeping one watchful eye on the crocodile as he searched for an escape.

"Stay the fuck away from me!" William roared.

Sensing victory, the predator squared itself to William, methodically creeping forward, backing its prey into a corner. As the creature shuffled forward, pressing William into a dire situation, it left a trail of slick blood behind it. William inspected the scattered debris and discovered a smear of blood and torn skin on the jagged boards. Wounded animals became aggressive. Without warning, the creature lurched forward.

"Shit."

William sprang to the right toward the center of the room, giving himself space to run. The crocodile crashed into a pantry shelf stacked with dishes, toppling it with a clatter of shattering glass. Out of the corner of his eye, William spotted a tight crevice between the far wall and a deep freeze. He dashed forward, hoping that he would fit between them. With a sliding skid, he twisted onto his side and crammed himself into the tight space, needing a second effort to squeeze all the way to the back wall.

The crocodile rammed the deep freeze, slamming it straight back into the wall with a thundering crash. Cement shattered from the impact, cascading over William in a shower of dust and crumbling pieces. A fierce growl rumbled from the beast's throat as it drove its body into the facing of the deep freeze once more. This time it shifted toward William, compressing his shoulders until he didn't think he could take it.

Not ready to give up, the crocodile tried to stuff its snout into the crevice. A putrid stench poured from the pit of the creature's stomach, wafting over its diseased gums as its jaws snapped shut. The massacred eye-hole faced William. With its claws dug into the softened cement floor, the crocodile shoved itself forward, forcing itself further than William would have thought possible.

William wriggled his way to a standing position, his knees and elbows knocking off the wall and side of the freezer as he struggled. When his hand found the top of the deep freeze, he hauled himself up, dragging himself over the lid. Once the predator figured out what William had done, it backed away. With a heavy scrapping shriek, the freezer slid across the cement floor along with the creature as it retreated.

Suddenly, the freezer stopped skidding across the floor. William lost his balance and rolled forward toward the edge. Somehow, he braced himself before falling over the edge. The crocodile circled back, giving itself room to make another strike. William scrambled to his feet and jumped toward the back wall, reaching for the slits in the wall. His fingers curled around the iron bar and his feet curled into the wall just as the crocodile struck the deep freeze, ramming it into the wall. The lid popped open and slammed into William's back.

"Goddamn it," William cried out.

He pushed the lid back down with his feet and stood up, sucking in the ocean air. the taste of brine soiled his mouth and soured his stomach. Water sloshed against the wall outside before it spilled over the ledge, ran down the wall in a steady stream, and splashed to the floor. The grate below had already reached its capacity, the excess water overflowing over the floor now. If he didn't think of something soon, the crocodile could swim up and grab him right off the lid of the deep freeze.

And the crocodile must have realized the same thing because it lay in waiting, its one good eye fixed on William.

CUT OFF

Harold rushed forward as the narrow corridors filled with shadows, enclosing him in a tomb of darkness. A shrill scream shattered the methodical rhythm of the storm, ringing out from somewhere within the warehouse. His boots sloshed in the rising water, the cement floor leaving nowhere for the surging water level to drain. As he turned the corner, a slate-gray sky offered a trickle of dull daylight, into the building. He found himself paused in-between two offices. Even though the situation left him vulnerable, he compelled himself to push deeper into the building toward the light. In the remaining darkness, Harold's feet tangled in something beneath the water, and he fell face first into the filthy liquid with a resounding splash.

"Christ," he groaned, pushing himself up from the frigid water. Water-logged wrappers and other garbage clung to his rain slicker. Kneeling in the water, he swept the debris from his coat and recoiled as his hand brushed against a used condom. He gagged and wretched as acidic bile burned his throat.

"Look out!" a screaming warning filtered through the wall.

Harold didn't heed the warning. "Stay put. I'll get you out of there." He trudged through the floating garbage, the water level reaching over his rubber boots.

"There's something in the water," the voice called out, clearer this time.

That froze Harold in his tracks. *Something in the water.* He leaned against the door frame that led into a warehouse. A woman sitting on the top shelf drew his attention. She tucked her legs beneath her and sat against the back wall below a narrow window, allowing a sliver of gloomy daylight into the room. The woman's shoulders trembled as hitching sobs shook her body.

"You're going to be alright, ma'am." Harold tried his best to sound calm, but his voice wavered with fear. A growl, gurgling and filtered through phlegm, rumbled from within the darkness. "What the hell?" Harold muttered, fumbling on his belt for his flashlight.

"Run!" the woman yelled, forcing the word out between her choking sobs.

A shelving unit along the far wall teetered. Dust-covered cardboard boxes tumbled into the water with a rumbling crash that sent ripples racing along the surface. Bursts of brownish-white foam sprayed in all directions, splashing the gritty liquid into Harold's eyes. He stumbled backward as he wiped his eyes with a gloved hand, and his shoulder slammed into the door frame. The woman was crying out, her words lost beneath a jumble of incoherent, panicked warnings.

The water splashed as something moved gracefully along the surface toward Harold. Hardened dark green scales reflected the faint light from the window above the stranger from behind the cluster of fallen boxes. A row of gnarled teeth erupted from the water amidst a guttural growl roar.

"Jesus Christ." Harold tripped over his feet and dashed into the hallway. He raced toward the open door, toward daylight. His eyes fixed on the outside, he never saw the mangled gazelle half submerged in the flooding waters, and his foot snared in its rib cage, sending him face first into a slick puddle of blood. Another roar boomed against the hollow walls. The creature's tremendous stomping legs shook the cement foundation of the building.

Harold scrambled to his feet as the ancient creature's skull emerged, the top-half row of filed teeth hung open, its bottom teeth submerged beneath the blackish-brown liquid. From deep inside the building, the girls' panicked cries rang out in a fury of short bursts. The creature snapped its jaw shut with a boisterous snap, sending a splash of water high into the breeze before being carried away. Years of instinct and a sense of duty guided Harold's actions. Not wanting any harm to befall the girl, he stomped his feet in the gushing water and shouted at the creature. If it disappeared inside again, there would be nothing for Harold to do. He couldn't get close enough in the tight confines of the building to fight the reptilian beast without anchoring himself to danger. All he could do was lure it outside and pray that he'd outrun the predator.

Under the cover of marshy water, the monster slithered into the abandoned parking lot, giving chase to Harold. With the wind driving the rain into his face, he struggled to find an opening in the fence. He heard the creature slithering through the gushing water. It moved with unfathomable grace and agility. The sounds demanded his attention. He glanced over his shoulder and let out a terrified gasp. Prowling beneath the surface, the armored torso glided with purpose toward him. A formidable tail swept from side to side, sending large ripples through the rushing water. From head to tail, Harold estimated the beast was over twenty-five feet. Fear swept over him, willing him to draw his weapon for the first time in his career. He pulled the trigger without hesitation. Bullets plunged into the water in a series of dull thuds. If the bullets were finding their mark, they did little to discourage the beast.

***

"The eye of the storm will settle over the Florida Keys just before sunset today, and we expect the worst of the storm will pass after as Hurricane Rose shifts over the Gulf this evening. The strength and speed of the storm will mean a quick but devastating blow to the Keys."

Daniel leaned in toward the speaker, trying to pick out the weather report over the cackle of the radio and the soft snoring from the seats behind him. It didn't take long for those living inside the abandoned building to fall into a deep sleep, enjoying the comforts of a cushioned seat instead of the cement floor.

"We expect wind gusts to top over 200 miles an hour, and the ocean water levels have already risen four feet and will continue to rise until Hurricane Rose shifts back out to sea."

Daniel took out his cell phone and held it up, trying to get a second bar, hoping that he could get in touch with William while he waited for Harold. A high-pitched blaring alarm came through the speaker, drawing a few disgruntled groans from the people trying to sleep.

"If you are able, head to the mainland as we expect wave surges to reach over thirty feet. We are urging anyone living south of Long Point Key to get to the emergency shelter at the Big Pine Sportsplex just outside of Big Pine Key if you cannot reach the mainland. Once again, we urge residents to make their way to the Big Pine Sportsplex. The Seven Mile Bridge will be closed to all traffic."

Daniel glared at his phone, realizing time was running out. "Where is that fool?" he whispered to the radio.

The air conditioner was losing its battle against the humidity. Frigid air spewed from the vents, dying before it reached Daniel's face. Impatiently, he opened the door to the bus. Wicked winds hissed, whipping drops of rain into the bus as the gales forced their way inside the bus. Daniel cupped his hands over his mouth, trying to funnel his voice into the shrieking racket. He called out to Harold but knew his voice had died on the wind, unable to travel to the front door.

"Stay here," he said. No one paid him any attention. After years on the force, he knew better than to leave anything to chance. He locked the door behind him out of habit.

He zipped up his rain slicker and dashed toward the building, his rubber boats splashing in the water puddled on the cracked cement walkway.

"Hey, Harold!" Daniel yelled, his voice booming inside the warehouse. "We need to get moving!" His frustration grew as his patience dwindled.

A thunderous series of rapid bangs erupted from outside. Daniel's hand dropped to his side. His thumb found the hammer of his pistol as his fingers worked to unlatch his holster. With his weapon drawn and readied before he reached the end of the hallway, he readied himself to take action. Left open, the outside door slammed against the brick wall, punctuating a woman's shrill scream. Terror riddled her voice, warning Daniel to run away. Daniel ignored her cries and raced toward the exit. Harold stood back on, his weapon raised, his free hand working to reload his pistol. Even from a distance, Daniel couldn't ignore the tremor in Harold's body as his arms shook.

Just as he reached the opening, something tackled him to the ground, driving the wind from his lungs. A woman wrapped her arms around his waist, and they tumbled back inside the warehouse. Daniel landed hard on his backside. The woman's weight crashed down on top of him.

"What's wrong with you?" Daniel shouted, staring back at the woman with rage burning in his eyes.

Tears streamed down the woman's face, tracking over dirt, leaving visible streaks behind. "There's a monster out there!" she cried, her arm trembling. "Don't go out there."

"There's a bus out front." Daniel stood up, brushing himself off. "Get on it if you want a safe place to sleep for the night." His hand gripped the door frame, and he hauled himself outside.

Outside, Harold dangled over the rickety chain-link fence, which wavered beneath his weight. The wind tossed it around, the metal rings banging off the sturdy poles. The fence buckled inwards from the bottom, sending Harold careening over the top bar. He landed on his backside, a splash of water shielding him from view momentarily. Somehow, he got to his feet before the water settled back down.

Daniel called out to Harold, but the blustering gales stole his voice. He stepped outside into the storm, the winds urging him back inside. With his hand raised to shield his face, he leaned into the wind, trudging through the parking lot.

The boisterous sound of the fence collapsing caught Daniel off guard, and his heart leaped into his chest. When he looked up, Harold was standing on the hood of a gray truck, waving his arms over his head. He was shouting at Daniel, but his words were inaudible, cut off by the storm. Daniel pressed on, moving closer to the collapsed fence.

"Stop!" Harold's hoarse voice reached Daniel. "Get back!"

"What is going on?" Daniel called out, struggling to see through the torrential downpour.

"Crocodile!" Harold screamed.

Confused, Daniel laughed. "Calm down, Harold, let's get out of here."

A hand spun Daniel around. "My daughter isn't on the bus. Where is she?"

Daniel brushed her hand off his shoulder, smacking it away. "I don't even know who your daughter is, ma'am. I'm going to ask you to calm down."

"Calm down?" she snorted, her facial expression twisting into disgust. "Look at that thing."

Another clamorous bang rang out, demanding Daniel's attention. When he turned around, his jaw dropped. A gigantic saltwater crocodile emerged from the blackened waters. Its hard scales gleamed a dull greenish-black in the dying daylight as it raised its massive skull toward the grill of the truck. Harold fired another shot. The bullet made a sickening sound as it slammed into the creature's tough hide. A small bloody circle oozed black blood, the rain working to wash it away.

"There she is!" the woman shouted toward Harold.

Daniel squinted, trying to see another person in the distance. "Where?"

"Behind that other officer."

In the truck's pan, a young woman huddled against the cab. The wind tossed her soaked hair around. Angry, the crocodile let out a snarling growl. Frustrated with its inability to climb the hood, the creature stalked the truck, using its snout to probe the tires. A vicious scream rose from the young girl as the croc rammed its head into the rear tire. It would only be a matter of time before the beast figured out a way to get to its prey.

"Harold!" Daniel yelled.

This time, Harold caught the source of the sound. The young girl reached out for his hand, catching him off guard. His foot slipped out from beneath him, and he landed on the hood. The deafening racket of aluminum buckling beneath his weight added to the clamor of thunder approaching. Thankfully, Harold slid into the pan of the truck.

"I got to go get them," the woman said, sprinting toward the truck.

"Wait!" Daniel called out, stretching out to grab her arm. He spun her around and locked eyes with the woman.

"Get off of me!" she screamed, pushing him back.

His grip on her t-shirt held fast, the collar ripping as she struggled against him. "That's my baby girl over there," she sobbed.

Daniel paused, his mind racing toward a plan. "I'll distract the croc, grab its attention. That should give Harold a chance to get across the block. I'll circle back in the bus and pick them up."

"I'm coming with you," she said, her tone firm.

"Stay close to me and try nothing rash," Daniel said, leaning in close, making sure she heard every word he said. "I don't need anyone getting hurt. I'm in control."

She glared at him with anger in her eyes but never replied. Daniel approached the truck. The chain-link fence clanked and clattered as they walked over the fallen section.

"Harold," Daniel said. He was close enough that he didn't have to raise his voice above a shout. "I'm going to get that beast's attention. You get that girl over to Young Street. I'll pick you both up on the bus outside of the strip mall."

"What if there are more of these fucking things around?" Harold asked.

"Head to the apartment buildings just past the mall. Where we responded to the domestic violence call on the corner of Fifth and Young." Daniel watched as the crocodile's massive head emerged from the gushing, muddy water. Its tail slapped against the surface of the water on the other side of the truck. Daniel shuddered, realizing the creature's gigantic size. "If you're in trouble, you can get up on the balcony around back. They all had ladders if I remember," he added.

"Don't be late," Harold said, nodding his head.

"Hey, fucker!" Daniel stomped in the water, demanding the crocodile's attention.

With a snarl, the saltwater crocodile snapped its head toward Daniel. Drawn to Daniel and the prospect of an easy meal, the beast slapped its tail off the pavement, sending up a wide arcing splash of water. It moved with surprising agility, clawed nails scrapping over the asphalt as it made its move toward Daniel, who staggered backward, narrowly avoiding tripping over the girl's mother.

"Get on that bus," Daniel ordered, guiding her toward the back door to Labrynth Oils. He pressed the bus keys into her hand and squeezed her fingers closed over them so she wouldn't drop them. "I'll be right behind you, I promise."

With the wind at her back, she dashed across the parking lot, her boots slapping through the growing puddles. The guttural growl demanded Daniel's attention. He shifted his gaze back to the fearsome creature, finding it much closer than he expected. But at least Harold and the young girl were out of danger—at least any immediate danger. Daniel could only imagine the hidden horrors that roamed the city during this hurricane, climbing over the brick walls separating the properties and vanishing into the concrete jungle. But for now, he had to focus on getting back to the bus safely. He didn't care what the beast did anymore.

"Fuck off," Daniel said out loud, not caring if the creature could understand him or not. He raced toward the dilapidated red-bricked building. As the adrenaline wore off, he could feel his leg muscles fill with lactic acid. Every stride caused his quadriceps to cramp. And for the first time, he noticed blisters had formed on his left heel.

Caught in a race that he had no prayer of winning, Daniel curled his fingers around the butt of his handgun once more, giving him a sense of hope. Without hesitation, he drew it from its holster and fired three shots at the beast. The impact produced a sickly, dull *whumpf*. But it didn't deter the crocodiles' brutish advance. Blackened blood oozed from the wounds, washed away by the torrential downpour. The creature stared Daniel down.

Daniel pulled the trigger again, but a hollow click echoed repeatedly as his finger pumped the trigger. "Fuck!" he shouted as he stumbled over something beneath the flood water. A jolt of pain shot up his arms as his wrists absorbed the brunt of the impact.

The crocodile crept toward him, its body low to the ground, half-hidden beneath the rainwater. It sent ripples through the water with every powerful movement of its massive frame. With a throaty growl, its jaw unhinged, revealing a snout filled with jagged teeth. The rain hammered off the beast's hardened scales, the hunter green skin almost black in the dull daylight.

A hand grabbed Daniel by the collar and yanked him to his feet. "Let's go!" a man's voice screamed in his ear.

Daniel holstered his weapon as he stumbled to his feet, the stranger forcefully guiding him toward the double doors. The ground shuddered as the crocodile dashed toward them, closing the gap quickly as it sensed its prey getting away.

"Lord save us," the stranger cried out as they raced across the loading dock.

They were too far away from the door. They'd never make it. At the last moment, Daniel spotted a ledge that ran along the loading bay doors. He yanked on the stranger's arm and darted toward the higher ground. With all his effort, he leaped toward the ledge, hauling the man with him. His abdomen crashed into the edge, driving the wind from his body with a deflating grunt as his upper body slammed hard onto the cement; his legs dangled over the side, his boots skimming the surface of the flood water.

The stranger hit his shins off the edge, tripped forward, but somehow stayed on his feet. He yanked Daniel away from the edge, pulling him onto the landing just as the crocodile slammed into the ledge. The concrete splintered and cracked from the force of the impact. Daniel scurried away from the edge until his backside collided with the brick wall of Labrynth Oils.

"Now what?" the stranger asked, his voice raspy.

Daniel kept his watchful eye on the edge of the landing, refusing to look away for a moment. "We need to find a way out of here."

"No shit," the man said, his southern accent thick. "And we'd best figure it out before he does." He pointed toward the crocodile.

A yellowish-orange eye stared at them from just above the water, its snout concealed below the surface. The apex predator studied them, processing the surroundings. With a swift swipe of its tail, it sent a wave of water toward the ledge, trying to formulate a plan to conquer the obstacle in front of it.

"Check the windows on that side," Daniel said, pointing to the left. "And I'll check over here. Maybe we can slip inside one of them."

"Don't waste your time," the man replied. "All the windows on the first floor have bars on them."

"How can you be sure?" Daniel watched the crocodile as it moved through the parking lot, searching for a way up. Its snout bumped a car. The hinges squealed with a high-pitched, metallic twang as the frame bounced up and down.

"All the buildings on this block have them barred off," the stranger said, his eyes wandering up and down Daniel's uniform. "Ain't you a cop or something? First time in this part of town?" The man laughed, shaking his head as if in disgust at Daniel's ignorance.

Sighing, Daniel examined the window next to him. Bars ran across in a criss-cross pattern, leaving no room for anything larger than a rat to climb in. But he didn't bother to respond to the man's comment. He could hear the crocodile sloshing through the water behind him. Every sound made his heart flutter. "What's your name?"

"My friends call me Frankie."

"Well, Frankie, let's figure out a way to get out of here before that thing finds a way up here," Daniel said.

"Couldn't we just run like hell?"

"It's too fast. You'd never outrun it, trust me," Daniel said, his heart thumping hard in his chest. "Besides, I got a bus full of people on the other side of this building. And if I can't get back to them soon, they may end up in huge trouble like us. I can't let that happen to them."

"I knew I should have told them to run away," Frankie said, wrapping his knuckles off his forehead. "If only I'd known you wanted to play hero. Why did I have to listen to Janette?"

"Who's Janette?"

"The mother of that little girl you saved. She ran back on the bus and shouted hysterically about some monster trying to eat her baby girl." Frankie paused. "Man, why didn't I believe that woman? I'd still be on that damn bus if I'd just minded my damn business." Frankie continued to speak to himself in a muffled fashion.

"If you didn't believe her," Daniel said, "why did you come back here?"

Frankie ignored him with a dismissive wave and said, "The same reason any man does anything. To impress a girl."

Daniel couldn't help but laugh. "Well, you saved my life, and I'm eternally grateful. I find myself in your debt. Is there anything I can do for you?"

"Last chance to escape down through the back gate," Frank offered with a crooked grin.

"It would take too long to backtrack to the bus," Daniel answered.

"Fine, whatever," Frankie grumbled. "But you still owe me one."

***

"Jump down to me," Harold called out to the young girl.

Sitting atop the fence, the girl straddled the brick facade, her legs dangling over each side. "There's no way I'm going to jump that far," she whimpered, gripping the cement wall with both hands.

Rain beat down all around them, driven by the wind.

A sheet metal advertisement absorbed the brunt of the storm, protecting Harold and the girl while offering low discounts on used cars. The sound reminded Harold of machine gun fire on fully automatic.

"What's your name, sweetheart?" Harold asked. "If I remember correctly, it's Laura, right?"

The girl rolled her eyes toward Harold. "My name is Lilly."

Harold laughed, shaking his head. "Right, Lilly. You need to jump down."

"I told you I can't do that," she snapped back with a shrill snarl.

"Trust me, I'll catch you," Harold said, holding out his arms to demonstrate.

She eyed him suspiciously, years of distrust clear on her face. With a deep sigh, she swung her left leg over the top so that both legs dangled out of Harold's reach. The wind lashed out all around them, driving the rain against her backside. "You better not miss," she said, clenching her eyes shut, her nose scrunched up with anxiety.

"Wait!" Harold cried out. But it was too late. She shoved off, and he lunged forward to catch her. Her weight slammed into his shoulder, knocking him off balance. She landed on top of him, driving the wind from his lungs as his rib cage compressed. "On the count of three," he gasped.

Lilly giggled. "Three."

"Let's get going," Harold said, fumbling his way to his feet.

"Will my mom be there?" Lilly asked, her sad eyes studying Harold for the truth.

"She will," Harold answered without hesitating. If Lilly didn't think her mother would be there, she would run off. Harold believed Daniel would meet them there; he just didn't know if they'd make it. In the park just ahead, only 100 feet away, Harold could see three more saltwater crocodiles stalking the fields. Not wanting another confrontation, Harold stuck to the middle of the main street. If traffic came, he'd deal with it.

THE BLUE HOLE

"On the count of three, we lift and pivot the tree that way," Erin said, using her finger to show which way to move the fallen tree branch.

Sharon peered over her shoulder, her eyes scanning the dirt road for obstacles that may get in her way. Satisfied that the coast was clear, she nodded her head in agreement.

"One,

"Two,

"Three!" Erin shouted out the last number.

They strained to pick up the thick branch and shuffled their feet toward the far shoulder of the road. With the tree slipping from Erin's grip, her forearms strained from the effort, the veins bulging over her wrist. Their movements got into a rhythm, and they swung the tree far enough to let the jeep pass. They both dropped the branch at the same time with a loud grunt.

Overhead, a long, low, rolling clap of thunder grumbled. Winded, Erin placed her hands on her hips, sucking in deep gulps of air. Before she could catch her breath, Sharon stood beside her, rubbing her back. "Come on," Sharon's voice raised over the rumbling thunder, "let's get back in the jeep. Something about all of this is giving me the creeps." She urged Erin back to the jeep, guiding her by placing her hand on the small of her back.

Back inside the jeep, Erin hoped for a sense of relief. But she still felt eyes watching her from the jungle, concealed within the dense foliage. For a moment, they sat in the jeep in complete silence, listening to the sound of the rain falling and the wind gusting through the palm trees. Normally, Erin would have experienced peace out here in nature, but a terrible vibe hung over the entire jungle.

"Can you turn on the radio?" Sharon asked, breaking the silence.

Erin fumbled with the keys, her hands quivering with unplaced fear. For a moment, she expected the engine would refuse to turn over. And they'd have to walk the rest of the way. With a sputtering, hungry growl, the engine roared to life on the first turn. Static blared from the speakers. Erin surfed the channels until she found one with old country music playing. "Do you think you could tolerate this the rest of the way?"

"I just want to hear something besides the weather," Sharon said as she reached out and turned the volume up.

Erin shifted into first gear and let the jeep roll forward at a snail's pace as she navigated around the fallen branch. The left tires sank into the soft shoulder, and the jeep jerked toward the ditch. Correcting her course, Erin chose to drive closer to the branch, and after a tense moment, they were back on the road with the fallen tree behind them. Erin let out a deflated sigh and loosened her grip on the steering wheel.

After stepping down on the gas and speeding down the dirt road, she tried leaving that atmosphere of dread behind.

***

The Blue Hole National Key Deer Refuge came into view as the jeep rounded the corner. Nestled against a luscious green backdrop, they had designed the wooden huts to blend into the scenery. It would have worked if they didn't place bright red tin roofs on all the buildings. But Erin had explained that they had built them that way as a safety precaution; anyone who got lost would know to look for the distinguishing feature.

Sharon scanned the visitor's parking lot—empty. "Looks like we are going to have the place all to ourselves," Sharon said.

"As soon as we can get rid of Jacob," Erin said, pointing toward the staff parking at the trunk of a Pontiac Sunfire pulled up alongside the building. Rust and dents riddled the deep purple paint of the car. "If you stumbled across this car, you'd think someone had abandoned it there and left it to disintegrate."

"Who knows? Some day an archaeologist will study it. You know, like they do with dinosaur bones." Sharon couldn't help herself. Erin's first car had been a Sunfire, long before they first started dating. She always laughed at the picture of Erin sitting on the hood of her car, an Eagle painted on the hood.

"Is that another joke about my car?" Erin groaned.

They made the turn toward the staff parking. This part of the road had been all but forgotten for years, deep ruts and holes displaying the level of neglect. The government had funneled all the money for the park toward the visitors. The jeep hitched and rocked over the dirt road. Years of exposure to the elements left craters in the hardened path. Erin leaned over the steering wheel, her butt lifting from the seat as she navigated through the puddles and potholes. She let out an exasperated sigh as a bump sent the steering wheel into her diaphragm. The jeep lurched forward, the front left tire dipped into a deep rut, and the back tires spun, flicking up an arc of mud behind them.

"I think this is close enough," Erin said. "We'll deal with this in the morning when Ted gets here. He has a wench on his truck. Shouldn't be a big deal."

"Sounds good to me." Sharon unbuckled her seatbelt, letting the tension yank it back, the metal clip clanging off the plastic. Erin gave her an annoyed sideways glance, letting her eyes do the talking. "Sorry," Sharon added.

"I'll get the stuff out of the trunk," Erin continued, not bothering to acknowledge Sharon's apology. She leaned to the left, reached for her keys attached to her belt, and unclipped them with a metallic jingle. "You run ahead and head inside. I don't know if Jacob's taking a nap, so I'll give you the keys, just in case." She handed the key ring over to Sharon. Without another word, Erin jumped out of the driver's seat and ran around the jeep, her shoes squelching in the puddling water building up on the road.

"Damn it," Sharon muttered then pulled her hood over her head and threw the door open. As she moved to get out, the wind tossed the door back at her, banging the hard plastic off her knee. A cry of pain escaped her lips, and she braced the door with her shoulder, squeezing out as the wind pressed the door firmly against her.

She slipped through the crack, and the wind slammed the door shut behind her.

As a gust of bitter-cold wind swept through the jungle, ripples raced through the groundwater. With a metallic drone, the rainfall hammered off the tin roof overhang. She tried the handle and found it unlocked. The door swayed inwards. Stumbling inside, Sharon lowered her hood and called out. Her voice echoed in the emptiness.

"Jacob!" Erin hollered as she forced her way in, dragging the luggage behind her as she entered. "Are you in here?"

No one answered.

"Do you think he ventured outside in this?"

Erin shook her head. "It's hard enough to get him to go out on a sunny day. He's got to be around here somewhere."

"You think he's hanging out in the main visitor's auditorium?" Sharon asked as she helped Erin with the luggage.

"I doubt it," Erin laughed. "Do you want my guess? I'd say he's been struggling to start the backup generator and is toiling to get it running. He's not a very useful person to have around, but he shows up on time and does not creep out the patrons, so management keeps him around."

Sharon wandered into the sleeping quarters and found the contents of Jacob's bag detonated over his unmade bed. She giggled at the sight of Jacob's Scooby-Doo boxers and matching socks. A glob of toothpaste rested on top of the nightstand, the toothbrush rolled onto its side, and the worn bristles smeared with the blue goo. Not wanting to get her suitcase contaminated with anything Jacob might have, Sharon headed back into the living quarters and left the luggage by the side of the love seat.

"Can you make sure he cleans that room before he leaves?" Sharon paused, then added, "It's absolutely disgusting in there." She pinched her nose to punctuate her point.

Erin stood in the doorway, her hand resting on the handle. "I'm just going to go out and help him with the generator. He'll clean it up before he goes. Probably just got tangled up with a project in the shed when the power went out." A gust of wind forced its way inside as Erin cracked the door. "I shouldn't be too long," she said as she made her way out into the blustering storm. Her dull, wet footsteps faded quickly as the howling winds boomed against the building.

A volley of fierce wind struck the door, pushing it open. The sudden clamor made Sharon jump and curse under her breath. When she gained control of herself, she headed over to the porch and shoved the door against the powerful winds until she heard it latch shut with an unmistakable clunk. She hung her rain jacket up on the rack, an instant puddle forming on the floor beneath.

Wandering around the tiny room, Sharon started opening drawers and cupboards, rummaging around inside to see if she could find anything interesting or useful. Old issues of *National Geographic* and a deck of playing cards would help pass the time if they couldn't get the generator started. Beneath the sink, she found an open package of candles and a red BBQ lighter.

Already dark, the drab daylight would soon vanish, and the night would stretch longer than normal during the storm. She found some coasters above the sink and placed the candles throughout the room. For now, she held off on lighting them. Preparing for an emergency, she placed the BBQ lighter on the dinette table next to a stack of candles where she'd be able to find it even in the dark with her eyes closed.

A flicker of light and a momentary buzz of electricity raced through the circuits as the generator grumbled, but it didn't last long. The generator sputtered and choked as it died. Erin wandered into the bathroom, having to squeeze into the meager space between the toilet and sink, and made her way to the window used to ventilate the tiny room after a shower. She yanked the curtains aside, revealing the utility shed just off the edge of the line of trees. The door swayed open and shut in the blustering winds, offering glimpses of Erin as she knelt in front of the generator, pouring gasoline into the reliable Honda.

From outside, a plodding thump approached, drawing Sharon's attention toward the front window. She wandered over to the front window and pulled the curtains aside. Raindrops pounded the asphalt, splashing back into the air in a mesmerizing display. Obscured by the palm trees swaying side to side against the path of the wind, something moved toward the parking lot.

A mechanical growl roared as the lights flashed on. Static buzzed from the speakers of the radio lodged on the window ledge, the antenna stretched toward the far corner of the window, searching for a signal. Sharon turned the volume down to get rid of the awful noise. She didn't bother to search for a station, realizing the storm had probably knocked them all out.

Erin burst through the door, out of breath and soaking wet. "It's really coming down out there," she panted.

"Did you see Jacob?"

"No sign of him anywhere," Erin answered without hesitation. "Probably caught a ride home with a friend. His Sunfire isn't the most reliable automobile ever made. Even when it first came out." Erin hung her coat up on the rack and kicked her shoes off into the corner of the mat. "I'll try to call him." She searched her jacket pockets, the wooden rack rattling as she patted down her raincoat pockets.

Sharon stared out the window, scouring the edge of the road for any signs of movement. Palm leaves swayed violently in the wind, the trunks bending toward the ground at a sharp angle as Hurricane Rose made her presence known. Shadows swayed amongst the foliage, darting from one hiding spot to the next. A terrible feeling of dread filled the pit of her stomach. "Maybe we should head back into town?"

"Too late for that now," Erin sighed. "The roads are treacherous. No, we are better off staying put and riding out this storm here. I promise you we're safe here."

Sharon glanced outside the window at the empty parking lot and enveloping bush. Jacob's car remained vacant besides the building. They were alone, but she sensed something outside, stalking them from the leafy foliage.

THE BEAST

Kyle lunged down from the ledge and into the tidal water as it surged past his knees. He scanned the cave, but every shadow threatened to leap out at him. "Come on, Tim," Kyle urged, keeping his voice as low as possible. The surging waves roared, crashing into the cavern with tremendous force. Vibrations ran up Kyle's leg, urging him to hurry. A faint trickle of daylight was the only hope remaining. "If we don't go now, we're going to get trapped in this cave with whatever is out there."

"Can you see it?" Tim asked, his voice wavering.

"No," Kyle answered. "But I can hear it." He stretched his arms up, helping Tim over the edge. Braced and ready to shoulder the burden, Kyle eased Tim down.

Tim yelped as his entire body twitched when he tried to take a step on his injured leg. Kyle supported the brunt of his friend's weight, driving his shoulder into his armpit. "I can't make it," Tim whined.

"Shut up," Kyle ordered. "You're getting out of this damn cave now."

Slowly, they made their way toward the light. Every noise felt like a threat. The constant shriek of the raging storm grew louder near the entrance to the cave. Funneled by the tight confines, Hurricane Rose's power was magnified beyond anything Kyle had ever seen in his life. Swift currents ebbed and flowed into the cave with ferocious intensity. The water level was already past his knees as the water gushed out of the cave. The retreating waves grew dangerous with enough force to rip you off your feet and drag you out to sea. If he didn't time this right, there would be no way out of the cave within the hour.

A wave crashed into the mouth of the cave, tearing shards of rock from the face. With a sense of irony, Hurricane Rose tossed debris from the shipwreck they had come to investigate at them. Splintered boards rode the waves into the cave, hurtling toward them.

Kyle screamed and his heart ascended into his throat as something cold and hard beneath the surface thumped into his calf muscle. He reached down into the churning water but found nothing. A flood of relief slowed his heartbeat into a gentle rhythm.

"Ready?" Kyle asked, the tide retreating.

"Let's go," Tim answered, sounding confident despite his labored voice.

Without hesitation, they raced toward their escape, following the receding water. They stumbled over debris left behind by the ocean as they crept toward safety. But just as they reached the mouth of the cave, the water rushed out, revealing a hideous sight beneath the filthy ocean waves. A jaw lined with jagged, filed teeth, hung wide open, waiting in ambush for them. As the water receded, they glimpsed the dark green reptilian scales that stretched all the way outside the cave, the flooding waters hiding the tail and the beast's gigantic serpentine torso from view.

"Jesus Christ!" Kyle screamed, stumbling backward, pulling Tim with him. Both men's legs tangled, tripping over each other to get away from the fearsome beast laying in ambush. Without communication, they turned in unison, scurrying back toward the ledge.

The beast's growl rivaled the roar of the ocean. A giant splash of water followed them into the cave. Kyle glanced over his shoulder. "Fuck me," he moaned. He doubled his efforts to reach the ledge, hauling Tim along with him.

No longer supported by Kyle, Tim's leg buckled, sending him toppling to the ground. The predator moved with surprising agility, closing the gap between them with ease. Brown-stained teeth lined the sinister abyss as its jaw unhinged. Tim lay in the flooding water, his eyes clenched shut, not willing to watch the freakishly colossal beast devour him.

The ground trembled beneath Kyle. He could feel the immense weight of the fiendish predator. There wasn't enough time to get them both to safety. Forced to decide, the captain realized there was only one option. With a fierce howl, he lunged forward to protect his fallen comrade.

***

Trembling, Tim closed his eyes, unable to watch as the beast raced toward him, its thunderous footsteps pounding a direct line toward him. A fierce howl pierced his ears as the next wave crashed into the cave. The boisterous racket joined to form a sickening symphony of destruction.

"Get up!" Kyle screamed, his words gurgling through

blood.

Tim opened his eyes. Concealed within the darkness, a massive, shadowed figure loomed feet away from him. As his eyes adjusted to the faint trace of light, a horrific scene emerged. Blood oozed from the beast's fearsome jaw, the crimson liquid pouring from the ragged wound on Kyle's thigh. With its filed teeth deep into the muscle, it flicked its head up. Kyle's vertebra snapped in half with a sickening pop, his insidious screams a sickening testament to the creature's power.

Kyle dangled from the leviathan's monumental jaw like a rag doll. His hands submerged beneath the retreating water, fighting to hold his head out of the water. "Run!" Kyle cried out, blood bubbling over his parted lips.

Tim stumbled to his feet, the pain of his ankle throbbing. Intense waves of pain gripped his entire body. But he forced his mind to shut it out, pushing through the agony. The beast rolled to the left, giving Tim enough space to escape the cavern. Not wasting Kyle's sacrifice, Tim hobbled past the death roll. Kyle's intermittent screams caused a chain reaction in Tim's brain, flooding his nervous system with adrenaline and quickening his pace.

The sound of Kyle's bones popping and cracking echoed in the cave. After the second roll, his screams ceased, replaced by the beast's ravenous growl.

Tim didn't wait at the entrance to time the tide. Luck was on his side, the retreating tide favoring him. The hip-high water tugged at him, guiding him along. He plunged into the surging water, swimming fast out of the entrance of the cavern, making his approach toward the shore. The next rolling wave crashed over him, sending him spiraling head over heels. He fought to regain his balance, kicking his legs and probing with his arms, trying to find the bottom. Caught beneath the waves, his lungs ached and he felt the pressure build up, his head ready to burst. His hand found purchase in the sand as his fingers clutched a jagged rock, allowing him to orient himself as the tidal force relented.

He broke the surface, gasping mouthfuls of fresh air. The sight of Cheryl's police cruiser within sight supplied a second flood of adrenaline that carried him forward. With the pounding waves chasing after him and the wind at his backside, Tim ran up the beach. A wave crashed into the barricade just as he lunged over, driving him into the passenger door of the police cruiser. Now, with the pavement beneath him, he breathed a sigh of relief. His hand fidgeted with the door. It groaned as he tugged it open, using the seatbelt to haul himself inside the vehicle.

Considering himself safe inside the car, Tim sprawled over the seat. His chest inflated and deflated as he drew in deep breaths. Beads of water dripped from his jacket onto the paper bags below. Outside, the wind howled, shaking the car. Rushing water sloshed against the bottom panel of the cruiser. Raindrops assaulted the window, hurled at the car by Hurricane Rose, her fury a reminder he wasn't safe yet.

Once the adrenaline was worn off and he was finally able to catch his breath, Tim dragged himself into the driver's seat. He flipped the driver's side visor down, and Cheryl's keys tumbled into his lap. The car started on the first turn, the engine rumbling to life. Tim allowed himself to smile, shifting the gear into reverse. The pain in his ankle throbbed as he pressed down on the gas. But he ignored it. Glancing over his shoulder, he maneuvered his way around the captain's truck, spinning around to face the road. Determined to get to safety, Tim headed toward the turnoff that would lead him to the Big Pine Sportsplex.

A wave of nausea hit him hard as the pain in his ankle radiated. For the first time since he left the darkness of the cave, he stared down at his ankle. The makeshift bandage was a bloodied mess. Barely holding on, he forced the car up to the top of a small hill and pulled over. He turned the dial to the emergency channel, praying that someone would answer his desperate plea for help. A voice rose out of the static to respond on the other end.

"I'm at the Golden Sands Beach," he mumbled. He didn't know if he pressed the send button before sinking into oblivion.

AROUND TOWN PART THREE

Amy sprinted across the dining hall as the massive creature stalking her crashed through the window, sending shards of razor-sharp glass clattering against the marbled floor. A gust of wind swept into the dining room. Napkins flew into the air and empty glasses tumbled from the tables and exploded on the floor.

The maître d' ushered Amy toward a set of double doors with a distinct shove. "Into the kitchen now," Darrell shouted, "Hurry!"

Jessie took charge, grabbed Amy by the wrist, and lead them toward the safety of the kitchen. A sign hung over the door warning "*Employees Only*." She pushed the door open with a crashing bang. From behind the counter, the cook stared blankly at them, a cleaning rag gripped loosely in his hands as he wiped down the stainless steel surface in a circular motion. A giant metal hood hung from the ceiling, cutting the kitchen in half, leaving a slim gap that exposed a counter for the orders to pass off to the servers. With a dazed expression on his face, his jaw dropped open and his eyes grew wide. Before he could say anything, a guttural growl accompanied Darrell's war cry. He burst through the double doors, slamming them against the wall with a calamitous clang.

"What is going on?" the cook asked with a hint of fright cracking in his voice.

"They're coming for us," Darrell said, huffing.

Before anyone could answer, the crocodile exploded through the double doors. Its devastating jaws snapped shut over Darrell's pants, tearing the fabric as Darrell fought to free himself. Amy jumped onto the counter that separated the kitchen from the serving line. A stack of plates and mugs tumbled to the floor and smashed into a thousand pieces of jagged artillery. In the confusion, the cook raced toward a thick metal door. A sign hung from the frame with the word **RECEIVING** printed in bold letters. He threw the door open and slammed it closed behind him with a clamorous bang, his hollow footsteps fading away as he raced down the unseen corridor.

Jessie tried to chase after Darrell as he rounded the corner. She slipped on a grease stain oozing out from the deep fryer. Her feet came out from under her, and she slammed hard on her backside. Glass shards drove into her backside, shredding her blouse into thin strips of dyed red fabric. But she miraculously avoided cracking her skull open on the hard floor. Dazed, she sat up and propped herself against a cabinet door, rubbing the back of her head. Brilliant streaks of scarlet stained her fingernails and sullied her palm.

Another crocodile lumbered into the kitchen, crawling over the first one. The beast on the bottom snapped at the other, hissing at its foul brethren. Amy bellowed out to Darrell to help Jessie. With the predators keeping themselves occupied, Darrell made his way back and hauled

Jessie to her feet, tugging her around the corner, her high heels clacking over the cracks in the tile. Jessie mumbled something incoherent before a silent scream choked off her words.

Amy tried to squeeze her leg through the tight gap between the front half of the kitchen and the back. Her leg slipped through until the gap closed over the middle of her thigh. A pair of hands grabbed her by the foot and pulled. Amy screamed for them to stop, bracing her upper body against the hood, her palms pressing into the aluminum hood, the sheet buckling beneath the pressure but not giving.

Below her, the crocodile rammed its jaw into the metal cabinets. The clamorous bang thundered in the tight space, rattling the pots and pans on the shelves. One creature scurried across the tiled floor, sharp nails digging into the tile as it raced toward Darrell and Jessie.

"Jesus Christ!" Darrell screamed, letting go of Amy's leg.

Amy's leg jerked free, and she toppled onto her backside. Her head dangled over the edge. As she struggled to get up, she turned her head to the side and found herself caught in the beast's gaze. Its venomous orange eye, filled with hunger and desperation, bore a hole through her. Caught in a trance, Amy stared at the predator with a sense of awe. The armored torso gleamed in the harsh light. Thousands of scars and scratches decorated the blackish-green scales. Crammed into a tight space, the crocodile's body coiled into a massive heap of ferocious claws and jagged teeth.

"I'll come back for you," Darrell called out as the receiving door slammed shut with a hollow thump. His voice faded into oblivion.

"Wait for me!" Amy screamed, her arm outstretched helplessly.

Trapped inside the confines of the kitchen, the foul reptilian odor festered amongst the overpowering scent of fryer grease and garlic. The two creatures hissed and growled back and forth, communicating as they explored the kitchen. They snorted, inhaling the scents of the kitchen, their appetites turned to eleven. Amy found her way to a standing position, her knees knocking as she gripped the hood, the metal wire holding it from the ceiling creaking as she leaned her weight against it.

With no way to close the double doors behind her, Amy decided the only safe way out of the kitchen would be through the receiving door. Cautiously, she made her way toward the edge of the counter. As she neared the edge, she cursed out loud and pounded her fist against the aluminum. It buckled beneath her blow, leaving a dent in the hood.

The hood jutted out over the counter a foot, forcing Amy to risk hanging off the hood to round the corner of the counter. When she searched for the second crocodile, she spotted the tail curled around the corner, slithering through the grease puddle that Jessie had slipped into earlier. Streaks of blood smeared across the tile as the beast dragged itself through the kitchen. Amy tested the hood, directing her weight toward the edge of the hood. With a little force, the hood swayed outwards, the wire groaning from the strain. Dust and debris fell from the ceiling and settled over the counter.

The crocodiles banged their snouts off the metal cabinets and clawed their nails at the tiled floor. Amy drew in a series of quick, shallow breaths, hyperventilating as the room closed in around her. "Fuck it," Amy cursed out loud as she decided to make a quick leap to the floor to round the corner and hop back up on the ledge. She needed to act fast before the predator could maneuver its mighty jaws back around.

Not wasting any time, she pushed away her fear and allowed adrenaline to carry her forward. With a burst of speed, Amy slid off the counter and her feet glided across the bloodied grease stain. As she landed on the floor, her toe jammed into the creature's hardened skin. But she didn't allow panic to control her. Instead, she stepped onto the beast's armored back and used the rough surface to brace herself as she jumped for the other side of the counter. Angered, the crocodile twisted its neck and snapped its jaws at Amy, but its teeth came nowhere close to snagging her. As the predator adjusted its body, a clamorous racket rose from below the counter.

"You've got to be kidding me," Amy sighed, staring down at the crocodile's massive frame lodged between the tight confines of the shelving. Its fearsome snout and watchful eyes blocked her path through the receiving door. "Why can't you back up out of my fucking way and let me leave?"

The predatory eyes glared at Amy, watching her every movement, taking in every slight twitch of muscle, judging her next move. It thrashed its tail against the cupboards, producing a rolling thunder that bore into Amy's skull. She slumped against the hood and slid down to the counter, grabbing at her hair with both fists. Deep, hitching sobs rattled her body as tears streaked down her cheek and rolled down her neck. A series of angry screams erupted from the pit of her stomach. She beat her fist against the counter and enjoyed the throbbing pain.

Exhausted, Amy tilted her head back and stared up at the ceiling. A long aluminum shaft ran along this side of the kitchen, emitting a soft blue light from a vent above. Amy made her way to her feet, stretching for the grate. It propped open and shifted in place, dropping at an angle toward her face before getting caught along the frame by the same loose screw that allowed her to open the vent. She yanked the grate the rest of the way out and tossed it at the crocodile. An angry growl retaliated against the harmless blow.

Amy placed her hands in the vent and transferred her weight to the ventilation shaft to see if it would hold. When it held, she let herself drop back to the counter. She searched the serving area for anything she could use to boost herself up into the shaft. A stack of plates was the only thing she could find. She dragged them over and balanced her right foot over the stack. With only one chance, she measured the leap and timed her actions. When her foot hit the plate, she drove herself up with her hands outstretched. The plates flung out from beneath her and smashed over the floor as she lunged upwards.

The edge of the vents dug into her armpits as she used her elbows to prop herself up. Her legs dangled out as she inched forward and pulled herself into the ventilation system. "I feel like Bruce Willis in that Christmas movie," she joked, trying to settle her nerves.

A faint blue light illuminated the humid shaft. It stretched far past the kitchen and turned toward the receiving bay. With enough room to crawl on her hands, she moved away from the hideous growls of the defeated crocodiles. The aluminum buckled beneath her with every movement, the sound echoing in the tight confines. Sweat streaked down her forehead, and she found her shirt clinging to her backside from the excretion. With the power out, the air had grown stagnant, pressing down on her with a festering stench of rotten garbage and compost.

As she rounded the corner, the shaft sloped upwards. A stiff breeze greeted her as the air flowed from the kitchen toward the outside of the building. She struggled to climb up the shaft, digging her heels into the sides of the shaft. Every movement was slow and deliberate. Amy didn't want to double her efforts. When she made it to the top, she rolled over onto her backside to catch her breath. Below, she could hear voices arguing back and forth. A faint trace of white light shone up through a vent ahead. Amy rushed forward, energized by the sound of people in the receiving bay. She peered down through the grate at Darrell, Jessie, and the cook, who was using his body to block the entrance, his arms and legs spread out over the frame.

"We have to try," Darrell yelled, trying to pull the man away from the door. The cook's fingernails were dug into the molding, his grip relentless.

"Those savage monsters cornered that poor girl in the kitchen," Jessie added.

"You'll get us all killed," the cook said, refusing to give

in to their pleas.

"It's alright," Amy screamed from the vent.

They all stopped, gazing around the giant receiving area, their eyes wandering from place to place, trying to determine the source of the noise.

Amy cupped her hands and called out. "I'm in the vent. Stand back." Without waiting for them to respond, Amy jammed the heel of her palm into the grate. It buckled, slipped out of position, and crashed to the floor with a high-pitched metallic bang. Amy turned around in the ventilation shaft, and backed herself toward the gap, wanting to drop from the shaft feet first.

Darrell raced under her and held up his hands. "Don't jump. It's too far and you'll hurt yourself."

With her legs dangling over the edge, she lowered her stomach and shifted her weight forward. "I can't stay up here forever. It's way too hot up here."

"Do you know where there's a ladder or something we can use to get her down?" Darrell's voice was urgent.

"There should be one in here somewhere?" The cook's voice came out unsure. "I don't receive the orders, but they must keep one around here close by."

A wave of nausea washed over Amy, the edge of the opening digging into the pit of her stomach. "Can you guys hurry?"

The sound of cardboard scrapping over the cement rose from below.

"You'll have to lower yourself down as far as you can," Darrell called out. "Hopefully this box of flower will break your fall enough."

"You have got to be kidding me?" Amy shouted.

"Come on," Jessie answered, her voice calm and reassuring. "You can do it. Just trust us. The three of us will catch you if you miss the landing."

"I feel so much better," Amy sighed. She took a deep breath, held it, and exhaled it slowly. When she felt calmer, she eased herself out over the edge. Inside her chest, her heart thrashed as her legs lowered into nothingness. The edge cut into her bony hips, then drove the wind from her as she balanced on her stomach. As she transitioned most of her body weight over the side, her grip threatened to give. She knew she wouldn't be able to hold on for very much longer. Staring straight ahead, unable to see over the edge, Amy clenched her eyes shut and let go.

Her vision blurred as gravity tugged her down toward the floor. The racks and shelves blended into one giant wall of mismatched colors. A silent scream escaped her throat, and her legs thrashed wildly as she plummeted toward the unknown. She slammed hard into the stacked flour, the bags tearing open from the impact. White powder exploded into the air, swirling around the receiving bay in a thick haze. When the cloudy haze settled, Amy could see Jessie, Darrell, and the cook covered in flour. She couldn't help but laugh. For a moment, everyone remained silent before they joined in the laughter.

"Can somebody help me out of here?"

Darrell stepped forward and stretched his hand out for Amy. "You made quite the entrance, young lady."

"So now what are we going to do?" the cook pouted, slumping against a pole and sliding down to the floor.

"We wait for the storm to pass," Jessie answered, taking charge of the situation. "And then we call the police or

fire department from the office to come get those crocodiles out of the hotel."

"What about our other guests?" Darrell asked.

"There's only a handful still checked in," Jessie said.
"We just have to hope that they stay out of the lobby
and..."

"They're stuck," Amy interrupted.

"Yes," Jessie acknowledged, "stuck in their rooms."

"No," Amy said, motioning toward the door. "The
crocodiles are stuck in the kitchen. I don't think they can
back up."

"Are you sure?" Darrell asked, concern and excitement fighting for control of his voice.

"Not 100 percent. But I'd be willing to make that bet."

"Then we should be able to go around the building
and stroll in through the front door."

"It's worth trying," Jessie added her opinion. "And the
worst-case scenario is we come back in here."

A quick snort escaped the cook's throat. Once everyone turned their focus to him, he said, "That door doesn't
open from the outside. If you're looking for volunteers to
stay behind to let you back in, I'm your guy."

"Sure thing, Gary," Jessie said, her tone abrupt. "Only
problem is, I don't trust you enough in here by yourself to
let us back in. We'll split up into two teams."

Gary shook his head and grunted his displeasure, but
he didn't bother to mount any further protest and pressed
his back into the wall, cementing his place on the home
team.

"I'll go," Amy said, stepping forward. "You guys
brought me off the street and showed me kindness when

you didn't have to. If it wasn't for you, I'd still be out there. It's the least I can do."

"Are you sure?" Jessie asked, stepping forward and placing her hand on Amy's shoulder. "You don't have to do that. I'll go."

Without hesitation, Amy answered, "I insist."

Darrell nodded his head in agreement. "Let's do this quickly, shall we?"

***

Everyone gathered in the front lobby, the storm outside drowning out the nervous chatter as the residents of Sunrise Apartments fueled the rumor mill. Exhausted, Jake slumped in the chair behind reception and watched the wind-driven rain spatter against the front doors. He laughed, watching Ms. Shelton attempting to find a signal as she held her phone up against the window. She muttered under her breath, cursing technology for never being there when you needed it.

Mr. Marshall made his way toward the reception desk, his gaze fixed on Jake. Before he could speak, Jake stood up and said, "I told you there's nothing I can do about that damn crocodile. There's no way to get in touch with animal control. We're just going to wait it out until the power comes back on."

An angry scowl crossed Mr. Marshall's face, deep creases forming on his brow. "I'm sure if you and one of the young chaps head down into the basement," he said, waving his hand with a flourish at the gathered crowd. No one seemed to pay him any attention, going about their collective conversation without skipping a beat. Mr. Marshall continued as if he had everyone's full support.

"You could corner that crocodile and get that generator up and running."

Annoyed by the old man's persistence, Jake shook his head. "You need to start listening. I've already told you twice. I'm not going down there with that beast…"

A quick burst of condescending laughter cut Jake off. "That animal you're so terrified of is only ten feet long," he snorted, then added, "Don't be a chickenshit."

Jake thumped his fist off the desk. "Not in my job description. And they don't pay me enough to deal with shit like this." Jake thrust his finger toward Mr. Marshall with enough enthusiasm to drive his point home. "Now, if you and one of your friends would be so kind as to deal with this creature, I'd be glad to start the generator."

Mr. Marshall scoffed, sticking his nose up into the air. But he remained silent and made his way back to the crowd. He shoved past the new girl in apartment 3B without uttering a single apology. For a moment, Jake thought the old man was going to make his way up the stairs. Instead, he leaned against the rail and glared at the door leading to the basement, considering his options and devising another scheme for Jake to attempt.

Jake watched as the new girl made her way to the couch, taking a seat on the arm of the chair. The hem of her black-and-white striped dress slid up her thigh, revealing a deep golden tan above her black nylon stockings. She ran her fingers through her bleach blond hair, twirling strands around her index finger as she chewed on her bottom lip. Her lipstick, a glossy pink, glistened with saliva.

Ms. Shelton grumbled something as she approached

reception, her high-heels clacking off the tiled floor. "Young man, are you able to get a signal on your phone? You young people are always better at technology. Have I ever told you about my grandchildren? And about how they were born knowing how to operate these damn things?"

"Sorry, the problem isn't with anyone's phone. I expect the towers are down and until this damn storm passes, no one's going to get a signal." Jake leaned back in his chair and stared up at the ceiling, wishing that everyone would leave him alone.

"Have you tried the roof?" Ms. Shelton asked, clutching her phone against her chest.

"You must have the keys," Mr. Marshall said, joining the conversation without being invited. "I demand that you try to get a signal from the roof."

Jake sighed and rolled his eyes. "Tell you what," he said as he unclipped the key ring from his belt, tossing the heavy metal clump onto the desk with a heavy thump. "You're welcome to try yourselves. But if you think I'm going to be your gofer, you've lost your fucking mind."

"What do we pay you for, anyway?" Mr. Marshall grumbled, making no effort to hide his contempt.

Neither of them made a reach for the keys. Angry, Mr. Marshall stomped off out of sight, making his way around the corner, his footfalls echoing down the corridor. A gust of wind rushed into the foyer as he threw open the back exit and stepped outside. Jake knew the old man was gone out for a puff of a cigarette. And if it had been anybody else, he would have joined them. If Lady Luck came over to his side, he could sneak out with the new girl later.

After spotting her outside several times with her vape, he made sure to carry his on him at all times.

"Are you listening to me?" Ms. Shelton interrupted his train of thought, her shrill voice snapping him back to reality. After an awkward silence, Ms. Shelton repeated herself. "I said, do we all need to stay in this lobby? The chairs down here are atrocious and offensive to all five senses."

Jake waved his hand and said, "Be my guest. You're free to go back to your apartment or stay down here. It makes no difference to me. I'm not in charge of things around here. I'm just the caretaker. And to be honest, I don't care about any of this."

With a deep grunt, Ms. Shelton furrowed her brow and headed off toward the elevators. She stood there for a full minute, pressing the button repeatedly before remembering the power had gone out hours ago. Several of the residents joined Ms. Shelton as she made her way up the staircase, including the girl from apartment 3B.

"Hey, Jake." A man Jake recognized from the fourth floor jogged over to the desk. "Now that all the stiffs are gone, want to come with me to Jessica's room for a draw?"

"Who's Jessica?" Jake asked.

"The new girl that moved into the apartment on the third floor."

A wide grin crossed Jake's face, and he whispered "Jessica" to himself. Without making it obvious, Jake thumbed through his work binder, remembering he did some work for the man in front of him just last month. "Hey, Albert, did you want to help me get the generator going?"

"Do you mean it?" Albert asked, curiosity giving his voice a new sense of vigor. "I thought you weren't going down into the basement with that alligator."

Jake put his palm on his forehead and sighed. "Crocodile," he moaned.

"What?"

"Nothing," Jake replied with a shrug. He hoped that getting the generator working would impress Jessica and, if nothing else, at least get the two geezers off his back for eight hours until the gas ran out. "There's a bunch of lawn tools in the maintenance shed out back, should be some metal rakes and shovels. Good enough to keep the creature at arm's length. If you're up to it, you can hold the creature back while I get the power back, and then we can head upstairs. Once everyone has power back and can finally leave me alone, we can head on upstairs in peace. And we'll have a great story to tell Jessica about how we faced the crocodile."

"Could be an alligator," Albert said.

Jake shook his head and rolled his eyes. "After seeing it with my own eyes, all I can tell you is that it's one mean son of a bitch." He patted his pockets, feeling the cigarette pack. "We can sneak in a smoke before we grab what we need from the maintenance shed."

Albert nodded his head and they started toward the back door. Mr. Marshall's shadow leaned against the frosted glass. Albert pushed the door open. The wind grasped a hold of it and slammed the edge into Mr. Marshall's arm with a dull thump. A pained yelp escaped his throat that was briskly whisked away by the howling wind.

"Fucking idiot," Mr. Marshall grumbled. Holding the cigarette down low near his thigh, the tip burned bright orange, sheltered from the harsh winds.

"Sorry, mister," Albert apologized. "The wind snatched it from my hand."

"Whatever," Mr. Marshall snapped, discarding the butt to the ground and snuffing it out with his heel.

Jake stared at the butt, considered reminding Mr. Marshall of the apartment's no-littering policy, then decided against it. Mr. Marshall made his way inside, hauling the door shut behind him, the pressure defeating his attempt to slam it closed. Jake leaned against the building, the overhang doing little to keep them dry. Rainwater poured down the brick façade soaking through his shirt. He struggled to light the cigarette. Albert pitched in, cupping his hands around Jake's. They both turned their backs against the blustering wind but still couldn't get it lit.

"Come on," Jake called out over the wind, "the hell with company policy. We can smoke inside the maintenance shed."

They raced across the walkway and headed straight for the side door to the garage. Jake fumbled blindly for the maintenance door key, knowing them by the jagged edges. As soon as they reached the door, Jake had the key in hand and unlocked the door in a flash. The door opened inwards, and they stumbled inside and slammed it shut behind them. A stale stench of diesel and grease hung in the air in a heavy fugue. Jake thought twice about lighting the cigarette, then decided he didn't care anymore.

"Should you light that in here?" Albert asked, his voice full of caution.

Jake lit the cigarette, inhaled a deep puff, and blew a ring of smoke toward the rafters. "If you don't want to join me, that's fine with me."

Albert held out his hand. "Don't hog the whole thing."

Jake searched through the maintenance shed, poking around in the dark corners. He found a metal rake, the head wide and the teeth long but dull. "We don't need to kill it, just keep it away. Does this work for you?"

Albert let out a puff of smoke and shook his head. "Got anything else? Maybe something sharper or sturdier? I don't think it's that's going to cut it for me."

"If you don't want to do this, we could just head up to Jessica's room and play cards in the dark."

"No," Albert answered, his tone sharp. "I'll do it." He made his way around the lawnmower and rummaged through a pile of tools along the far wall.

"Find anything?" Jake called out as he opened the tool chest.

"Not really."

Jake lifted a plastic container filled with sockets and drill bits. A wide smile crossed his face as he stared down at the yellow and black drill. He picked it up and appreciated the weight. With a flick of his finger, he tested the battery. The motor sprang to life with a whir and a beam of light shined from below the tip. "This might scare it off. And if it doesn't, we can just drill into its brain."

"What's in this cigarette?" Albert laughed, taking a deep puff and then exhaling a ring of smoke.

"Come on," Jake said, putting the biggest bit into the drill. "Grab that rake as backup and let's go get that generator running."

Albert leaned against the door frame, holding out the cigarette for Jake. "Do you watch scary movies?"

"They're my favorite."

"Don't you find the heroes are always making the wrong decisions at the worst possible time? Why do they go back for their friend who's captured by the murderous villain instead of going to the police and letting them do their job?"

Jake laughed, leaning the rake against the wall. "Every *Texas Chainsaw Massacre* movie would have a runtime of ten minutes if people just did the right thing." He pulled the trigger of the drill one last time before placing it back in the toolbox. "What the hell was I thinking?" he discarded the butt on the cement floor and snuffed it out.

Albert patted Jake on the back. "Let's go get baked and ride out the storm."

"That's a better plan than what I got cooked up," Jake answered, shaking his head. "I'll just double check the lock to the basement, so no asshole tries to go down there."

"You mean Mr. Marshall?"

Jake nodded his head, mentally adding a few more names to the list, but keeping them to himself. Empty-handed, both boys headed toward the back entrance.

***

Rainwater choked the streets, gushing over the pavement, churning up clumps of dirt and pollution as the filthy rivers coursed throughout the city limits. Amy stared down, her legs dissolving into the swampy water, granting an avenue for a concealed predator to ambush its prey undetected from beneath the murky surface. Her knees went weak as her feet turned into cinder blocks, cementing her to the ground. Darrell tugged at her wrist, guiding her through the parking lot, weaving in and out of the vehicles. With nothing but asphalt for a mile in all directions, the dreary water puddled in the parking lot, sloshing around in between the tire wells.

"Something doesn't feel right about this," Darrell yelled. Despite standing next to her, the wind made it seem like he was calling out from the distance.

Amy sensed something lurking beneath the surface, the same disturbing presence she had perceived earlier that morning. Each vehicle presented a hiding spot for another hideous crocodile, every shadow a chance for a slithering reptile to pursue them. And every square inch of the parking lot offered a hiding place for another one of those fearsome predators to strike out from the muddied shallows.

Taking the lead, Darrell yanked on her arm. A searing pain radiated from her shoulder as it inched out of its socket. With intense cramps crippling her thighs, she couldn't match Darrell's lengthy strides. Jerked forward, she collapsed and plunged face-first into the floodwaters. She gagged on the gritty flood water, gasping for breath as the rain mocked her.

Darrell pulled Amy to her feet, patted her on the shoulder, and offered her an apologetic smile. When she caught her breath, she shook his hand off and pointed toward the grand entrance to the hotel. Nothing stood between them and the fancy stone archway that gave the architecture an old-world flare that reminded her of a school trip to London.

Their feet thrashed through the gushing water as they raced across the front walkway and toward the front door. As they reached the entrance, Amy expected to find it locked—or worse. But when Darrell reached out, the door sliced through the rushing water with ease. A flood of water gushed into the lobby, stretching out across the marbled floor in an instant. Amy's eyes wandered to the dining hall. The tables and chairs were overturned, dishes floated along the surface, and a path of destruction led toward the kitchen.

Without a word, Darrell headed toward the front desk, made his way around, and pulled a drawer beneath the counter open. "Here," he called out, producing a room card. "Take this and head upstairs. It's the suite on the first floor. If you take those stairs, get off on the fourth floor. Then you take a sharp right, and you'll see the room at the end of the hallway."

"What are you going to do?"

"I'm going to pull the gate across. It's held up against many hungry guests over the years, should hold up against those creatures for the time being." He strolled over to the gate casually, as if it were the end of the dinner rush.

The gate clicked and clacked loudly on its tracks as Darrell walked it closed. Water gushed between the metal bars that ran from floor to ceiling. He slid the lock into place with a dull thud and turned back toward Amy. With the danger behind them, Darrell's face eased into a weary smile. Exhaustion seized control of his eyes, extinguishing the light that had stayed lit long enough to get the job done.

"Go on upstairs," he said, sleep creeping into his

voice. "I'll lock the staircase, grab the others, and check on you in the morning." For seemingly no reason at all, he laughed.

"What's so funny?"

"I was going to say, I hope you enjoy your stay."

Amy burst out laughing as Darrell made his way back outside. She thought about waiting for him to ease her conscience. But she found her legs carrying her up toward her room. In a few minutes, sleep would take her until Hurricane Rose made her exit from the Keys.

AWAKE

Raindrops hammered the roof and splattered off the windshield, wrestling Tim from a restless state of unconsciousness. Every muscle in his body ached and a dull throb pummeled his temples. Tim groaned, smacking his tongue off his dry lips, the moisture stinging deep into the cracked skin.

Confused, Tim stared out at the bleak horizon, his mind wandering through the strange surrounding, trying to piece the situation together. He rubbed his temple and tried to recall how he'd ended up in Cheryl's squad car. His feet shuffled through a pile of discarded takeout food bags and napkins. He found a half-eaten jelly donut in the cup holder, the red paste gelled over the dusted pastry in thick ribbons.

Suddenly, it all rushed back. Alert, his eyes scanned the area for the man-eating beast that had killed Kyle and Cheryl. Tim hunched over the steering wheel, his hands fumbling for the keys. He rocked back and forth in his seat as he turned the key. The engine grumbled to life as the headlights cut through the drab daylight. With his heart thundering against his ribcage, Tim drove down the highway. Once the car accelerated over sixty, he felt safer.

A burst of static crackled through the speaker. The sound chimed in his head, reminding him he should request help. Tim snatched up the receiver. "Dispatch, this is officer Robichaud. Do you copy?"

Another crackle of static erupted, then dispatch came through. "This is Emma from dispatch. Go ahead, Tim."

"Oh, thank God," Tim said, not knowing why. "The captain is dead."

A long pause filled the radio as Emma held the button down. He heard her stumbling over her words and staggering through mumbled sentences. "Say again?" she said after several broken attempts at a coherent phrase.

"Captain Krusneski is dead," Tim repeated. "And Officer West."

"When?"

The car sped down the winding highway, storm water surging over the pavement. Tim had no clue how long he had passed out. The sky was a dreary gray that could have been dusk or dawn, or anything in between. He stared at the dashboard, not sure he trusted Cheryl to adjust for daylight savings or even to have it set to the correct time.

"What time is it now?" Tim felt foolish asking.

"It's four o'clock." A burst of static cut in as the car rounded a mountain. "How did it happen?"

As Tim crested the hill, the road wound down into the valley. The tide cut through the asphalt, washing away the highway and leaving a gaping, muddy hole, forcing him to stop. "Fuck," he muttered to himself. He glanced over his shoulder and backed up slowly.

"Tim," Emma's voice broke over the radio, "where are you? I'll send a unit to you."

"No!" Tim shouted. "Don't send anybody out there." He spun the wheel all the way to the right. The front end of the police cruiser swung around, as the tires slid over the wet asphalt, sloshing water up the side of the door.

"What happened out there?"

Tim laughed. "You wouldn't believe me if I told you."

"Tim, the family are going to want to bury the bodies. They're going to demand to know what happened." The radio went silent. Emma kept the button depressed. "It's procedure, Tim, you know this."

"There's no point in sending anyone out," Tim sighed. "They won't find anything, and it's too dangerous to recover their bodies." With the car turned around, he headed back the way he came, and a deep fear grew in the pit of his stomach. He slammed on the brakes; the prospect of facing that creature terrified him.

"Did they get caught up in the current and swept out to sea?"

"That's what we are going to tell the family," Tim answered, lowering his head to rest it on the steering wheel.

"What are you talking about?" Emma demanded.

"I just need a minute to reflect, Emma." He closed his eyes. Outside, the storm raged, the boisterous racket making it nearly impossible to think. Tim added, "I'm not trying to cover anything up."

A booming crack of thunder sent vibrations through the metal frame of the police cruiser. He stared out at the horizon with a sense of dread at the slate gray sky. Overhead, the dying daylight faded into a black chasm that hovered over the ocean. Rolling waves churned the water into a roiling rage along the coast, pounding the shore with a relentless fury. With Hurricane Rose arriving soon, he couldn't just sit here and pray that he would survive. But what else could he do?

"Are you still there?"

"A crocodile killed them," Tim said, finding it difficult to accept his own words.

"What?" Emma snapped, her voice riddled with static.

Tim took a deep breath, counted to five, and exhaled. "A massive crocodile fucking ate them. And I don't think there's anything left of either of them. At least, nothing worth risking more lives for." He inhaled another long breath, holding it until it stung his lungs before releasing it.

"Jesus Christ," Emma's voice trembled with fear. "What the fuck is going on out there?"

With nowhere else to turn and time running out, Tim started driving along the coast. His entire body trembled as the fear grew, taking hold of his senses. A prehistoric reptile rendered years of training at the police academy useless. Unable to control himself, he laughed out loud at his miserable situation.

"Is something about any of this funny to you?"

"Not laughing at that," Tim snapped, a flare of anger flushing his cheeks.

"Sorry," Emma apologized, her voice timid. "I guess I'm just in a state of shock."

"That makes two of us," Tim said, his tone softened. "Wait, did you ask what's going on out here?"

"I've received several reports of crocodiles and alligators throughout the Keys today. I received hospital statements being faxed in and dispatch was taking the strangest calls. We don't have enough bodies to cover all the incidents. It's a shit show out there."

"Are you serious?" Tim's heart sank deep into the pit of his stomach.

"Dead serious. But this is the first reported death," Emma said, her voice distant.

Tim spotted an old access road that cut into the jungle, the canopy of palm leaves casting the trail in a shroud of darkness. Puddles of rainwater filled the potholes and ruts. He eased his foot off the gas and slowed down to take the turn, not really caring where it led. Anywhere far from the surging waves, and that diabolical beast would suit him. Static buzzed through the speaker as he made the turn. Before he lost communication, he told Emma that he was heading toward the Sportsplex, not knowing if the road had already washed out or had become impassable because of fallen trees.

"Emma, I just turned off the 44 and took the access road to the Blue Hole National Key Deer Refuge." The car rocked up and down as he traveled over the weathered road. "I may lose you for a bit once I enter the jungle."

"Why in the name of God are you going that way?"

"The highway washed out about twenty minutes south of Golden Sands Beach. And I can't risk going back through there. I can't face that damn creature on my own."

Tim waited for Emma to respond. But the radio crackled static as he drove down the old access road and the lush green vegetation swallowed the police cruiser.

THE STRIP MALL

Daniel craned his neck back, staring up at the warehouse's brick facade. Drops of rain pattered off the building, producing deep, percussive drumming. He checked his wristwatch, worried about the bus full of people parked out front.

"Hey officer," Frankie called out, ushering Daniel over with an excited wave of his hand. "I think I have a plan."

Filled with hope, Daniel joined Frankie near the edge of the loading bay platform. "What is it?"

"That pickup truck over by the sign," Frankie said, pointing toward the far edge of the parking lot. "When the crocodile makes his way behind that truck, we can throw some rocks at that sign. If we're lucky, the booming sound will confuse the croc. I don't figure it has much room to maneuverer around between the fence and pickup truck."

"How do we get it over there?"

"The only thing we need to do is wait for it to happen," Frankie said, his voice trembling with excitement.

"Goddamn it, I can't stick around and hope that creature just wanders back there," Daniel sighed, rolling his eyes in frustration.

"Never said we'd have to hope," Frankie retorted.

"You're suggesting that one of us tries to lure that fucking thing over there?" Daniel paused. "Are you offering to get down there with that freakish monster?"

Daniel scanned the parking lot, finding the crocodile's tail sweeping back and forth, sending a ripple of waves out from behind a white cube van. "Haven't you been paying attention to that croc?"

Daniel shook his head. He had been following it, not paying attention. Instead, he had searched for a way out.

"The thing is patrolling the perimeter," Frankie pointed to the front of the cube van. As if on cue, the crocodile lumbered out from behind the bumper. "If you keep watching, he's going to come straight across us, then make his way back along the far wall. And if we wait till it makes its way around the backside of that black pickup, we can throw rocks behind it. Should confuse it long enough for us to make a break for the door."

It didn't take Daniel long to find crumbled pieces of cement in the corner of the loading bay door. He bent over, scooped up a handful, stuffing some into his pant pockets, and handed the extra to Frankie, who stuffed them into the pockets of his ragged coat. They examined the crocodile as it stalked toward the ledge, its reptilian eyes fixed on them as it made a sweeping pass of the entire ledge. With a twist, the predator probed for a soft spot in the cement with its snout as it passed.

"Get ready," Daniel whispered. He tossed a chunk of cement up into the air and caught it in the palm of his hand, gauging the weight; it didn't feel right. He discarded it into his pocket and retrieved another, repeating the process three times before he found a suitable hunk.

Frankie got into a pitcher's stance, holding the chunk of cement behind his back, his fingers rolling the misshapen piece over, probing for the perfect grip. When he found it, he stopped fidgeting and said, "Make sure your throw doesn't end up falling short. If it lands close to us, you might draw him straight toward us."

Aided by the rain, sweat rolled down Daniel's forehead and into his eyes, the stinging pain drawing tears to his eyes. He used his sleeve to wipe away the tears and water, clearing his sight. Despite years of pee-wee baseball, doubt flooded Daniel's conscious, his throwing arm encased in lead. The crocodile waddled along the far wall, heading toward the pickup truck. Daniel raised the rock up beside his cheek, tilted his wrist back forearm back over his shoulder, and squatted down.

"The fuck are you doing?" Frankie demanded with an outraged expression on his face. "Ain't you ever watch baseball?"

"Shut up," Daniel said. "Don't fret about me. Just worry about making your throw count."

"Kinda hard not to worry when I look over at you." With Frankie's accent thick, it came out as *achoo*. "On my go."

The crocodile rounded the corner, pausing for a moment, wedging its snout into the corner. Chortled grunts blared from the creature's nostrils. Daniel cursed internally, their plan taking an unexpected detour. "Now what?" Daniel snapped, his patience spent.

"Steady now," Frankie said, his voice soothing.

"Why am I even listening to you? You're probably just

some guy who watches too many nature shows on the Discovery channel." Daniel wound his arm back, getting ready to throw the rock as far as possible.

Before his arm sprang forward, Frankie grasped his wrist. "Wait," he snapped.

The crocodile continued to investigate something beneath the water. When it cured its curiosity, it resumed its sentry path, lumbering toward the black pickup.

"Get ready...not yet...just let it get a little further... now!" Frankie barked.

They heaved their chunks of cement toward the far wall. Daniel watched as the pitch sailed through the air and clanked off the wall well short of the truck. "Fuck," Daniel yelled.

Frankie had already leaped down, tugging at Daniel's pant cuffs. "Let's go," he ordered.

Daniel jumped off the ledge, landing on the cement with a loud splash. Twisting his head toward the pickup, he found the crocodile scampering beneath the undercarriage. The hardened scales caught on the exhaust, tearing the muffler off with a crunching metal roar. Frankie wrapped his arm around Daniel's waist, guiding them toward the door.

Their footsteps splashed through the puddles as they raced toward the door. Daniel glanced over his shoulder at the crocodile as it struggled to pass its massive frame beneath the pickup. The truck rocked on its axles, the hinges bouncing up and down with a metallic screech. As they rounded the corner of the loading bay, the door leading through the warehouse stood open, waiting for them. When they reached the door, Daniel's shoulder slammed into the metal frame, sending a jolt of pain coursing through his chest. But he didn't let the impact slow him. Once they were both inside, Daniel slammed the door shut.

"Let's get the fuck out of here," Daniel said, panting.

Too out of breath to respond, Frankie doubled over as he headed down the hallway.

***

The deserted strip mall sprawled over a city block, with rows of shops all living in one long slab of industrial cement. Rainwater gushed down the gutters, sloshing into the empty parking lot in rivers. The rain dampened the cement, turning it a drab gray, not the usual inviting appearance you'd expect from a mall. As they walked along, Harold tried each storefront door, hoping to get out of the elements until Daniel made his way here.

The metal door frame rattled as Harold tried the door to a used clothing store. "Damn it," he muttered in frustration. He leaned his face against the glass window, peered inside at the racks of clothing, and thumped the glass door. All the lights were off. If anyone remained inside, they weren't about to let him in. "Come on Lilly, let's keep moving."

Lily glanced over her shoulder, her feet scuffing along the asphalt as her concentration wandered. By mistake, Harold tugged her sleeve and Lilly stumbled forward. He steadied her before she took a tumble. She stared up at him with a vacant, far-off expression. Ever since her mother left, Lilly had slipped into a shell, refusing to talk. Harold knelt down in front of her, resting his hands on her shoulders gently, and tried to make eye contact with her, but she refused to match his attempts. Instead, she stared down at her feet as she rubbed her toes with the heel of her feet.

"Lilly," Harold said, using her name as often as possible. "Everything is going to be just fine. My partner and your mother are on their way to pick…" A booming crack of thunder interrupted Harold in mid-sentence. Beneath his grip, he felt Lilly tremble and shrink from the clap of thunder rolling over the clouds. When it died off, Harold continued. "They're going to be here soon, Lilly. I promise you that."

Lilly shook her head, her eyes glued to her feet. Harold stood up, straining his ears for the distinct grumble of the bus, but the howl of the storm drowned everything else out. He couldn't hear a single car on the streets. No one would be foolish enough to be out in this weather. He glanced down at his watch, having to raise his arm to see the hands through the beads of water on the face.

"Where are you, Daniel?" he asked himself in a hushed whisper.

Across the street, a crackling pop rang out as a transformer exploded in a fury of white-hot sparks. All at once, the lights went out in the apartment building across the street. An eerie darkness fell, replacing the drab daylight. Shadows grew deeper and loomed nearer. Lilly yanked Harold's sleeve, tugging at his arm. When he finally tore his eyes off the exploding spectacle, he found a wide-eyed Lilly staring up at him.

"What's wrong?"

Without saying a word, Lilly pointed at a truck down the street, jabbing her finger toward it repeatedly. Beneath the lifted undercarriage, a greenish-yellow reptilian eye stalked them. Lilly started in the opposite direction, hauling Harold along with her. Compelled by fear, Lilly found her voice and said, "We need to get out of here."

"Wait," Harold said, holding up one finger. From this distance, Harold didn't sense any immediate threat from the predator. "I think it got a fright from that explosion. And now that we've spotted it, we've prevented it from ambushing us."

Lilly pulled on Harold with all her might, bending low to the ground, trying to get some leverage to aid her efforts. Tears of fear tracked down her cheeks, rolling off her chin before the wind whisked it away. Deep, hitching sobs shook her entire body, stifling her attempts to get his attention. Hysterical, she screamed in a high-pitched, terrified wail. The crocodile perked up at the sound, poking its snout out from underneath the truck.

"Shit," Harold cursed.

With time running out, Harold searched the strip mall for a place they'd be able to hide from the predator. At the far end of the building, Harold saw a sign for McDonald's. "Come on," he said as he continued to process his plan.

With no time, Harold couldn't count on Lilly's legs to carry her fast enough. He scooped her up into his arms and ran. Her lower legs draped over his arms and bounced uncontrollably. Heavier than she appeared, Harold struggled to carry the girl the short distance across the parking lot. After twenty feet, he slowed, gasping for air. As he got closer, he scoured the property, searching for a hiding place.

When they reached the parking lot, Harold turned

around, his eyes falling on an empty street. Fear gripped his heart as he methodically scanned the area—there were too many hiding places. And with that crocodile lurking nearby, panic settled in over him.

Unable to contain his fear, Harold repeated "Fuck" under his breath repeatedly. He glanced down at Lilly, finding her face turned into his chest and her eyes clenched shut.

"Think Goddamn it," Harold swore, the overwhelming stress eating away at him, deteriorating his better judgment. His eyes wandered aimlessly back and forth over the same locations, hoping for a new discovery that would lead to a miracle.

Far off in the distance, the boisterous grumble of the bus droned on the empty streets. He had to make sure that they remained visible to Daniel and kept that creature away from them long enough so that they could reach the bus when it arrived. He staggered backward, pressing his back against the large pane glass window. With his strength drained, Lilly slipped from his grasp. He laid her down gently. "Stand up," Harold said, gasping for air.

Lilly clasped onto Harold's leg, pressing her face into his thigh muscle. Her eyes remained shut. The glass felt cool and soothing against his backside as he leaned into it. His chest heaved as he sucked in gasps of air. Rain beat against the glass all around him, droning in a maddening crescendo, making it impossible to think. A deep, hungry growl caught Harold's attention. When he glanced up, the crocodile stood thirty feet away in the parking lot.

To the right, a giant cement wall bordered the parking lot, and he couldn't find anything to help them over it.

If he didn't have Lilly with him, he'd leap over the fence and rid himself of this nightmare. He couldn't leave her to fend for herself, but maybe he'd manage to hoist her up to the top.

"Lilly," Harold said, without taking his eyes off the creature. "Stay close to me and do as I say."

Harold knelt down so that they were at eye level and pointed toward the corner of the parking lot. From her vantage point, the wall became a daunting mountain. "When I say, run as fast as you can toward the wall..."

"I can't climb that," Lilly said, her voice timid and trembling.

"Don't worry, sweetheart, I'll get you up there. Then I'll be right up there." Lilly nodded her head in an unconvincing fashion. "Can you hear the bus?" Harold pointed toward the boisterous grumble. "It will be here any moment."

The crocodile crept toward them, producing a low, hissing noise as it approached, closing the gap to twenty feet. Suddenly, the predator stopped, lifting its head toward the rumble of the bus. Interested in the noise, the creature's tail swung back and forth in the water, sending ripples through the parking lot. For the second time today, Harold drew his service pistol in the line of duty outside of the training range. He prayed years of practice would transfer to him now when he needed it the most.

"Now," Harold said in a hushed tone, trying not to draw the crocodile's attention away from the bus, giving Lilly a head start on the beast.

Lilly raced toward the wall, her boots splashing in the puddles as she crossed the parking lot. With a twist of its mighty neck, the crocodile shifted its gaze toward Harold. Frozen, the crocodile flared its nostril and shut its eyes, using its sense of smell to determine where to focus its attention. And when the eyelids opened, the black pupil shifted directly toward Lilly. The predator launched toward the girl with tremendous speed.

Forcing himself to remain calm, he repeated the mantra he used on the range. "Steady pressure," he said out loud as he took aim. "Now."

BANG

The gun barked with a sharp report as he squeezed the trigger, a deafening boom that reverberated off the concrete walls. As the bullet found its mark, a dull thump echoed and a splat of blackened blood splattered over the creature's head. With an agile turn, the crocodile changed directions in an instant and faced Harold. Its claws scraped off the pavement as the creature pumped its tiny legs, its momentum still carrying it toward Lilly as it corrected its path. Harold didn't waste his opportunity.

BANG BANG... BANG BANG BANG

The hammer made a dull thud as the clip emptied. Riddled with bullet holes, the crocodile lunged at Harold. Glass exploded inward as the crocodile collided with the window. Shards of jagged glass rained over Harold as he landed on his backside. The crocodile lay still in the restaurant. Its upper torso crushed the table in a flat pile of debris. The metal pole holding up the chair bent toward the table, the seat digging into the yellow underbelly.

Woozy, Harold called out "Lilly!" as he labored to his feet, sharp slivers of glass tearing away at the flesh on his palm. When he tried to stand, he toppled over, landing hard on the glass-covered cement. He glanced over his shoulder and screamed, his left leg missing from the knee down. A slick trail of blood oozed over the parking lot, the rainwater spreading it everywhere.

The sound of twisting metal from inside the fast-food joint grabbed Harold's attention. He expected to see the crocodile stalking him, but the chair lay in a crumpled heap, the metal pole cracked off from the stress of the mighty carcass. The dead beast lay motionless and flat atop the debris.

"Lilly!" Harold tried to call out, but his voice was weak and wavering.

He dragged himself away from the scene of destruction. His vision faded to black, and he drifted into oblivion.

***

Daniel climbed into the driver's seat. A chorus of questions rose from the crowd, all the voices blending into a chaotic buzz. The engine grumbled and roared as Daniel turned the key over; the wipers streaked and skipped across the windshield. Without an answer, the voices grew louder. An electric current of rumors raced through the crowd of passengers behind him. He could feel the tension on the bus growing out of control. But he didn't have time to address them now, so they would just have to sit patiently and wait. He couldn't think straight, and he needed a minute to process what had just happened.

Frankie took the seat behind Daniel. A gush of air escaped from the tore fabric as he collapsed into it. He held up his hand, motioning for silence. No one paid him any attention. Instead, the barrage of questions came at full speed now.

"What's happening out there?"

"Why aren't we moving?"

"Do you think there are more of those creatures out there?"

"How did that crocodile catch your partner?"

"Where is the other officer now?"

"Is my little girl going to be okay?"

Daniel twisted in his seat, shifting his gaze to Frankie. "Tell them I need a minute. I just need to get to the strip mall over on Fifth Avenue..." He paused, taking a moment to find the time on the dashboard. "I'm already late and I can't afford to leave my partner hanging. He's got a little girl with him. And see to Janette, make sure she's holding up. I'm sure she's worried sick about her daughter. Let her know we are on our way to get them right now."

"Man," Frankie groaned, "whatever you say, boss. But you owe me two favors now. Don't you think I'll be forgetting about them, either?"

With a deep groan, Frankie stood up and turned to face the crowd. He raised his fingers to his mouth and whistled. A hush fell over the crowd. "Listen up, everyone."

"What moron decided to put you in charge?"

"Nah, it ain't like that, Peter," Frankie said, offended.

"Then tell us what you doin' up thar, acting all big," Peter retorted.

"I don't know if you all realize it, but we are in this together now. There's no going back out on the streets until those crocs are gone." Frankie paused as a collective gasp sucked the air out of the bus.

"You mean those things are out there?" A panicked expression rose from the rear of the bus.

"Bitch, I told you I ain't crazy," Janette snapped.

Daniel made a quick turn onto Jackson Avenue. Not expecting it, the passengers all shifted to the side by the centripetal force. Angered complaints rose from the crowd. Ignoring them, Daniel continued down Jackson Avenue. Normally, this would be the long way to the Fifth Avenue strip mall. But with the streets clear and no need to concern himself with the red lights, Daniel pressed down on the gas and sped down the road, making record time. That thought reminded him of William. If he were here, he'd make a joke about making the Kessel Run. He promised himself as soon as they picked up Harold, he would try to get in touch with William.

"Calm down, everyone," Daniel called out from his seat, keeping his eyes focused on the road ahead. Cars lined either side of the street, narrowing the two-lane road. "Let Frankie finish." His voice was authoritative, it boomed off the windshield in front of him. A hush fell over the bus. From the rear-view mirror, Daniel caught Frankie giving him a nod and a mock salute.

"Janette, we are on the way to get Lilly now."

"Oh thank God," Janette burst out, relief raising her voice and mood.

"So…" Peter trailed off, the drone of the engine drowning him out. "Those monsters are really out there."

The bus flew through an intersection, the massive tires sending walls of water splashing over the cars parked along the side of the road. Staring down at the speedometer, Daniel eased off the gas. He slowed the bus to fifty and continued through the next intersection, where the light waited for him in his favor.

"Those monsters," Frankie emphasized the phrase before continuing, "are crocodiles."

"What are they doing here?" An unseen voice asked from the middle of the bus.

"My guess," Frankie paused, lifting his hat to scratch at his scalp. "Storm's got them riled up and confused."

"Are they dangerous?"

"Of course they're dangerous," Frankie snapped. "But if you leave them alone, they'll leave you alone. Get along to get along, you know."

Bang

Confused silence fell over the bus as a sharp boom cracked outside. Everyone turned their head in the sound's direction. Daniel recognized the sound immediately and pressed down on the accelerator. He shouted, "Hold on!" just before he made the turn onto turn onto Fifth Avenue. The bus tires skidded off the slick asphalt, tossing a torrent of water over the sidewalk. A collective groan rose from the passengers as they struggled against the centripetal force generated by the sudden turn. The rear end of the bus swerved out and slammed hard against a parked car. Glass shattered and metal crunched from the impact.

Behind him, a terrified scream rang out. Daniel pulled the wheel away from the accident without easing on the gas. For a moment, the mangled metal dragged the car along behind them before the fender of the car ripped off and the bus lurched forward with a jolt. In the distance, Daniel could see the sign for the Fifth Avenue strip mall.

"Hold on, Harold, I'm coming."

***

"Over here!" Lilly's voice called out from far away, rousing Harold from the abyss.

Harold rolled over onto his back, droplets of rain hammering him, forcing him to roll onto his side. "I can't," he cried out, his voice a hoarse whisper. His check rested along the rough edge of the curb, as the sound of rushing water roared past his ear.

"Please hurry," Lilly pleaded, "this way."

Harold tried to find her through the torrential downpour, his vision blurred with pain. Reddened rainwater washed past his face as the wash-off carried the blood from his leg down the culvert. He stared down at his knee, finding his belt tied off just above the vicious wound. A trickle of blood seeped out and over the cement. He couldn't recall taking off his belt. "I can't, Lilly. You need to run someplace safe."

"I'm over here," Lilly yelled, "can't you see me?"

Frustrated, Harold banged his fist off the pavement, forgetting about the glass, driving a sliver into his hand. A muffled cry rose in his throat and died on his lips. Hauling himself over the curb, he dragged himself forward on his elbows, his right leg helping push himself along. The sound of a child's footsteps running through the water faded away from him.

"Time's running out. Hurry."

Lilly's voice echoed in his ear. Stars danced in his vision, the horizon spinning on a strange axis. Driven by the overwhelming need to protect Lilly, Harold fought back against the encroaching blackness. Somehow, he balanced himself on his right knee, crawling awkwardly forward toward the sound of her voice.

"I'm coming," Harold said, coughing up blood that splattered against the pavement below.

The sound of thundering paws hammering the cement charged toward him. Another crocodile coming to finish what his dead brethren started. He mustered all his energy and screamed, "Run, Lilly!" Red spittle flew from his mouth, dangling from his lips in thick crimson cables.

Helpless against another attack, Harold hoped that his body could provide a distraction to the new predator long enough for Lilly to escape. He laid face down in the parking lot and closed his eyes, hoping death would take him before the crocodile inflicted a fresh round of suffering.

"Get over here now," Lilly said, her voice demanding.

The hollow echo of her tiny footsteps approached, trampling through the puddles. A shadow fell over Harold as Lilly reached down, nudged his shoulder, and gave him a shake. "Get up," she pleaded, her voice urgent.

"No," Harold choked out. "Run far away."

"He's here," she cried, her voice shrill and cracking.

Footsteps galloped toward him. Out of the corner of his vision, he saw black rain boots splashing through the puddles. "Harold," Daniel's voice called out. When Harold opened his eyes, he found Daniel standing over him with a false smile on his face. "Everything is going to be just fine."

Harold coughed up spats of blood. "Don't lie to me."

Daniel scooped his arm beneath Harold, raising him to a seated position. "Frankie!" Daniel called out. "I need your help."

They hauled Harold to a standing position. Parked at the edge of the lot, the bus waited for them. The idling engine soothed Harold. As they dragged him toward the waiting bus, his right foot scrapped over the ground. He shuddered at the gruesome sight of his left knee, thick globules of blood falling to the ground at a steady pace.

ONE WAY OUT

William stared down at the deep crimson stain on his right leg, the blood having soaked through his jeans and the rag he used to staunch the bleeding. A dull ache radiated from the wound, a constant reminder of the crocodile's vicious strength. As he patted the rag with his hand, bright red liquid squelched outwards from the fabric. Once more, William pulled his phone out of his pants pocket, the wet fabric clinging to the leather case, making it an arduous task. He pressed the power button, praying it would power up. A black screen stared back at him.

A foot of murky, sullied water covered the basement floor. At this rate, it'd soon be deep enough for the crocodile to swim through it, giving the predator the ultimate advantage. Tepid, the air filtered into the room in a hazy fog, Hurricane Rose pushing the chilled deep sea air over the land. Droplets of mist soaked through every layer of clothing, making him miserable. Soaked to the bone and exhausted, he had to fight off sleep with every ounce of willpower. His brain struggled to comprehend a solution out of this basement. With his feet aching and his legs drained of strength, William sat on the freezer's lid, slumped against the wall, as the rainwater gushed over his backside, sloshing over his shoulders.

Perched in the corner, the crocodile stared at William with its one good yellowish-orange eye. Unblinking, the beast studied William, scrutinizing his every movement, biding its time. A sliver of uncoiled intestines floated on the rising water, the waterlogged innards bloated, oozing brown bile. Even though they were both wounded, deep down, William realized he couldn't wait for the creature. If the croc didn't devour him, he would eventually bleed to death waiting to die in this basement. Actually, he prayed he would bleed out before the crocodile got to him.

William matched the crocodile's glare and said, "You're a real asshole. Did you know that?" Even though speaking to the creature made him appear crazy, it felt good to hear his own voice; it grounded him. "When I write a novel about all of this, I'm going to make you out to be a real idiot."

Unblinking, the crocodile stared at William.

"A bumbling buffoon," William grimaced as the pain in his stomach flared. "Really, nothing more than a punchline and punching bag for the main character. Would you like me to teach you about the Harmon Story Circle?"

William paused, waiting for the prehistoric predator to respond.

"I won't even charge you for it." William hesitated, waiting for a snort or grunt. "You're not even the slightest bit interested in any of this, are you?"

A howl of wind thundered against the side of the house.

"Anyway," William continued as the weather outside

intensified. "There's always a part in the story where the protagonist has to defeat a bad guy who's not the chief antagonist. Kinda like a minion who wants to be the big bad wolf but is actually just a toy poodle. That's going to be you." Despite the suffering, William couldn't suppress his laughter.

Bracing himself against the wall, he pushed himself to his feet. Although he'd already examined every square inch of the basement, he had nothing else to do, so he figured he'd may as well search again. Maybe he'd missed something the first time.

"I'm getting out of here," William said, speaking to the crocodile. "Even if it means I have to go through you."

The crocodile scowled at him, as its eyelid clenched shut and opened. Its pupil, a tall, slanted oval, grew fuller as the light trickling into the room dried up. Seemingly, as if in answer to William, the crocodile thrashed its tail, daring William to get down from the high ground.

"You'd like that." William coughed into his palm. diluted blood stained his palm a bright red. "Haven't you ever learned of a fair fight?" William laughed, but it hurt too much. He wheezed and cringed as an agonizing warmth spread throughout his abdomen. Bile raced up his throat, causing his stomach muscles to clench, the searing pain dropping him to his knees.

Sensing William's moment of weakness, the crocodile bolted forward. Thrashing water drowned out the roar of Hurricane Rose. With a crushing blow, the monstrous beast rammed its skull into the deep freeze, sending William hurtling forward. The snout of the creature loomed closer as William rolled toward the edge. Somehow, William braced himself with an outstretched arm. Reaching back, his palm scraped over the rusted metal. Bits of flesh tore off in strips as he teetered over the edge. As the creature snorted, a rush of rancid air from its nostril supplanted the sour odor of fear.

"Jesus Christ," William wheezed, hauling himself back onto the lid before the crocodile could nab him. He rolled over until his shoulder connected with the far wall with a vigorous smack.

Enraged, the alpha predator tried to force its way up the side of the deep freeze, jagged claws grinding the metal in a hurried frenzy. The creature smashed back down into the water with a thunderous boom that shook the entire foundation of the house. Defeated, the crocodile crept back to the corner and turned to face William.

William laughed breathlessly. "Not yet, pal." He coughed and wheezed, then added, "Soon."

***

"There's got to be something in here I can get to," William said, growing frustrated with himself. "You will not die like this. Not on the day you find out you're going to be rich and famous." He glared at the crocodile in the basement's corner. "You can't take that away from me."

The crocodile ignored William's outburst, watching him through tight slants between the green scales, one pale yellow eye peering out at him from behind. A clap of thunder boomed in the sky. The entire foundation of the house trembled, the vibrations rattling the cement wall, debris tumbling from the weakening structure. Agitated by the clap of thunder, the crocodile lashed its tail against the wall and emitted a low, grumbling growl.

"What's wrong?" William guffawed. "Are you scared of a little thunder?"

The crocodile scurried from the pile of debris and swam toward the deep freeze. William stared down at the black water, as the choppy waves lapped halfway up the metal container. Realizing time was running out, he swallowed a lump in his throat.

A bright flash of light shone through the slits as a crack of lightning slashed across the drab horizon. Gales boomed against the side of the house, causing worn beams to creak and groan. Outside, the intensity of the rain picked up. Raindrops pelted the windows and siding with a hammering crescendo. Water gushed in through the slits carrying broken branches and rocks in its current. Debris built up against the slits, blocking out the light and dimming the room. Water sloshed into the basement, cascading down the wall in buckets. William reached the grate, trying to clear a path for the light, claustrophobia settling in with the darkness. As he leaned forward against the grate, it shifted forward beneath his weight. He laughed uncontrollably. William pushed the grate again. It budged an inch before coming to an abrupt halt. In the corner, a rusted screw jutted out of the wall. A deep crack in the paint revealed a frame around the grate.

William grasped his hands around the iron bar. Bracing himself, he shifted his feet to the wall, applying his weight to the frame. The screws groaned, grinding through the cement as William labored to haul the grate from the wall. He pulled himself up and let his weight drop, jerking the grate loose. Debris and dust pelted him as the metal ripped away from the wall. Lurking beneath the surface, the crocodile sent a ripple through the surface as it approached the deep freeze.

"Come on, you bastard," William growled as he threw his weight back.

With a boisterous, crumbling crash, the grate ripped from the wall. William fell hard on his backside with a solid thud. In a state of disbelief, he stared up at the gaping hole in the wall. Despite the drab horizon, the light shone as bright as any beacon. An uncontrollable fit of laughter erupted from deep within his belly. He turned around and waved, "See you ya later, Alligator. But I guess, in this case, it'll be in a while, crocodile."

William stretched out, his fingers digging into the earth outside the newly formed opening. Mud dug in beneath his nails as his fingers curled into the muck. Digging deep, William gathered all the strength left in his body and jumped up as he hauled himself forward. He gouged his shoulders on the rough edge, the cement carving out scratch marks that would leave scars.

Hurricane Rose greeted him, pelting him with a barrage of enlarged raindrops. The wind spattered the house with a rolling, percussive pounding of frigid precipitation. William sucked in giant gulps of the fresh, salty air, filling his lungs with the newfound freedom. Exhilarated, he found an additional source of energy that had laid dormant until hope appeared, getting to his feet with ease and moving around the corner of the house. He stepped through the splintered front door, taking his time to search the closet for the keys to the Chevrolet, finding them hung on the hook beneath Mr. Burke's baseball cap.

"Marlins fan," William said to himself. "Always been

a Rays fan myself." He pulled the hat on over his head. The worn fabric rested on his head awkwardly, the front bib dragging the hat down, giving it an odd slant.

With the keys grasped tight in his fist, William glared out at the approaching storm. The sight of seagulls tossed through the air by the relentless mercy of the gales demanded his attention. He watched as they tumbled up and down in flashes of white and gray as they struggle to reach safety. Beneath the cliff, the Atlantic Ocean rose in majestic peaks rolling toward the shore; anger expressed through water. Above, the clouds were the color of a rock quarry. Brilliant bolts of lightning snaked down from the heavens, lashing out at the sea.

William hung the keys back on the rack and limps back into the house, not liking his chances on the open road in this storm. He staggered through the dining room and into the kitchen. Without thinking, he rummaged through the cupboards for something to eat. A package of Ritz crackers caught his eyes. Hung on the wall, a landline called out to him. He wandered over to the phone as he fiddled with the box, tearing open the top and popping the thin plastic pouch, releasing the rich, buttery aroma into the air. His mouth watered at the prospect of food. When he collected the receiver, there was no dial tone, so he slammed it back into the cradle with a curse.

Disappointed, he mindlessly placed a cracker into his mouth. He savored the salty taste. Drool filled his mouth as he chewed. Craving more, he stuffed a handful into his mouth, crumbs and saliva flying everywhere. He couldn't control himself, cramming fistfuls of crackers until they were gone.

With his fists on the counter, he stared out the kitchen window at a rapid burst of lightning that tore the horizon into a hundred pieces. Outside, the wind howled, tossing a thick spattering of rain at the window, leaving a series of round blotches on the glass. He turned around and headed straight for the fridge, yanking the door open. The inside light was out, the refrigerator giving off only a faint trace of cool air. Not willing to risk soured milk, he grabbed a two-liter bottle of off-brand soda. He unscrewed the cap and flung it to the linoleum floor, chugging the carbonated beverage, belching in between gulps. Finished, he tossed the empty plastic bottle into the sink. It rattled around inside the metal basin, taking a minute before settling.

"Mr. Burke, you are such a glutton," William said to the fridge, spying a container of half-eaten rocky-road bars behind the milk. The lid rested on the top, not even sealed.

He pushed the milk aside and hauled out the container. Before he dug in, he grabbed a chair from the kitchen table and pulled it over to the doorway leading down to the basement, the wooden legs scraping over the tiles.

"How are you doing down there?" William called out to his erstwhile adversary.

The crocodile waited silently, glaring at William with its one good reptilian eye. For a moment, he thought the creature had actually died until it blinked. The water sloshed around the creature, debris floating around in every direction as the drainage churned around the room.

"What's the matter?" William said, staring down at the crocodile with a wide grin. "Are you a sore loser?" He stuffed a rocky-road cookie into his mouth. A flood of chocolate and sugar wreaked havoc on his stomach, giving him a gratuitous rush of adrenaline. "You want one?" He waved a cookie in the air before tossing it down into the basement. It landed in the water will a dull *plop*.

Uninterested, the crocodile didn't budge an inch. A deep, guttural growl demonstrated its displeasure in the tiny morsel.

"Suit yourself," William laughed and licked his fingers before taking another bite.

BIG KEY PINE SPORTSPLEX

"We need to get him to an emergency room," Frankie insisted. He ripped off a swatch of his shirt and used it to tie a tourniquet above Harold's knee. Frankie was a former combat medic, so Daniel felt blessed to have crossed paths with him. If he had to be the one to take care of Harold, he wasn't confident he could have kept his friend alive.

"The hospitals are too far," Daniel replied as he drove the bus through the narrow city streets. "There's a medical team at the Sportsplex who can take care of Harold. They have all the emergency medical equipment."

"If you say so," Frankie grumbled. He rummaged through the first aid kit that lay open on the floor beside him. Pill bottles rattled around inside the plastic tin while bandages and gauze spilled over the side as he searched through everything.

Periodically, a soft whimper or groan escaped Harold. Daniel fought back a tear at the gruesome sight of Harold's maimed left knee draped over the edge of the seat. The bandages were soaked through with blood, dripping to the floor in thick, viscous droplets. Focused on saving Harold's life before he bled out, Daniel drove with reckless abandon through downtown. Nothing would prevent him from getting Harold the help he required.

"Can somebody hold this for me?" Frankie turned toward the other passengers. "Come on now, this man is going to die if I can't stop the bleeding now."

A hushed silence lingered over the bus. Everyone was in shock at the horrific sight. Curiosity had gotten the better of them earlier, but now they avoided Frankie's gaze, not wanting to see the terrible injury up close.

"Please," Daniel pleaded, "you can't just let him die. He put his life at risk to save all of you. And when shit hit the fan, he risked it all to rescue that little girl. Every damn day he put on that uniform to keep everyone safe. He's a great man and needs your help now."

A woman stood up, stepping forward gingerly with her hand raised to her face to cover her mouth. "What do you need?" she asked from behind her palm, her words muffled. Her eyes widened, taking in the gruesome scene with a sympathetic gaze.

"Just take this," Frankie said, holding the roll of gauze out for her to take. "Make sure you keep it clean, keep it off the ground, and try not to let it touch anything. I don't want his wound getting infected."

The woman gave a timid nod, but her eyes remained glued to the floor.

"What's your name?" Frankie asked, trying to engage her.

"Hailey," she answered in a faint whisper.

"Alright, Hailey," Frankie said, softening his tone and using her name. "Thanks for your help. And remember, it's important you keep this bandage off the floor. Can you do that for me?"

"Yes," Hailey said, confidence creeping into her tone.

As Daniel escaped the towering buildings downtown, the brunt force winds, no longer blunted by the towering cement structures, pounded against the bus. He struggled to keep the bus straight, swerving and adjusting to combat Hurricane Rose.

"Hey, man," Frankie grumbled, "can you try to keep us straight? I can't do anything with the bus going all over the road."

"I'm doing my best," Daniel snapped, growing frustrated with everything. Even the sound of the wipers gliding over the windshield was driving him wild with anger, each thump another nail driven deep into his cerebellum.

"Well, you're going to need to do better," Frankie shot back.

Waves hammered the coastline, crashing in thick plumes of white foam that sent shivers along the shore. Rolling mountains of water raced toward the shore, towering eight meters high and devouring the land with greedy intent. Daniel knew that passing over the highway along the coast would be a treacherous gamble and considered taking the inland route. But that meant backtracking through downtown and taking the long way around. Harold didn't have enough time remaining to make that trip.

Forced into danger, Daniel punched the steering wheel and screamed, "FUCK!" A searing pain radiated from his knuckles. His foot eased off the gas, the bus slowed to a crawl.

"What's wrong?" Hailey asked in a timid voice, frightened by Daniel's outburst.

"I should have gone to the damn hospital," Daniel cursed at himself.

"Why are you slowing down?" Frankie asked, his expression riddled with concern. "Your friend here doesn't have much time left in the tank."

"The road's going to be impassable further up the coast," Daniel waved his hand out toward the bleak horizon as it rolled toward them. "I've wasted too much time already. I'm going to turn us around and head back." Daniel eased off the gas as the wind threatened to push the bus off the road. The tires skidded across the pavement and a collective scream raised from everybody.

"There's another way around the hill," Frankie said, his hands busy tying off the tourniquet. "There's an access road through the old park. My old man used to maintain the road for the city before he retired."

"Where?" Daniel asked, his eyes darting up and down the road, searching for the road sign.

"It's just after the turnoff to the Golden Sands Beach parking lot."

Daniel nodded his head as he pushed the pedal to the floor. The engine revved and roared as the bus lurched forward. "I'll have us there in no time," Daniel said with renewed enthusiasm.

Frankie stared down at Harold, cut off another swatch of gauze, and said, "You're going to be in better hands soon." He wrapped the white fabric over the blood-stained layer covering the stump where Harold's knee ended. With a deep sigh, he watched as a crimson blossom bloomed on the fresh gauze.

***

Tim cursed as the back tires sank into the muck, spinning and kicking out an arc of muddy water behind. He punched the steering wheel and slammed the gear into reverse. The tires squealed as the car lurched in place, sliding toward the ditch as the front end swung out. Through the torrential downfall, he could see a Jeep just ahead, but he couldn't tell if anyone remained inside. The motor died with a choking rattle as he killed the engine, removing the keys and stuffing them into the visor.

Reaching down, Tim pulled the lever and popped the trunk, hoping to find some useful gear before he set off. The hinges screeched as the wind tossed the open trunk up and down. Every thunderous impact threatened to shatter the rear window, the violent banging sending shuddering vibrations throughout the vehicle. With a deep sigh, Tim pushed the door open and made his way around to the back, the rain hammering against him, his uniform affixed to his body. When he opened the trunk, he chuckled at himself for being so foolish. Locked behind a stainless steel compartment built into the frame, a riot shotgun for emergencies waited to be used.

"Goddamn it," Tim cursed at himself. "You know, I could have used your help earlier."

Not needing the weapon now, Tim snatched the roadside kit, tucked it underneath his arm, and slammed the trunk down with a dull thud. The pounding rain dampened the noise. He approached the abandoned jeep from behind, finding it empty. Driven by years of training, his hand graced the hood as he passed, finding it cool to the touch, the occupants having abandoned the vehicle long ago.

Nestled amongst the verdant foliage, a bright red roof jutted out of the jungle. With nowhere else to go, it seemed the only logical place to go for shelter. As he made his way toward the building, he could see a blur of movement coming from within the building, the rain obscuring his view. He held his hand up to his forehead to block the rain, but he still couldn't make out the figure in the window.

Picking up his pace, Tim jogged toward the building, his boots falling into deep ruts concealed by the murky water building up inside the worn tire tracks. Beneath him, his boots ripped out clumps of muddied road, his feet slipping and sliding in all directions, making him work for every step. As he neared the building, the shape in the window came into focus. A young woman frantically waved her hands over her head. Not understanding, Tim nodded his head and waved back.

"I saw that red tin roof long before I ever saw you, lady," Tim mumbled to himself.

Overhead, booming claps of thunder rolled across the horizon. A rumble coursed through the earth. The road trembled as the sound passed directly overhead, disguising the approaching creature. The wind howled through the jungle, forcing the palm trees to bend toward the ground at a threatening angle with a collective groan. The raucous clamor drowned out the banging sounds as the woman pounded her fist against the window, trying to grab Tim's attention. If he had taken notice of her frantic attempts to get his attention, he would have broken into a full sprint sooner. But he didn't know the ancient predator was chasing him until he heard the terrified cry that tore through the storm. It took him a moment to register what she had been screaming. Then it came through loud and clear.

"Run," the voice screeched.

Tim turned around as the sound of crunching metal erupted behind him. Cheryl's police cruiser rocked on its hinges as a massive reptilian snout slammed into the driver-side door. Covered in greenish-gray scales, the crocodile's length dwarfed the cruiser, and its girth was as wide as the police car. Driven mad by the storm, the creature growled and hissed at the sight of Tim. The wind tossed thick ropes of saliva from the rows of gnarled teeth against the side of the car with an audible splat.

When Tim turned to run, his feet tangled together, throwing him off balance. He stumbled forward as he tried to regain his balance. His hands scuff through the mud and grime, hauling himself along. Fueled by adrenaline, his heart hammered against his chest as he found his stride, carrying him toward the open door. Screaming hysterically, the woman waved Tim forward with the frantic motion of a third base coach waving the runner home at the bottom of the ninth.

Tim refused to look back at the enormous monstrosity. Instead, he kept his eyes focused on the murky waters, doing his best to avoid tripping over a rut. Any mistake at this point would prove fatal. His eyes searched frantically for safe footing, the rain making the job arduous and dangerous. As he approached the house, guided by the dull glow of the electric lights, the rumble of the generator grew into a steady droning buzz that coursed through his body.

Beneath him, the ground trembled violently, the vibrations registering deep within his limbic system, unleashing one last wave of adrenaline into his limbs. The muscles in his legs tightened and pumped, carrying him across the last twenty feet in the blink of an eye. As he reached the doorway, the woman snatched his collar, yanking him inside as she slammed the door shut in one fluid motion. Tim careened into the room and smashed his hip against the dinette table, tipping it over with a crashing bang.

The younger woman at the window howled, turning away from the glass pane just before the crocodile hurtled its massive frame against the shack. In a thunderous crack, the beams bowed inward. The wood snapped as drywall showered the living room. The window exploded, sending shards of razor-sharp glass over the floor as the wind swept into the shack, bringing the torrential rainfall with it.

Outside, the predator heaved itself against the door, the wood splintering against the mighty blow. Everything clattered to the floor with a crashing bang. Picture frames shattered, the radio exploded in a spray of plastic and electronic components, and books thumped against the hardwood. The reptilian eye glared at them, peering at them through a crack in the door, the large oval pupil a black chasm against the diseased yellowish iris. Tim jumped to his feet and pulled his savior back into the room with him. The vein in his neck pulsed as his heart broke into a gallop.

"What the hell is that thing?" Sharon shrieked. Her hands tangled her hair as she slumped into a chair. With a quick tug, Sharon pulled out a clump of matted hair and threw it to the floor.

"Does anyone know what the hell is happening here?" Tim asked no one in particular, his eyes fixed on the wall as the beams bowed inward. Another crushing blow rattled the shack. The hinges cringed as the bottom of the door tore from the frame and dangled from the top hinge. Everyone in the house gasped as the crocodile let out a rumbling growl that rattled the floorboards.

"Get behind me," Tim yelled, waving his arms in a frantic motion. Sharon and Erin scuffled across the floor and got behind Tim. Erin pressed herself into Tim. He could feel her shallow, rapid breathing against the back of his neck.

The crocodile lashed its tail against the wall, rocking the floorboards with a wood splintering crack that tore through the shack. Imploding from the savage blow, the window sent a shower of glass flying through the room. Tim raised his forearms to shield himself from the deadly barrage. Erin pressed herself closer, their bodies mashing together in a tangle of limbs. If Tim didn't know any better, he'd swear she was trying to wear him as a protective layer of body armor against the predator.

Sharon let out a pained gasp. Tim spun around and saw a jagged shard of glass sticking out of her throat. Sharon dropped to her knees with her hand grasped around the object embedded in her throat. Thick gouts of blood seeped through her fingers and fell to the floor. Erin rushed over, easing Sharon to the floor, using her own body to prop the dying woman up. Deep, hitching sobs rocked Erin's entire body as tears tracked down her cheek.

"Help her," Erin begged, her hands fumbling over Sharon's body, trying to hold her in place. Sharon's eyes rolled into the back of her head and rolled over onto her shoulder as she lost consciousness. Her skin turned parchment-paper white. Her blouse was soaking wet and stained maroon, trickling drops of scarlet down her jeans. Erin's fingers ran through Sharon's hair, entwined in the tangles of soaking wet chestnut brown curls.

Tim knelt down in front of Sharon, searching for a pulse. "Her pulse is faint," he said, trying to calm himself down, "but she still has one. If we can stop the bleeding and get her to the squad car, we should be able to save her life."

As if in reply, the crocodile hissed and struck the side of the building. Tim's heart froze for a moment before surging into a sprint. Erin was screaming, but the sound of her voice blended seamlessly into the chaos that swirled around them. With the window smashed out, wind and rain whipped into the cottage, accompanied by the fetid stench of reptile, pungent and overpowering. Tim's stomach contracted, forcing a mouthful of bile up into the back of his throat.

Erin moved her hands toward the shard of glass lodged in Sharon's neck. Tim snapped out of his trance and grabbed her by the wrist, harder than he meant to. "Leave it in or she'll bleed out," he ordered. She stared at him wide-eyed and trembling, but she obeyed.

From outside, the distinct grumble of a diesel engine hummed into existence, growing louder with every passing moment. The ground thundered as the massive predator lumbered away from the shack, drawn by the approaching noise. Tim allowed himself to catch his breath, his mind wandering toward hope.

"What do we do?" Erin said, drawing Tim's attention back.

"Find something to put around the wound to stop the bleeding."

"There was a first aid kit in the bathroom," Erin said, pointing across the small room to the door.

Without a word, Tim sprang to his feet and hurried toward the bathroom, jumping over the jumble of chair legs and broken glass. The droning roar of the engine drew near, demanding Tim's attention. He took a quick peek through the broken window and saw the crocodile lurking along the edge of the road, working to conceal itself in the thick bush. With time running out, he ducked into the bathroom and scanned the cabinet over the sink for the first aid kit. He snatched it from the bottom shelf and ran back out into the common room.

Erin stood over Sharon, her bloodied hands balled into fists at her side, frustration and fear writhing the soft features of her face. Sprawled on the floor, Sharon lay on her back, her chest moving in shallow breaths. "Help me move her to the chair over there," Erin said. Without waiting for Tim, she knelt behind Sharon and cradled her upper body, hoisting her into a seated position with a strained groan. Tim picked Sharon up by the legs, and with Erin's help, they carried Sharon to the love seat and propped her up in the corner. Erin snatched the first aid kit from Tim, rummaging through the mess inside. "Where is the fucking roll of gauze?"

Tim reached out and placed his hand over Erin's.

"Calm down," he said, his voice steadied by years of training. He held out a roll of white gauze for Erin. "It fell on the floor when you opened up the kit."

Erin worked the gauze around the glass shard, careful not to bump the jagged sliver and cause more bleeding. Blood sullied the paper-thin fabric instantly. With deftly experienced hands, Erin continued to work the bandage until the bleeding remained contained.

Outside, the diesel engine's grumble shifted down into a rumbling hum. Tim stared out in disbelief as the station's bus pulled up behind his squad car. Absent-mindedly, he wandered toward the broken window. Rain assaulted him as he neared the shattered remains of the window scattered over the floor. Behind him, Erin soothed Sharon, ensuring her it was going to be alright. A man ambled off the bus and ran toward his squad car. Instinctively, Tim's hands patted his jacket pocket, feeling the keys dig into his palm. "Shit," he muttered to himself, turning to face Erin. "I have a plan. Don't go anywhere. I'll be right back." He unclipped his flashlight from his belt and turned the bright LED bulb on and headed outside, determined to make his way to the trunk of his squad car to grab the shotgun from the trunk.

***

The bus rocked on its hinges, the giant tires finding every pothole and rut on the old access road. Surrounded by palm trees on all sides and a slate gray sky overhead, some passengers panicked as claustrophobia settled in. Unable to keep up with the torrential downpour, the wipers struggled to keep the window clear enough, forcing Daniel to lean over the steering wheel and peer through the thick raindrops spattering over the windshield.

Swampy puddles littered the road, concealing their depth from Daniel. He did his best to avoid the ones he believed to be the deepest. With every bump, Harold let out an agonized groan, reminding Daniel of his dire situation. But there was little for Daniel to do but push forward and hope they made it to the Sportsplex in time for the medical team to help Harold.

"Up ahead," Frankie said, appearing out of nowhere. "Do you see that?"

Daniel raised his eyes from the road and squinted ahead. A vivid red square nestled into the wall of jungle green ahead immediately drew his attention. "What do you think it is?"

"That's the visitor center for the deer refuge and the ranger's shack," Frankie answered, his voice bursting with excitement. "That means we're almost there. The road should bend to the right and make its way up to the Sportsplex from there." He slapped Daniel on the back, his palm slapping off the vest beneath his jacket. "It's a narrow path, but we should be able to make our way up the hill as long as the road hasn't washed out."

In the distance, two derelict vehicles appeared through the veil of rain. Daniel eased his foot off the peddle, allowing the bus to roll forward. "Jesus Christ," Daniel said out loud to no one in particular.

Frankie leaned toward the window, trying to get a better view. He scrunched up his face, a confused expression set deep lines running across the bridge of his nose. "Is that a police car up ahead?"

"Yes," Daniel replied, shocked to see the telltale florescent yellow strip running between two blue ones.

"What's it doing all the way out here?"

"No idea," Daniel muttered to himself. No matter how hard he tried, he couldn't make out the squad number through the falling rain. He could also see the jeep just ahead of the abandoned squad car, the tires sank deep into a rut. "But we're going to have to move it out of the way." He pulled the bus up behind the squad car and let the engine idle. "I'll head out and move it."

"You think the keys are in the ignition?" Frankie asked, blocking the stairs down to the door.

"If they're not, my guess is the officer driving the car is just up ahead," Daniel stood up, staring down at Frankie, motioning for him to move out of the way.

"I'll check it out for you. You stay here and keep these people safe." Frankie turned and headed down the stairs. When he reached the door, he tried to push it open, but it remained locked.

"You're the medic. I need you to monitor Harold. I can't afford to have something go wrong with you out there."

"Something about this is giving me the shivers." Frankie turned his gaze toward the window and continued. "There's something awful in the air. Can't you smell it?"

Daniel shook his head. "No, I don't. But if you insist on going out there, you make it quick. If the keys aren't in the ignition, you come on back in here and I'll go. Do we have a deal?"

Frankie said nothing. He simply nodded his head in agreement and turned to face the door. When Daniel turned the lever, the door opened with a metallic thunk and a gust of air forced itself onto the bus, blowing Frankie's baseball cap off his head. He turned around, picked it up, and dusted it off before heading out into the elements. Daniel watched as Frankie sloshed through the puddles toward the squad car, tossing the driver-side door open and vanishing into the vehicle.

A hushed murmur ran through the passengers behind him. Daniel turned to face Harold for a moment, watching as he drew collective shallow breaths, confirming he was still alive before turning his attention back to Frankie. The dreadful pang of anxiety reared its ugly head, gripping Daniel and twisting knots in his stomach, that awful feeling Frankie mentioned making itself known. When he turned toward the road, Daniel could see Frankie inside the car, searching the visor for the keys.

In the distance, a series of flashes caught Daniel's attention from below the red roof. He peered through the driving rain, his focus drawn to the distraction. The faint reflective strips that ran down the officer's pants shimmered faintly in the dim daylight. Waving his arms over his head, the other officer endeavored desperately to get his attention. Daniel's heart sank into the pit of his stomach as he watched a blackish-green blur rush from the side of the road toward the squad car.

"Everyone sit tight," Daniel said before he opened the door. He didn't want the gusting wind to drown out his words.

Before he reached the road, he heard the crunch of metal over the storm. As his eyes found the squad car, he couldn't fathom the size of the beast crawling over the hood of the car. Frankie scrambled out of the driver's side and collapsed onto the road just as the creature's weight collapsed onto the roof. The sound of shattering glass and twisting metal clamored as the biggest crocodile Daniel ever saw crept off the car, dwarfing the vehicle beneath its yellow belly.

Frankie scurried to his feet and raced toward Daniel, but the creature swept its tail across the road, cutting Frankie's legs out from beneath him. The tail curled toward the car, dragging Frankie through the mud before crushing him into the side rear tire of the squad car. From the roof of the car, the *Deinosuchus* let out a phlegm-filled roar that Daniel felt deep in his chest.

A familiar voice called out to Daniel. "There's a shotgun in the trunk!"

The *Deinosuchus* rolled off the roof of the car, demolishing the driver's side in a crumpling roar of crunching metal. It landed on the road with a heavy thud and continued its roll, exhibiting a ferocious death roll.

"Frankie!" Daniel screamed.

An agonized groan answered Daniel, his voice shaken and muffled. Daniel searched the area for any sign of Frankie, but the rolling beast demanded his attention, the armored torso displacing muddy water in exaggerated arcs. Out of control, the monstrosity rolled straight across the road and into the bush, flattening the underbrush and splintering tree trunks. When Daniel tore his eyes away from the unearthly display of raw power, he discovered a leg sticking out from beneath the squad car.

"Frankie," Daniel called out as he raced toward him.

"Daniel," the familiar voice carried through the storm.

"Get the gun."

"Tim?" Daniel said, confused. "What the fuck?"

Tim raced toward the edge of the road where the *Deinosuchus'* destructive path led into the jungle. Before he entered the dense foliage, he turned to Daniel. "There's a shotgun in the trunk and an injured woman in the shack. I'll lead the beast away and you get them out of here now."

"I can't leave you here to face that creature alone," Daniel called out as Tim rushed into the jungle without giving Daniel a chance to change his mind.

"Goddamn it," Daniel cursed, staring up at the slate gray horizon. Out of the corner of his eye, the edge of the storm turned a dismal black as the eye of the storm neared. He could see the daylight bleeding away. A pink-ish-orange horizon stood out against the dismal clouds that dominated the skyline.

"Help!" Frankie's plea snapped Daniel back to the horrible reality around him.

Daniel got down on his hands and knees to crawl toward Frankie, finding his leg broken just below the knee, his shin bone protruding from the skin and out through his jeans. "I'm going to pull you out on the count of three," Daniel said, giving Frankie a moment to brace himself.

"Are you going to pull on three or count to three then pull?"

Ignoring the question, Daniel began his countdown. "One,

"Two,

"Three."

Frankie let out a pained scream as Daniel yanked his

body out from beneath the squad car. A clap of thunder drowned out his pitiful sob.

"I'm going to get you to your feet and help you to the bus," Daniel said as he helped Frankie to a seated position.

Frankie bit his lip and nodded his head. A pained expression highlighted his face, draining the color from him. Daniel placed his shoulder under Frankie's armpit and eased him to a standing position. A woman from the bus appeared beside them and, without speaking, bared some of Frankie's weight as they dragged him to the bus and up the stairs.

"Let's lay him down next to Harold," Daniel said, nodding his head toward his injured comrade. They eased him down and Daniel leaned toward the stranger. "I need you to do everything you can to get him comfortable."

"I'll take care of Frankie," the woman acknowledged. "You just get us out of here."

"I need someone to help me," Daniel announced. "There's an injured woman in that cabin and we need to get her out of there."

"I ain't going out there," a man spoke up from the crowd. A murmur of agreement swept through the passengers.

"I'm going to drive this bus right up alongside the door. Once I'm there, I expect someone to help me. I don't care who," Daniel snapped, "but somebody better be willing to give me a hand."

Without speaking another word, Daniel got back in the driver's seat. He threw the gear in reverse and eased on the gas. For a moment, the tires spun, and he thought the bus would get stuck before ever getting started. But with a sudden lurch, the tires kicked out a spray of mud and rolled backward. When he figured he was far enough back, he placed the bus in neutral and let the engine idle.

"Grab on to something," he called out.

A panicked cry rose from the crowd behind him as he slammed the gear into first and put the pedal to the floor. As the bus accelerated toward the squad car, the engine grew louder, gaining speed as the tires tore up the road. The sound of screaming voices rang out as the bus slammed into the squad car. As the squad car flipped over, the bus shuddered from the impact. Daniel swerved to avoid the jeep, but the bumper clipped the rear end of the vehicle. With a jerking lurch, the jeep rolled into the ditch alongside the road as Daniel fought with the steering wheel to keep the bus on the road. For a moment, the tires dug into the soft shoulder of the road before Daniel got them back on track.

With a clear path ahead of him, Daniel drove the bus up to the front of the damaged shack. All the windows were shattered across the road, the frame was fractured and splintered, and what remained of the door hung on for dear life. Without saying a word, he pulled the lever and got off the bus. He heard footsteps following him as he made his way into the disheveled shack.

EYE OF THE STORM

Sharon's limp body melted into Erin, radiating waves of heat as her chest swelled and sank in shallow gasps. With her hands clutched around Sharon's waist, Erin allowed the tears to fall freely down her cheeks, spattering onto her blouse. Suddenly, the bus engine revved, growling over the storm. Then, the boisterous crunch of metal, followed by a crashing bang, rang out as the wind died off. Erin allowed a wave of relief to wash over her as the bus pulled up alongside the shack, driving over a section of collapsed fence.

"Everything is going to be alright," she said.

The sound of Erin's voice roused Sharon. Her head shifted toward Erin and her eyes fluttered open. When she tried to speak, a coughing fit rocked her body. Her eyes clenched shut and her cheeks flushed. As she raised her hand to cover her mouth, Erin guided her forearm away from the shard of glass protruding from her neck with a deft touch. When Sharon moved her hand, thick wads of frothy blood coated her palm and smudged her lips.

"I won't live to see another day." Sharon's voice was a weak whisper.

"Don't speak," Erin said, holding Sharon's hand.

"Save your energy."

The mangled door creaked and groaned as it swayed into the shack, pushing a pile of debris against the wall. Another police officer Erin didn't recognize shoved his way through the door, ripping the broken door from its hinges and tossing it aside. "Ma'am, let's get you and your friend out of here."

Permeated with joy, Erin grinned as the officer and another man carried Sharon onto the crowded bus. She followed close behind, ready to spring into action at a moment's notice. They laid Sharon down next to a man with a grizzly appearance. Next to him, covered beneath a gray wool blanket, lay a man, the police officer in uniform stuck out from beneath the rough fabric. The blanket fell to the floor where the man's left leg should have been. As they readjusted the cover, Erin glimpsed the man's injured leg. A snapped-off shard of bone protruded from the gnarled wound. His paper-white face was covered in a slick layer of sweat despite the chill he seemed to be battling, no doubt a symptom of shock caused by the macabre wound. A woman tended to both men. She looked exhausted and overwhelmed, her eyes plunged deep in the sockets, swimming in a sea of worry.

"Can anyone drive this bus?" the officer called out as he stood up.

"I used to be a school bus driver before I lost my job," a man answered from the back, his voice timid.

"You're hired," the officer said, ushering the man to come forward.

The man maneuvered his way to the front, joining the officer at the front of the bus. With their backs turned to the crowd, they talked as the officer pointed toward the Sportsplex atop the hill. But the droning murmur of the passengers drowned out their words. When the officer finished, he turned back toward everyone else and cleared his throat.

"You'll be safe at the Sportsplex. A team of medical professionals will be there to take care of you. All I can ask of you is to help them if they need your help to get the wounded off the bus and into sick bay. There will be enough food and water for everyone, and other officers on site to keep you safe."

"Where are you going, Officer Grant?" a woman's shrill voice rose from amongst the crowd.

"You never leave a man behind," Daniel answered as he made his way down the stairs.

"Famous last words," Erin mumbled to herself. When the door closed behind him, Erin felt a lump form in her throat. She didn't expect to see Officer Grant again—at least, not alive.

Erin watched as Daniel raced down the road, running past her window. At that moment, she noted the rain had stopped falling. A swatch of bright denim sky broke the dreary gloom of the day and settled over the Keys, sweeping across the slate-gray storm clouds that dominated the horizon. When she glanced down, she noticed the officer had the trunk popped open. The mangled hunk of aluminum rested against the road, the bumpy edge digging into the softened mud. When Daniel emerged from behind the slab of aluminum, he held a shotgun across his chest. As the bus driver shifted gears and started toward the winding hill, the officer dashed off the road, following a deep rut that veered into the jungle and vanished into the dense sea of verdant.

***

Tim's voice had grown hoarse from screaming out to the sadistic predator to follow him. His shoulders ached from waving the flashlight in giant, sweeping arcs behind him as he maneuvered his way through the dense vegetation. He ducked under low branches and vaulted over fallen stumps as he made his way over the treacherous terrain, keeping ahead of the monstrosity that gave chase. He'd double back and make his way up the hill if he could lead the beast far enough away from the Sportsplex. But his energy was depleting rapidly, his muscles heavy with fatigue and his lungs burning.

The *Deinosuchus* barreled through the jungle with reckless abandonment, enraged by its prey's audacity. Tree trunks snapped in the creature's wake, splintering as the massive, armored torso shoved its way forward. Branches and sharp shivers of wood scraped the reptilian hide, gouging out sharp red rivers along the blackened scales. The predator's vicious claws tore up clumps of damp earth, its massive frame dispersing puddles of water as it gave chase to Tim. No matter how hard he tried, he couldn't put any space between himself and the beast.

Covered in deep shadows, the gnarled roots littering the jungle terrain lay half-buried in the mud and bush. Already on borrowed time, Tim's feet tangled in a root and sent him sprawling to the ground. The flashlight jumped out of his hand and spun around as it flew out of his grasp. It landed with a hard metallic thump against the ground, the bright white beam angled down at the ground and into a bush. Tim scurried on his hands and knees toward the light, his fingers probing blindly into the dense foliage, the canopy of palm leaves casting elongated shadows over the jungle floor.

Behind him, the *Deinosuchus* closed the gap with incredible speed. The putrid stench of rotting meat filled Tim's nostrils as the creature closed in. He could hear the throaty growl of the crocodile as it snorted and hissed, honing in on Tim's scent. Using all his strength, Tim dug his heels into the softened earth and drove himself forward in a lurching leap for the flashlight. When he reached it, he spun around and directed the beam of light toward his path. A wall of reptilian armor exploded through the dense foliage. With its sickly copper-toned eye locked on Tim, the predator's jaws hinged open with a bone-cracking creak.

Locked in a showdown with the wild animal, Tim had nothing to defend himself. With a deliberate pace, the *Deinosuchus* crept forward with its jaw wide open. Tim stared into a black chasm lined with razor-sharp teeth. Somehow, he found the fortitude to gather his composure and face the beast head-on. Without thinking, Tim directed the beam of light directly into the creature's eyes. It let out an angered growl, twisted its head away, and staggered to the side.

Not wasting his opportunity, Tim broke into a sprint through the dense jungle, his feet guided by luck as he ran toward the unknown. Bewildered, the *Deinosuchus* took a moment to realize that its prey was escaping. Enraged, the mighty beast doubled its efforts and made a frenzied dash for Tim. As Tim ran blindly through the uncharted jungle, he burst through a clearing, finding nothing but open space in front of him. A giddy laugh escaped his lips as the jungle floor gave way to a cavernous ravine. He crept toward the edge and shined the flashlight down into the darkness, the light falling on the jagged rocks of a steep cliff face. Overhead, the sky closed off once again and let loose a torrential downpour. The raindrops hammered the ground all around him as the eye of the storm passed. A grumbling snort demanded his attention before he found the bottom of the chasm with his light.

The *Deinosuchus'* horrendous snout stuck out of the jungle, and its piercing eyes locked onto Tim's with malicious intent. Camouflaged within the dense foliage, its tremendous frame vibrated with anticipation. With its tail thrashing back and forth, banging off tree trunks and flattening bushes, the creature emerged from the jungle. Bathed in the harsh glare of Tim's flashlight, the hardened skin cast menacing shadows behind it. Left with nowhere to turn, a series of incoherent screams escaped Tim's lungs as the *Deinosuchus* lunged at him. The beam of light illuminated the blood and guts caught between the creature's jagged teeth. Tim clenched his eyes and waited for death to strike him down. The thunderous roar of death answered his call.

***

The creature left behind a divergent path of destruction through the jungle. An extensive trail of trampled bush and toppled palm trees lay in its wake. Daniel aimed his flashlight down the trail, the beam bobbing up and down as he raced to save Tim. Beneath him, he felt the earth tremble as the enormous crocodile gave chase. Each drumming stomp sent a shudder through the earth. For a moment, the threatening sounds gave him the illusion that the ground would split open, devouring him whole.

Daniel cupped one hand over the side of his mouth and yelled out, praying to get a response from Tim. A savage roar acknowledged his pleas. Drawn by the horrible sound, Daniel pumped his legs, driving deeper into the jungle. He could only hope his friend was still alive.

A petrified scream ripped through the jungle, abruptly cut short by a roar that resonated with a deafening clap. The jumbled sounds of panicked calls for help, crumbling earth, trees splintering, and triumphant reptilian war cries rose from just ahead.

Exploding into a clearing, the light gleamed off the scaled backside of the deadly creature. Savage rivers of red crisscrossed the armored torso, the light glistening in globules of blood oozing from the cracks all over its body. Hidden somewhere behind the slithering reptile, Tim begged for mercy. Hunched on its hind legs, the crocodile coiled into a powerful stance, ready to spring forward.

Just as Daniel called out Tim's name, the pounding roar of rain drowned out his voice as the eye of Hurricane Rose raced past. Wind swirled, rattling the palm trees all around him, the leaves lashing out at him in the chaos. Daniel raised the shotgun. His finger passed the guard and rested on the trigger, aiming for the creature's skull. Just as he was about to pull the trigger, a flash of yellow reflective strip caught his eye, forcing a jerk reaction that raised his arms. A brilliant spark of flame erupted from the barrel as the resounding bang rang out.

In a jumbled blur of motion, the *Deinosuchus* became

entangled with Tim. An arc of red goop exploded from the creature's backside. Then, in an instant, they vanished from view, dropping below the ground as if hell had opened up and swallowed them into its depths.

"Tim!" Daniel screamed, racing toward the edge of the cliff.

"Help!" Tim's weakened voice rose from the darkness in a desperate plea.

Daniel directed the beam of light over the edge of the cliff, finding Tim clutching to a tangle of gnarled roots jutting out over the fall. Daniel eased himself down the outcropping, found a secure grip on a tree growing from the hardened earth, and reached out for Tim. Reluctant to let go, Tim stared down into the dismal abyss.

"Hey," Daniel called out over the storm, "don't look down. Whatever you do, don't take your eyes off me."

"Get me out of here." Tim pulled his gaze off the fall and held his gaze on Daniel. Blood flowed from a deep cut on his cheek then ran the length of his face.

Stretched out over the cliff, Daniel stared down at the bottom of the ravine. Flooded with rainwater, the river gushed, massive rapids churning up frothy mud as it snaked through the jungle and vanished into the darkness. For a moment, Daniel froze in place, struck by the powerful sight below, until Tim's hand brushed his own. Covered in grime and grit, Tim's hand nearly slipped from Daniel's grasp. But Tim braced his body weight against the mountain, allowing Daniel to yank him to safety. As they reached the top of the hill, they both rolled over onto their backs, panting from exhaustion.

"Let's get out of the rain," Daniel said.

Tim sat up and wiped his face. The rain rinsed away a scarlet streak tarnishing his cheek. "After this, I never want to see another crocodile again."

***

The sound of grinding metal cut through Erin's head as the bus driver tried to shift gears. In a jerky motion, the bus rumbled forward, plodding up the hill. A luminous, blaring light lit up the night sky as the bus rounded a corner, giving a gorgeous view of the soccer field and the Gulf of Mexico lying below. An uneasy cheer rose from the passengers as the lights of the Sportsplex came into view.

"We made it," Erin said, holding Sharon's hand.

Sharon's eyes fluttered open, a faint smile tracing her lips before opening into a reticent sigh of relief. She squeezed Erin's hand. An inaudible whisper escaped her parting lips.

"Don't speak."

The generators rumbled as they pulled up by the front door. A man wearing a blue rain slicker exited the Sportsplex and approached the bus. When he clambered up the stairs and turned to face the passengers, his hand raised to his face to cover an astonished gasp. Worried by the gruesome sight of the officer's missing leg, the man stood silent as his mind raced.

"We need help," the bus driver urged.

Brought back to reality by the hysterical tone of the bus driver's voice, the man shook the cobwebs. "I'll alert the nurses and get the stretchers." And with that, the man dashed off the bus and vanished inside the Sportsplex.

"I don't need a stretcher," Sharon said, her voice a

harsh rasp. She draped her arm over the chair, trying to pull herself to her feet. With Erin's help, she stood on unsteady legs.

"Are you sure you don't want to want for the medics?"

With a pained smile, she shook her head and said, "We made it."

Outside, the pounding of boots on pavement raced toward the bus. Erin turned her gaze toward the window. A group of paramedics carrying stretchers boarded the bus. With a calm demeanor, a female paramedic coordinated the group, giving orders and relaying information back to the nurses' station on her radio. They tended to Harold first, lifting him onto the stretcher. One paramedic strapped Harold down as another dressed the savaged wound. With an emphatic splat, he discarded the blood-soaked bandages onto the floor. Once stable, they rushed him inside.

"Let's get you inside and we'll get you fixed up," a female paramedic spoke to Sharon.

Together, they followed the paramedic into the Sportsplex and out of the horrific storm to wait out Hurricane Rose.

***

Daniel and Tim made their way back to the main road, stumbling toward the Sportsplex on exhausted legs. Tim's heavy, rasping breath worried Daniel as they walked along. He heard something on his chest and wanted to get him out of the elements and into the care of a doctor as soon as possible. But Tim couldn't keep up, his ankle swollen to twice its side, having struck it against the cliff on his tumble over the edge. Relentless, the rain hammered the jungle all around them, waterfalls cascading from the canopy of palm leaves overhead.

Harsh light spilled down from the top of the hill, basking the jungle in its warmth. From the distance, the steady drone of generators kept them on track. A sign alongside the road read *Blue Hole This Way*. With no other directions, Daniel headed toward the Blue Hole, hoping to find shelter or another way up over the hill to the Sportsplex. He knew that no matter how hard he tried, Tim wasn't about to step foot back in that jungle. "Come on, this way," Daniel said, urging his friend along.

Staggering, Tim's right foot sunk deep into a puddle, and he tripped. Trying to get himself out, he sprawled onto the road in a defeated heap. "You should go on without me," Tim said, coughing into the cup of his hand.

"There's no way I'm leaving you behind," Daniel snapped, anger fueling his every word. "Not after everything you've been through. You'll die in the middle of the road. And I won't be responsible for it. Now, get on your damn feet and keep pushing forward."

Tim grumbled under his breath. He reached out his hand, seeking help from Daniel to get him to his feet. When he stood up, he leaned into Daniel, placing his arm around his neck to brace himself. "Did anyone ever mention you're a cruel bastard?"

Laughing, Daniel nodded his head and said, "You're beginning to sound like my husband. I see a utility shed up ahead. Let's get you inside and rested, then I'll head up the hill and get a vehicle to pick you up?"

"I won't argue with you."

Together, they staggered toward a utility shed. When Daniel placed his hand on the handle, he expected it to be locked. When he pushed down, the door fanned inwards with a shuddering creak. A faint trace of light lit up the tight confines of the work shed just enough for them to make their way inside without tripping over all the tools scattered on the floor. Inside, the sweltering heat of the damp jungle greeted them, the stagnant odor of moss and dank mineral water filled the air. Rain hammered the rooftop. The wind howled against the side of the building, the foundation creaking with every violent gust. Daniel closed the door over, blocking out the storm, and unzipped his jacket.

With a cursory glance, Tim found a bag of soil and made himself comfortable. Glad to take the weight from his swollen ankle, he let a thin smile press his lips against his teeth. "If I'm asleep when you get back, please don't wake me up."

Daniel allowed himself to laugh, but he felt an uneasy shiver race down his spine as if something was watching them. Suddenly, he spun around, expecting to see that massive beast blocking the doorway. His line of sight fell on The Blue Hole. The lights from above twinkled on the water's surface, the pounding raindrops breaking the light apart, sending ripples throughout the pond.

"Here," Daniel said, handing the shotgun over to Tim. "I can't leave you here defenseless."

Tim held the shotgun in his lap, staring down at it with a questioning expression darkening his thoughts. "What if you need this?"

"Why would I need a shotgun? Do you think that

thing survived that fall?" Daniel said, trying to disguise the unease in his voice.

Tim's eyes spoke louder than his words ever could. "I can't lie. If you won't take it, I'll keep it, but it won't do much against that massive crocodile in my hands."

"I'll be as fast as I can. There's no way that lumbering reptile will ever catch me."

"Have you seen that creature move?"

Without answering, Daniel moved to the doorway. "Try not to fall asleep. I'll be back as soon as I can with help." Before Tim could mount a further protest, Daniel closed the door behind him.

Back out in the horrible weather, Daniel drew the collar of his jacket up to protect against the rain. As he reached the road, a low grumbling snarl caught his attention. His heart leaped into his throat. With the top of its head poking through the surface of the crystal clear water, the *Deinosuchus* glowered at Daniel with those evil reptilian eyes.

THE BLUE HOLE

Caught in the middle of the road, Daniel kept his gaze locked on the Deinosuchus and moved toward the crest of the hill, drawing the creature away from the utility shed. He kept his movements short and simple, fighting back the impulse to turn and run. The creature stalked Daniel from the water, its massive frame drifting beneath the surface, its top teeth biting into the water.

When the creature approached the edge of the pond, it dragged itself onto the bank with its mighty front claws, scrapping clumps of softened earth into the Blue Hole behind it. As its body emerged, Daniel saw that the creature's right hind quarter was a mangled mess, its limb dragging uselessly over the ground. Its stomach scrapped the ground, rocks and hardened earth tearing at the thin flesh of its stomach. Shredded innards dragged behind the creature, leaving a greasy mess in its wake.

Evident by the predator's injuries and the severe impact on its mobility, Daniel realized he would never have a better chance of killing the beast, but he still couldn't get close to the creature. He had to think of a way to outsmart the ancient predator. Now, regretting that he didn't take the shotgun, he scanned the area for an advantage. If he could get Tim's attention, he could distract the crocodile, giving Tim the opportunity to land a killing blow.

Fully emerged from the water, the *Deinosuchus* showed a surprising burst of speed and agility, closing the gap between them. With labored breath, the creature maneuvered toward the road, blocking the straightforward route of escape, pinning its prey into a tight corner within striking distance. Daniel drew his service revolver, firing two rounds before the hammer fell on empty. The bullets embedded into the scaled torso with wet *thwacks*, doing little more than enraging the beast further.

Trapped, Daniel circled toward the edge of the Blue Hole, doing his best to keep his stalker off balance by moving toward the injured leg. Along the edge of the pond, Daniel spotted a pile of jagged rocks. He bent down and picked one up, gauging the weight of the stone in the palm of his hand. It wouldn't do much against the *Deinosuchus'* armored scales, but he'd use it if all else failed. Daniel drew in a deep breath, wound his arm back, and heaved the rock toward the utility shed. His first attempt sailed high and wide left, landing in the foliage with a dull thump. The next attempt landed dead center on the roof with a thunderous bang.

Drawn by the calamitous clatter, the beast jerked its head toward the sound with a squealing hiss. The door swung open, and Tim wandered out of the shed and froze in place as his gaze wandered upon the *Deinosuchus*. Daniel snapped his fingers, calling out to the creature, demanding its attention. He heaved another stone at the utility shed without taking the time to aim when the creature took its first lurching step in Tim's direction. The impact rang out with a sharp thud, and the stone fell harmlessly into a puddle.

With a harsh scream, Daniel yelled at Tim to snap him out of his trance and get out of the way. But Tim ducked back inside the utility shed and slammed the door behind him as the crocodile made a macabre dash, using its skull as a battering ram. Wood splintered and collapsed to the ground with a tumultuous crash. Daniel cursed, staggering toward the beast, drawn forward by his duty to a fellow police officer. Standing on top of the pile of debris, the crocodile let out a triumphant roar, signaling victory to the jungle.

"Get away from there!" Daniel shouted, his voice hoarse.

Beneath the rubble, Tim's agonized moan escaped the debris, barely audible over the pounding rain. A glimmer of hope flashed in Daniel's heart, releasing a wave of adrenaline into his system. With a stone clasped in his fist, he charged the beast with a thunderous roar. Waiting with its jaw wide open, the putrid stench of rot poured from the creature's diseased mouth. At the last moment, Daniel got low and lunged to the predator's right side, driving the stone into the injured leg. A dreadful roar of pain escaped the beast's throat. Wild with an unfamiliar sensation of pain, the crocodile scampered away from Daniel for a moment to regroup.

Buried underneath a heap of rubble, Tim tried to make his way out from beneath the remnants of the collapsed shed.

"Where are you?" Daniel got down on his hands and knees, throwing shattered boards and toppled tools off the pile. A reflective strip of yellow caught Daniel's eye, drawing him toward the low moans of his injured friend. "Hang on, Tim, I'm going to get you out." Redoubling his efforts, Daniel tossed debris left and right, uncovering his friend, each board stained red with globs of blackened blood.

As the *Deinosuchus* regained its composure, Daniel struggled to free Tim. The creature's growl sent a shiver through him, forcing him to turn around and face the beast. Something cold and hard poked his calf muscle. When he looked down, he saw Tim holding out the shotgun through the debris. As he knelt to snatch the shotgun, the *Deinosuchus* lunged forward. Before he secured his grip on the shotgun, the predator drove its snout drove into Daniel's chest, sending him spiraling head-over-heels onto the ground, driving the wind out of his lungs. He landed awkwardly on his leg. His knee twisted hard to the right with an audible pop.

Sprawled on his backside, the creature stalked Daniel, climbing over the debris toward him, snorting and hissing. Suddenly, a glare of light flashed into the creature's eyes, stopping the beast dead in its tracks, if only for a moment. With nowhere else to go, Daniel scurried backward, unable to gain any distance between himself and his stalker as it continued its advance. The *Deinosuchus* reared back on its hind legs, raising its snout into the air, giving its jaw room to unhinge. Daniel clenched his eyes shut, waiting for the blackness to engulf him.

BOOM

An arc of blood splattered over Daniel in a wide arc. The creature slumped forward, crashing to the ground in a heap. A bloodied, gaping red hole stared at Daniel. The *Deinosuchus'* eye hung from its socket on a sinewy chord. Tim stood behind the creature, a trail of smoke billowing from the shotgun's barrel.

"Jesus Christ," Daniel muttered.

"Let's get out of here," Tim said, hobbling forward and offering his hand to Daniel.

An armored van with the windows tinted pulled up alongside the fallen *Deinosuchus*. With ingrained practice, soldiers dressed in black camouflage and armed to the teeth exited the SWAT vehicle. Weapons raised to the ready, they surrounded the beast with caution.

"It's dead," Daniel choked out. "Get us out of here."

Without acknowledging Daniel, a soldier turned his back to the group and spoke into his radio. The rain drowned out all but the cackle of static. When he turned around, he motioned toward the van with the butt of his assault rifle. "Get in," the soldier barked.

"Who the fuck are these guys?" Tim asked as they made their way toward the van.

"Our saviors," Daniel answered, not caring who they were. All he wanted was to get the hell out of here and someplace safe. Exhausted physically and mentally, Daniel helped Tim into the back seat without uttering another word. As they drove away, the soldiers closed in on the beast, their rifles at the ready.

Tim leaned in close to Daniel and whispered, "I don't think these guys belong to the military."

Daniel shook his head, staring at the vaguely familiar logo embroidered into the dashboard. "At this point, who cares who they are? We're safe, and that's all that matters."

AFTER THE STORM

Frankie hobbled down the corridor toward Harold's room, the IV cart dragging behind him. The wheels squawked with a high-pitched screech. He discovered five mobile beds set up throughout the conference room as he made his way into the makeshift intensive care unit. They had set all the beds up beneath a window to allow the daylight to shine through, raising the patient's spirits. Frankie remembered learning that trick during triage training. Machines hummed and blipped in a garbled symphony. In the far corner, an elderly woman sat up and stared out the window with a faraway expression on her face.

He found a nurse hovering over Harold with a clipboard in his hand. Frankie watched as the nurse checked the monitors and made his observations, jotting down all the vital stats. Reminiscent of his time in the core, Frankie vowed to get himself off drugs and back onto his feet. After last night, he knew he still had a lot to offer this world.

"Is he going to be alright?" Frankie cleared his throat when he recognized the nurse was searching for the source of the voice.

"Are you a family member or friend of someone in the

room?" the nurse inquired as he acknowledged Frankie standing in the doorway.

Frankie shook his head. "Not exactly. But I saved that man's life yesterday." He gestured toward Harold. "I just wanted to drop in and make sure he made it through the night. That's all." When he turned to leave, he heard the nurse clear his throat and call out to him.

"You don't have to leave," the nurse said, turning back toward Harold. "He would enjoy the company when he wakes up."

"So," Frankie hesitated, "he's going to come out of this unscathed?"

"Well," the nurse rolled his tongue over the roof of his mouth, pondering the philosophical implications. "He won't ever start in the outfield for the Marlins. And he may find riding a desk for the rest of his career. But he's going to pull through with no major complications."

"I guess that's the best we could have asked for?"

Saying nothing, the nurse nodded his head and turned his attention back to his chart, scribbling his pen across the page as he went about his duties.

"Do you need a hand with anything in here?" Frankie asked, his eyes wandering around the room. "I'm trained and can help while I wait for him to wake up."

The nurse laughed and nodded at Frankie. "I suppose you could monitor everyone in here while I make my rounds." He waved his clipboard toward a panel on the wall. "If anything comes up while I'm making my rounds, you can reach me on the intercom. It should reach all the conference rooms and the corridors where I'll be.

With a genuine smile, Frankie nodded and pulled a

chair up beside Harold's bed. He didn't notice when the nurse left. But he enjoyed finding his place again.

***

Rustled from sleep by the blazing morning sun, Amy rubbed her eyes with her knuckles. A stretching yawn whistled past her dried lips as she greeted the warmth of a familiar Florida day. Bunched up around her waist, the satin sheets soothed her aches, the pillow supporting the small of her back as she sat up. A metal tray with a dull orange dome waited for her on the nightstand. When she lifted the plastic, a whisk of steam billowed from the cup of coffee. The bouquet of nutty coffee and smoky bacon permeated her nostrils. She took a tentative sip, enjoying the smooth flavors dancing on her pallet.

Tucked beneath the plate, a note written on the hotel stationery caught her attention. She pulled it out and read it as she inhaled a piece of bacon. The chewy fat melted in her mouth, releasing a flood of flavor over her tongue and igniting her hunger. She did not know what time of day it was, but at some point the power must have come back on. Between each bite of breakfast, she read the note from Darrell with a grin on her face.

At the foot of the bed, a neat stack of clean clothes and a luxurious robe from Jessie waited for her, compliments of the hotel. She gulped down the coffee and stuffed forkfuls of food into her mouth as if she were a soldier eating in the field before a battle. After she finished every morsel, she planned to take a shower and get dressed. If she put her head back down on the pillow, even for a second, she realized that a deep sleep would take her once more. She was too curious to discover what had happened to those awful crocodiles in the hotel lobby. And she wanted to give Darrell an answer to his question before he came to his sense and changed his mind.

***

Sleep relinquished its hold over William. He awoke with a yawn, stretching his arms out over his head, taking in the unfamiliar surroundings. Rain spattered against the window softly, the gales reduced to a gentle sea breeze. Darkness filled the descending corridor in front of him, the staircase demolished. A whimpering growl emanated from the basement, eliciting the memories of his battle of wits with the crocodile left trapped below. He felt the sudden urge to get away from the stairs, afraid fate would tip him over the edge and take back the death it desired.

William wandered into the kitchen, opened the fridge door, and fumbled around the top shelf for the bottle of milk he had seen earlier. When he found it, he discarded the top onto the floor and drained the jug, chugging it down as fast as his throat muscles would allow. The cold liquid gushed over his face and dribbled down his neck. He stuck the empty bottle back in the fridge and wandered through the house until he found himself in the living room. Resting on the end table next to the chesterfield, William spotted a phone charger for the car. After checking the chord to make sure it fit, he headed outside into the calm morning.

Fallen trees and debris cluttered the lawn and driveway. William turned back toward the house, finding several broken windows and bare patches where the wind had ripped the siding from the home. When his awe over Hurricane Rose's power subsided, he made his way to the car. A fallen tree trunk blocked the car from exiting the driveway. But William only needed to charge his phone and call Daniel to hear his voice. After that, he would go back inside and sleep until help could arrive. William unlocked the car and hauled the door open. The hinges screeched as if in protest at the intruder violating Mr. Burke's property.

He turned the engine over. It grumbled and sputtered as it turned over. William plugged the charger into the car. When the charging icon appeared on the screen, a tear of joy streaked down his cheek. Unable to wait, he powered up his phone, the screen taking an agonizingly long time to load. It took even longer before he got a signal. He dialed Daniel's number, and he didn't have to wait long for his husband to pick up.

"Daniel," William said, his voice filled with relief, "are you alright?"

"I'm fine. Where are you?"

"I'm at Mr. Burke's." William stopped himself before he went any further.

"Are you ok? Did you find my father? Why are you at Mr. Burke's?" Daniel asked in rapid succession, then paused, waiting for the answers.

William waited for the interrogation to end before jumping in. "Your father wasn't home. I couldn't get in touch with him." On the other end of the line, Daniel grunted but allowed him to continue without interruption. "I'm going to need to visit the hospital, but it's not life-threatening."

"Do you need me to come get you?" Daniel interrupted before William answered another question.

"Can you?" William asked, staring down at his bandaged leg. A dull throb radiated throughout his entire body.

"Tim and Harold are both in stable condition. I'll head over and get you once they're loaded into the ambulance."

"What happened to them?" William asked with genuine concern.

"It's a long story," Daniel said, the exhaustion clear in his tone.

"Tell me about it," William paused. "I think I'm going to write a novel about all of this."

EPILOGUE

Hunched over his keyboard, Dr. Anders' fingers raced back and forth with a determined sense of purpose, the keys clacking at a rapid pace. A glimmer of harsh light reflected on the edge of his glasses, forcing him to squint against the glare from the computer screen, but it didn't slow him down. Words scrawled across the screen as he made his weekly report. And this had been a week for the record books. After years of hard work and dedication, it was finally paying off.

A sharp buzz broke his concentration. "Dr. Anders," his assistant's voice filtered through the intercom, "you have a visitor here to see you."

Annoyed, Anders furrowed his brow and pressed the button. "Are they on the schedule?"

A long pause. "No sir," static crackled. "Should I send them in or make them come back later?"

His finger hovered over the button as he considered it. "Let them in," he paused. "But clarify that in the future they will need to book ahead of time. I'm a busy man and won't have my schedule dictated by unannounced visitors."

Anders stared at his report, considered continuing,

then thought better of it. He saved the document, then closed the file, shutting off the screen. An Asian man wearing a slim black suit stepped through the doorway as Anders' assistant held the door open for him. "He'll be right with you," she said. The man gave a slight bow and entered Anders' office as the assistant drew the door closed. With impressive posture, the man's suit fitted his body in all the right ways. A brown leather briefcase dangled from his right hand.

"Please, help yourself to a seat." Anders offered the stranger his hand.

The stranger sized Anders up, staring down at his outstretched hand for a moment before reciprocating the gesture. His palms were dry and his grip firm, the signs of a confident man. After he sat down, the briefcase echoed a dull thump off the marble floor. With meticulous attention to detail, the man adjusted his tie and straitened his jacket. "Thanks for taking time out of your busy schedule, Dr. Anders."

Anders snorted. "I hope you can appreciate how busy I am. State your name and business."

"I'm Mr. Lao," he said with a curt bow of his head. "And I understand you'll be particularly interested in my business."

"And what makes you assume that Mr. Lao?" Anders grunted, showing his displeasure.

"You've recently genetically engineered a *Deinosuchus*…"

"How do you know about that?" Anders cut the man off. "Who are you exactly, Mr. Lao?"

"I'm the CEO of Labrynth Oils and we are very interested in your project," Mr. Lao responded without a trace of emotion in his voice.

Anders shook his hand with a dismissive wave. "I'm sorry to inform you, but you're too late. We have sold all our specimens and we don't have the required resources to produce more."

Mr. Lao rested his hands on the table and drummed his fingers against the hardwood. "We know that you abandoned the project once the federal government caught wind of it." He paused and smirked. "My security team has already retrieved several of your specimens from the Keys. We figure you ditched any incriminating evidence once you realized they were after you. Very smart, releasing them during the hurricane to cover your tracks."

Anders dismissed the comment with a curt flick of his wrist and said, "preposterous."

"Even if it is," Mr. Lao hesitated. "I have it under good authority that your stockholders aren't happy with your financial numbers."

"I've already told you," Anders snapped. "We can't engineer you another *Deinosuchus*."

"We aren't interested in the *Deinosuchus*," Mr. Lao said, holding up his finger. "What intrigues me is the process you've used to replicate the extinct creature."

Anders shook his head. "That's not for sale either. I'm afraid you're going home empty-handed. Now, if you'll excuse me, I have work to do."

Mr. Lao opened his jacket and pulled an envelope out of his pocket. He tapped it off the edge of Anders' desk. "You'll want to look at this before you send me away. It's a very lucrative offer that will make your investors rich. It will make us all rich. A real win-win situation for us."

"Do you have any idea the type of scrutiny my research gets?"

Mr. Lao bowed his head in agreement. "Almost as much as a multi-billion-dollar oil conglomerate."

Anders eyed him suspiciously. "Did you say Labrynth Oils?"

"Yes, I'm sure you've heard of us. We are a worldwide leader in sustainable oil solutions."

"I've heard of you," Anders chuckled. "But not for the reasons you want. Weren't you guys responsible for that disaster off the eastern coast of Canada?"

"That's what people want to believe, but that's not the entire story, Mr. Anders," Mr. Lao answered, his tone still void of emotion.

"Yeah, that's right. And there's been allegations of a cover-up and the whole nine yards. I didn't bother to read the entire article," Anders said, moving the mouse and firing up the computer screen. "Lost interest about the same time my eyes rolled over the word megalodon. Wait a second, is that why you're here? You want my company to engineer you more of the most pernicious predator that ever stalked the oceans?" A genuine fit of laughter overcame Anders.

"We've recovered some of the creature's teeth. But I'm sure if you wanted to reconstruct another megalodon, you'd have no problem getting your hands on a set of authentic teeth." Lao laughed. "You can purchase them off eBay nowadays."

Anders leaned back. His chair squeaked as he stretched his arms out and clasped his hands behind his head. "Now

I'm curious. What is it you came here to speak to me about, Mr. Lao?" He noticed the time at the bottom of the computer screen. "Cut to the chase. I have deadlines to meet and arrangements that require my full attention."

Lao reached down by his side and laid the briefcase on Anders' desk. The supple leather cushioned the sound on the teakwood desk. His fingers opened the metal clasp with practiced ease. Two metal rods secured the lid in the upright position. When he spun the briefcase around for Anders, the leather scuffed across the surface of the desk. A fragment of a sharp, ragged tooth lay beneath a hardened plastic shell, the sides padded with dense foam to protect the inner shell. Yellowish brown, the cracked tooth measured at least twelve inches and came to a razor-sharp point.

"What is that?" Anders asked, his fingers tracing the protective layer. He found it cold to the touch and wondered if that was by design.

"Have you ever read *Moby Dick*, Dr. Anders?"

"I believe so," Anders agreed and added, "when I was still a youngster if I'm not mistaken."

"This fragment of tooth is from a *Livyatan*. An ancestor of the bull sperm whale, this sea monster inspired the whale for that narrative."

"You want me to extract DNA from that tooth and incubate an overtly aggressive sperm whale?"

"That is correct, and we will pay handsomely for it," Lao announced, turning the briefcase back toward him and closing it.

"Let me get this straight," Anders said, leaning forward in his chair. "You want us to create a second, genetically enhanced sea monster..."

"We never created the megalodon." Mr. Lao spoke with an offended, harsh tone. "Evolution is the reason for that monster."

"Then what do you want from me?" Anders asked, growing frustrated.

"A means to fight against nature." Mr. Lao threw a portfolio of pictures at Anders. "She's winning, and it's bad for business."

Anders' eyes grew wide as he examined the photographs. "How much are you offering?"

"Whatever it takes," Mr. Lao said. "How soon can you begin?"

AFTERWORD

Once again, I find myself writing a book about an important animal on the earth. While the creature in this novel is an extinct, prehistoric predator, it is related to the modern-day saltwater crocodile. I want to make it clear that I've elaborated (if not butchered) the behaviours of these creatures to tell another salty dip. Crocodiles are an important part of the food chain. They should be respected, not feared. I hope that you understand my story was created and fabricated for your amusement, and that I have the highest respect for these reptiles. I am captivated by Crocodiles, and I hope I brought just a little of what makes them so special to the page. I tried to use as many of the facts as possible, but sometimes, fiction is more entertaining than the facts. Any errors in this novel about the behaviours of crocodiles, or anything else, are on me.

As always, thanks to my wife, Leah, for your love and support. I could not do this without you. Thanks to Dana and Rick, for your constant inspiration and energy. Thanks to my family and friends, your support means everything to me. Luckily for me, there are too many of you to name here.

An extra special thanks to my editor, Brad Dunne, for

editing another novel. Your guidance and expertise have been vital to my success. I can't thank you enough for everything that you do. You're the best editor and a better writer. I am eternally grateful. And of course, another special thanks to Ellen Curtis for this spectacular cover. Once again, I am in awe of your talent. Thank you, Jon Dobbin, for being a supporter, but more importantly, an inspiration in my writing endeavours.

Last but certainly not least, I want to thank you, the reader. Without you, I wouldn't be able to live out dreams. Thank you.

DARK STORIES FROM ENGEN BOOKS

THE HOWL BECONS

Growing up without his father, Tyler had no way of knowing the horrible secret that has plagued his family for generations. To free himself and find the cure, he will have to look beyond himself and into his dark history.

"A very ambitious novel… the horrors of everyday life can be worse than anything in fiction. The idea of using werewolves as a metaphor – to me this pushes the book a bit above much of what is out there… Brad [Dunne] is a very good writer and obviously has a deep background."
— Andrew Peacock

WESTON'S WAR

Something evil grows in the heart of Colorado. Bill Weston was a man of the West. He knew it – its land, its people, its stories. It was where he plied his trade, hunting men for money. His life wasn't easy, but it was predictable. That all changed when he captured Faraway Sue and he was led on a trip through the Colorado forests

"Take a little Zane Grey. Add a little Penny Dreadful. Read with Sam Elliot's voice. Discover Jon Dobbin's masterful The Starving."
— Darrell Power,
Great Big Sea

Did you enjoy the work of Paul Carberry?
Read his other short fiction in Engen's bestselling anthologies,
including *Terror Nova*, *Chillers from the Rock*, *Fantasy from
the Rock*, *Flights from the Rock* and *From the Rock Stars*.

The From the Rock series features short stories written by a
diverse mix of the best authors in Canada, including award-
winning veterans of their craft, and brand new talent.

Also featuring the work of Ali House (*The Segment Delta
Archives*), Matthew LeDrew (*Coral Beach Casefiles, The
Xander Drew series*), Jon Dobbin (*The Starving*), and more!

These collections showcases the talent, imagination, and
prestige that Canada has to offer. From stories of censorship
gone awry to sentient buses, global warming to corporate-
branded culture, these collections have it all!

ABOUT THE AUTHOR

Paul Carberry is a huge proponent of the horror genre and its place in literature. He has two children, daughter Dana and son Rick, with his wife Leah.

Previously, Paul has published six novels with Engen Books: the four-novel *Zombies on the Rock* series, *Carcharodon,* and *The Cottage Across the Lake*. He has also had numerous short stories featured in publication in anthologies such as *From the Rock* and *Terror Nova,* including The Light of Cabot Tower, Into the Forest, and Halloween Mummers.

The Last of the Dragons is his seventh novel.

www.ingramcontent.com/pod-product-compliance
Lightning Source LLC
Chambersburg PA
CBHW011424010726

47494CB00011B/2495